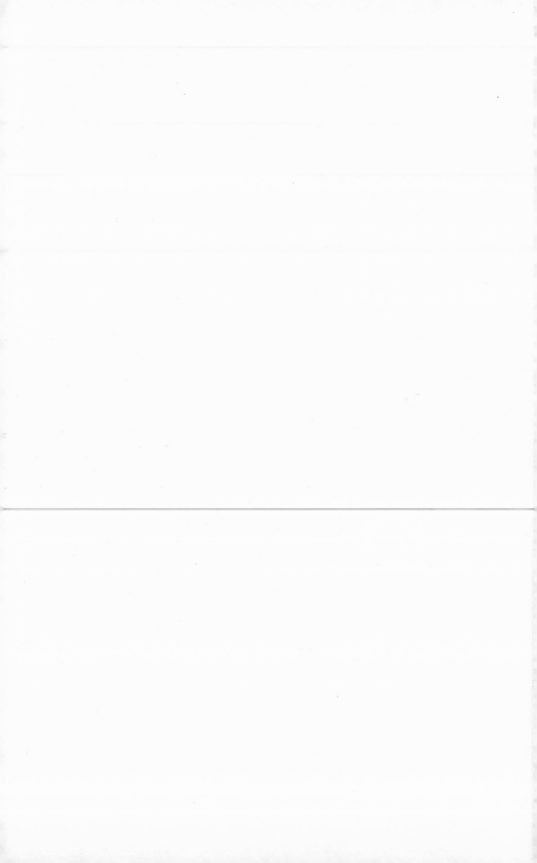

Every Man for Himself

Every Man for Himself

Orland Outland

KENSINGTON BOOKS
http://www.kensingtonbooks.com

KENSINGTON BOOKS are published by

Kensington Publishing Corp.
850 Third Avenue
New York, NY 10022

Kensington and the K logo Reg. U.S. Pat. & TM Off.

Library of Congress Card Catalog Number: 98-075067
ISBN 1-57566-418-6

First Printing: June, 1999
10 9 8 7 6 5 4 3 2 1

Printed in the United States of America

For Bill Hansen
. . . who already knows

CHAPTER ONE

J ohn woke up just before the alarm went off; he flipped it off before it could wake Harrison. He rolled out of bed and crept into the living room, turning on the TV at low volume and settling on the floor to do his crunches while Katie Couric burbled agreeably in the background.

The timer-activated coffee was ready by the time he finished his crunches, but he forced himself to flip over and do fifty push-ups before making for the kitchen. Once settled into the chair-and-a-half with his coffee and a muffin, he picked up the phone and dialed Patsy's number.

"Hello?" a voice grumbled on the other end.

"Wakey-wakey."

"Nooo. . . ."

"You make my job so hard, Patsy," John complained. This morning ritual had started a month earlier when Patricia's alarm clock had broken and John had volunteered to call her one morning to wake her up. Somehow, she had never gotten around to buying another one, and so the call had become a part of both their mornings. Since his own new life had begun, John had found that he had little patience with people who were not as apt to greet the morning as he was.

"I hate morning. I'm not conscious in the morning."

"That's why they make us go to work in the morning—if you waited until you were conscious to go to work, you'd realize what an awful thing you were doing and you wouldn't go."

"Give me my good reason to go today," she demanded. This had also become part of the ritual—it was up to John to lure her to their office each day with the promise of something she couldn't get at home. This usually involved bribery with some sort of baked goods, but this morning he had an ace up his sleeve.

"Tim, the incongruous computer hunk, will be coming in today," he said, naming the office computer consultant.

"Ooh! Oh, but we don't even know which side of the fence he's on."

"That's what I need your help to find out, Pats."

Patsy laughed. "Okay, I'll try and make it."

"See ya." He hung up and chuckled to himself. "I don't remember this being in my job description."

He showered and shaved and threw on jeans and a black polo shirt, thanking God silently for the advent of the casual office. He checked on Harrison again—still asleep. He called his partner's name, to no avail, then sat on the bed and shook him slightly.

"Mmmph?"

"I already had to wake Patsy up, don't you be a pistol, too."

"Time?"

"You have a final to administer in about an hour and a half."

"Everyone passes. Congratulations. Good night."

"Don't abuse the privileges of tenure too shamelessly now. There's coffee on; I have to go."

"I'll be up in a minute."

"I'll call you from work to make sure." He leaned over and kissed Harrison's brow.

"Mm-hmm," Harrison grunted, but since he reached for his

glasses and actually put them on, John decided his work here was done and he could go.

Their one-bedroom apartment was conveniently located just off Castro in the heart of San Francisco's gayest neighborhood. John used to take Henry Street to Seventeenth and then cut quickly across Castro to the subway station, avoiding the heart of the neighborhood, but no more. His morning saunter down Castro was one of the reasons he was eager to get out of bed these days. Men looked at him now, met his gaze and didn't look away. Things were so different now. . . . He felt like Sally Field, wanting to run up and down the street shouting, "You like me! You really like me!"

"Hi," said the toothy boy behind the counter at Starbucks. "What can I get for you today, handsome?"

John laughed. "An extra cup to hold all the flattery. And a mocha, with lots of extra whipped cream on top."

"Not flattery, just the truth." The counterboy winked.

John reappraised him—kind of cute, he thought, in a funny little way. The lopsided grin, that's what does it, he thought. "Well, thank you very much," he replied, laughing, making sure to tip the boy well.

A smile on his face, he finished the walk up Castro to the subway. He had made a rule recently: If a man looks at you, don't look away; if he smiles, smile back; and be the first to say hello. He had spent thirty years on the wrong side of the glass, and when it had become apparent that was about to change, he had made that resolution: "I won't treat people the way I was treated." He'd sworn that now that he was "good enough" for them that he wouldn't be like them, and so far he'd kept his promise. It was easy; the attention and the smiles he got still seemed like a dream.

At the age of thirty-two—well, thirty-three tomorrow—John was shockingly handsome. Shockingly, that is, to anyone who had ever known him before. There had never been anything wrong-looking about him, he had just been, well, out of shape and out of fashion and out of circulation. Men looked at him because he had become quite good-looking, in that sleek, to-the-minute look of gay trendies, but also because he . . . well, *smiled* more than most good-looking men do. He didn't walk down the street with a stern frown warning people off from any expectation of acknowledgment from the deity. Of course, he had every reason to smile now.

When he came out of the subway station at Market and Montgomery, he found Patsy idly perusing the wares at the flower stand, sipping a coffee and trying to discreetly palm her cigarette after seeing him approach.

"Naughty girl," he chided her halfheartedly. "Put it out or smoke it, but don't hide it from me."

She sighed. "I'm impossible, aren't I?"

"I have to get you out of bed, I have to keep you from smoking—jeez, Pats, I feel like your nanny."

She handed him the change from her coffee. "Here're your wages."

"Gee, Pats, fifteen cents, thanks. Can you afford it?"

"Sure; I'll just take it out of petty cash when we get upstairs."

"This is my only retirement fund, you know, so don't get caught." When they reached the Obelisk Building, Pats made her way up to the office to unlock the doors, while John stopped in the ground-floor mail room for the day's delivery. Mail in hand, he got on the elevator and just as the doors were closing a familiar voice rang out. "Hold that door!"

He waved his free hand between the doors to activate whatever magic wands detected such things. "Thanks, guy . . . hey, it's you! How are you!" John thanked his lucky stars he'd held the door, for his passenger was none other than Tim, the aforementioned incongruous computer hunk, who had been recruited to upgrade the systems and to provide Patsy with the day's inspiration.

"Great, how are you? You're awfully early."

Tim laughed, dropping a spool of cable and running a hand through his beautiful dark, curly locks. "Well, I was up all night— network crash at the Three Initial Corporation. So I thought I'd get this stuff done ASAP and get to bed."

"Ah," John said, dropping the ball at his end of the conversation at the thought of Tim and bed; Tim in bed; Tim by himself in bed, his beautiful sea-green eyes looking up at his approaching partner. . . . "Um!" he said, clearing his throat.

"Are you okay?"

"Oh yeah," he smiled. "Frog in my throat."

In the reception area they found Patsy on the couch, flipping through a magazine. "So when does the computer hunk come in?" she asked, hardly looking up.

"Hey, Patsy," Tim grinned.

She nearly fell out of her chair. "Oh shit! I—uh-oh—Hi! Can I get you some coffee?" she asked automatically.

"Thanks. I'll be right back, the rest of my stuff is still down in my car." He winked at John and disappeared.

When the elevator door shut behind him, Patsy jumped him. "What are you doing? Why didn't you volunteer to help him bring the stuff up?"

"Oh, I should have done that, shouldn't I? That would have been nice of me, anyway."

"Nice, hell! I want to see what kind of car he drives!"

"Pats! We really did pick the right name for you, didn't we?" She scowled but said nothing; the truth of the matter was that Patricia shared more than just a hairstyle with Patsy Stone of AbFab fame; though it was the hair that had gotten her the nickname, it had been her persona that had made it stick.

John made his way to his office and checked his e-mail. Tim interrupted his perusal. "Hey, I'm ready. Where do I start?"

John shut down his system. "Right here. Me first!" Today was a good day; he had finally convinced the boss to spring some money for decent computers.

"So you're pretty excited about this, huh?" Tim asked, getting down on the floor to start taking apart the old system to remove the network card. John watched him work, enraptured by the play of muscles in Tim's back through his tight gray rib-knit T-shirt. Tim was twenty-three years old, beautiful, friendly, with his own business and a client list a mile long. Everybody who liked men wanted him, though nobody at Obelisk & Associates had yet been able to pin down just which side of the fence he played. John's vote was for gay: "He dresses like a model; straight men will dress like that to go out but not for daywear." Patsy had voted for straight, because he was so flirty with her, at which John could only roll his eyes. Annabelle had voted for bi "because anyone that good-looking has had at least one offer he can't refuse from a member of the gender he usually refuses." It was hard to argue with that one.

"Yeah, I finally get Windows 98, now that it's 1999. It was like pulling teeth to get Mr. Obelisk to fork out for it." He lowered his voice to mimic the boss. " 'But we just bought new computers three years ago!' "

Tim laughed. "Wow, so you've been on 486s for three years, huh?"

"Off and on."

"Somebody's got a power machine you've been messing around on?"

"No. I mean, I haven't been here for three years—not continuous. I was on disability for a while."

"Ah." They looked each other in the eye and Tim went back to work, but John knew Tim had figured it out. "So what are you doing for lunch today?"

"Huh?"

"Ah-ha! A little ulterior motive there, eh?''

"Hell, yes. I don't see why you should stop getting presents for your birthday just because you're an adult. It's like, they congratulate you for living another year when you're a kid, and then all of a sudden you're an adult and that's when it starts getting hard to live another year, so . . .''

"Okay, okay. Listen, I'll meet you at Badlands at six. And if you really need to buy me something, you can go to Vibrant Health and get me some EAS products.''

"You want cosmetics for your birthday?''

"No! EAS makes bodybuilding supplements. You can get me HMB, or CLA, or V2G. . . .''

"Gee, you sure need a lot of initials to keep up that bitchin' bod of yours. Like you need any more help in that department. Just another queen spending every cent keeping up with the hot young gymbots. . . .''

"I will see you later, Ethan, goodbye.''

"Okay, okay. God, they're gonna look at my skinny ass and I'll have to say. 'It's for a friend,' like I was in the dirty bookstore buying a sex toy, and the scary thing is, they'll believe me!''

Ethan was a handsome guy, John thought, embracing his lanky friend, but he could use some beefing up. It wasn't the sort of thought he'd had before all this had happened, but he had found himself becoming more critical of other men's bodies, even harshly critical at times, even of friends.

"I went through the humiliation of walking in there for you, and *of course* there were like three muscle studs in there who all turned to look at me when I came in. So I played helpless and asked the counterguy for EAS products, and of course he asks me which ones do I need, and I say I'm buying some for a friend, I don't know, a bunch of initials—well, that was helpful—but he says everybody takes HMB so I got you this fifty-five-gallon drum of it," he finished, handing John a bag. "There's like 360 pills in here, so that oughta last you the rest of your life."

"Uh . . . not that long, but thanks." He hugged his friend again, feeling guilty about having criticized him, even to himself.

"Uh? What do you mean 'uh'?"

"That's a thirty-day supply, actually."

Ethan choked on his martini. "It was eighty bucks! On sale! My God, that's not muscle you're packing, it's gold. How do I get a piece of *that* action?"

"That's what revolving credit is for."

"You better watch it; that revolving credit's the reason you had to go back to work."

John sighed, sipping his orange Stoli. It was true—if he hadn't run up $20,000 in charge-card debt when he was sick, his Social Security disability would have been enough to live on comfortably, what with the absurdly low rent he and Harrison enjoyed by dint of Harrison's long residence in their apartment.

But then again, when he'd gotten sick there was no "miracle cocktail" and death had already been officially diagnosed as inevitable by all the "Powers That Be." Lacking actual funds with which to throw himself a giant farewell extravaganza, he had charged it, taking his first trip to Europe, several to New York, and admittedly using the cards to make frittery-frippery purchases as the mood struck him. The advent of the cocktail and a viral load changed from nearly a million down to undetectable, had meant either bankruptcy or a job. (Harrison had frowned deeply at even the mention of bankruptcy; now that John was going to live, they might be buying a house someday, and bankruptcy would make that nearly impossible.)

"I don't regret it," John said. "It made perfect sense at the time; it's not my fault my world got turned upside down overnight."

"But how will you ever pay them off if you keep charging these expensive supplements?"

John shrugged. ''Ed McMahon will pay them.''

''Okay, whatever.''

''So what happened to you that prompted this crisis?''

''Oh, right. Well, you know I've been waiting for a one-bedroom apartment in my building to open up—well, one finally came up and guess how much they want for it? *Thirteen hundred dollars!* For a one-bedroom apartment! Last year when I moved into a studio, the one bedrooms were six hundred, so the bastard more than doubled the rent, in one year's time!''

''That is unbelievable. You know, it's getting to be like those stories you used to hear about New York City, where a thousand bucks bought you a closet with a bathtub in the middle.''

''And I said to the landlord, how can you do that? And get this, he says, 'I'm just charging what the market will bear.' What the market will bear!''

''That's the first law of capitalism, kiddo—if you can find someone to pay more for it, charge more for it.''

''And it's rented! This guy who took it shows up in the office when I'm talking to the landlord, and I couldn't help myself, I asked him what he did and he said 'new media.' ''

''Uh-oh. Let me get another cocktail before I hear this one again.''

''But it's true! It's all these goddamn computer kids making eighty thousand dollars a year right out of college. They all work in the Valley but they're too hip to live there, they all want to live in San Francisco. So they come up here and they see a place and they don t even *blink* at the price. They just say, 'I'll take it,' and because they're willing to pay these highway robbery rents, they're driving the rest of us out. Did you see the *Bay Guardian* the other day?''

''No, why?''

''They've come up with the greatest line; do you know what they're calling them? The 'Silicon Implants.' Priceless.''

"Easy now, sport, I'm one of those computer kids."

"You're making eighty thousand a year?"

"Hell, no! I do desktop publishing, not whiz stuff."

"Then you're excused. But you don't have to worry, you're not moving. You guys have a great place. And how much do you pay for it?"

"Four-fifty a month. Split between the two of us, I pay two-twenty-five a month." Idly scanning the bar, John's eyes stopped on a man looking his way—very tall, very handsome, and pretty damn young. They held each other's gaze for a second before John tore away.

"Unreal. And you know what the downside is? You can never leave. I can never leave! You know what this town needs? A good earthquake to get the property values down. And another recession."

"That's sick."

"I know, but that's also the only thing that will get rents back to where normal people can afford them."

"Ethan, I'm not going to disagree with you, but your problems could be a lot worse. It's not the end of the world because you didn't get that apartment. You're getting along fine with Kevin, aren't you?" he asked, naming Ethan's roommate and their mutual friend.

The young hunk was looking his way again and this time he smiled and nodded. John looked away out of habit, out of a sense of "I'm not good enough for him," but he caught himself quickly and smiled back. *God,* he thought, *I am not equipped for this! I just don't know what to do with a good-looking guy.*

"John, it's not the end of the world because I didn't get that apartment, it's the end of the world because I'll never ever get another apartment unless I move to the burbs, and that, for an urban gay man, is the *kiss of death.*"

"Now you are really exaggerating."

"Do I have your complete attention?"

"Huh?"

"Oh, ah-hah. I see him. Much more interesting than me."

"Ethan, it's a bar. I'm just looking and so is he."

"And he's also just coming over here to say hi to you."

As the man got closer, he got better-looking, and John got more nervous. He wanted to shout, "I'm not ready!"

"Hey, I just noticed you across the bar and wanted to say hi." He extended his hand. "I'm Eric."

"Well, I'm glad you did. I'm John." He shook Eric's hand. "And this is my friend Ethan."

"Nice to meet you, I'm just leaving," Ethan said, getting off the bench.

"No, he's not," John said, pulling Ethan back by a belt loop.

"You need a protector? I won't bite, I promise. Unless you like that."

John felt weak. "Oh." *Oh?! He's getting all flirty and you're saying Oh!?*

"So what are you up to tonight?"

"Well, tomorrow's my birthday and my husband and I are going over to some friends' house."

"Ah. Wouldn't happen to be an open relationship, would it?"

"No, not really."

"Which one? No, or not really?"

"I mean, we haven't discussed it, but . . ." he trailed off. The fact of the matter was, there had never been any need for Harrison and him to discuss extramural activities—until recently. After all, nobody had been giving him the time of day. Confused, he broke off the engagement. "I'm sorry, but it's 'no' these days. But it was nice meeting you." He extended his hand.

Eric took it. "You too. Maybe someday you'll decide it's 'not really,' and we can . . ."

John laughed. "Maybe. See you later."

Out on Eighteenth Street, Ethan shook his head. "You're going to be single soon, you know that?"

"What do you mean?" John asked.

"Jesus, John, you've become like this . . . big pot of honey and . . ."

"And everybody wants to dip a finger in me!" He laughed.

"Exactly."

"You know, maybe it's possible to have it all. Just because I start getting . . . dipped doesn't mean I have to leave Harrison. Does it?"

"Is that what he says?"

"We haven't discussed it. So I don't know."

"It sounds like it's about time you did."

John watched Eric's retreating form. "Yeah . . . I guess so."

He spent the rest of the walk home trying to suppress the idiotic grin on his face. "Me!" he wanted to shout. "He wanted *me!*" The fact of the matter was, he enjoyed turning down the offers he'd gotten so far. He was too happy right now to be bitter, but he remembered what it had been like to be invisible to the very same boys who now regarded him with such interest, and, he had to admit, it was nice to see them denied what they wanted as he had been denied what he'd wanted. A dark cloud passed over his brow for a moment. Should he have that discussion with Harrison? *Shouldn't we make it clear what the terms of the relationship are?* But if a commitment to monogamy was the conclusion of the conversation, then there would be no adventures. And, he laughed to himself, as long as they never discussed it, they could never agree to that, so the door would always be open a crack just in case something . . . something really . . . something so . . .

He put it out of his mind as he arrived at their apartment building. The mailbox was full, but that didn't mean Harrison hadn't made it home first, just that he'd probably forgotten—again—to perform the one domestic chore John asked of him. "Absentminded professor" could have been coined with Harrison in mind, John thought, flipping through the mail. "Ugh!" he shouted involuntarily as a toothy face confronted him. He ripped the cover off the *TV Guide* and crumpled it into the lobby wastebasket. "I didn't need to see that," he grumbled.

"Avon calling!" he announced as he walked in the door.

"I'll take three of the red," Harrison called from the living room. John found him slumped in the easy chair, cat in one hand and a volume of Bruce Catton in the other. *Uh-oh,* John thought to himself. *More Civil War stuff.* John plopped the mail into Harrison's lap; the cat scrambled with a petulant *mrap* and Harrison started. "Oh, shit, the mail. I'm sorry."

"No matter," John said, not really meaning it.

"Uh-oh. No cover on the *TV Guide* again. Who was it this time?"

"Kathie Lee," John called from the kitchen.

"Thank you."

"Don't ever say I'm not looking out for you." He tossed back a glass of juice before flopping on the couch. "Oh, God. Must . . . get . . . shoes . . . off."

"How was work?"

"Fine, how was your day?"

"Excellent. Finals week is my favorite. I hand out test questions and spend three hours reading the paper and drinking coffee."

Harrison was a history professor at San Francisco University; in fact, that was how John had met him. While on disability, John had found himself with time hanging heavy on his hands and had decided to take a class on Ancient Rome as a lark. Harrison had proven to be a fascinating lecturer, encyclopedic in the field, and funny, to boot. He was no great shakes in the looks department, John thought, regarding him now—well, he looked all right, he'd look better if he'd apply himself a bit—but he hadn't been unattractive in his way. Hair over the ears, glasses not quite right for his face, rumpled, disheveled, and yes, absentminded, but when he looked straight at John with those deep brown eyes . . . John had made a lot of visits to Harrison's office after class, there had been some awkward moments, a little professor-student chemistry. John had been shocked to get a C as his final grade on the Roman Republic. Harrison had given him no quarter, treating him just as roughly as he treated the upper-division history majors who comprised the majority of the class population. Determined not to be put aside so lightly, he signed up for the Roman Empire the next semester, worked twice as hard, and got an A- and, after agreeing not to sign up for Ancient Greece the next semester, a date with Harrison. Three months later, they were living together.

"So what time are we supposed to be at Matt and Helen's?" John asked.

"Sevenish. Are you going to dress up?"

"Yes. I had an outfit come to me in a vision the other day." John's friend Helen loved to throw elegant get-togethers and insisted that her guests don at least a tie if not, preferably, a suit. John thought Helen had been exposed to too much Martha Stewart without sufficient lead shielding. While he had initially balked at having to go to all that trouble on his birthday, he'd found a beautiful gold Armani tie at Neiman Marcus during lunch one day that made a perfect match with his khakis and black dress shirt. It wasn t quite as piss elegant an outfit as Helen would have liked, but it was his birthday and he was determined to be comfy.

"How disturbing."

"What?"

"That higher powers have nothing better to do than plan your wardrobe."

"Just imagine all the trouble they'd be getting into if I weren't keeping them busy. How's that book?" He couldn't help asking, even though he knew consciously that it would probably be best to let this infatuation of Harrison's blow over.

"Excellent. Would you like to read it when I'm done?"

"I don't think so. Your reading material wouldn't have anything to do with a certain expedition, would it?" He didn't really want to have that conversation now, but their vacation plans for the summer had become a bone of contention for a while. John had advocated a California road trip, or a week in New York, or a Caribbean jaunt, or just about anything other than Harrison's proposal of two weeks pottering about old Civil War battlefields.

The problem had started when a colleague of Harrison's had foisted Ken Burns's Civil War documentary on him. Harrison had watched the whole thing in one weekend and John suddenly had an obsessed mate on his hands. Wandering about the rural Deep South in the middle of summer sounded about as exciting to John as a root canal.

"I really don't think you've given this a chance," Harrison complained. The fact was, John had tried to sit through some of the series with Harrison, but the long, lingering shots of old photos, the schmaltzy letters home from the front, and most of all, the irritatingly twangy banjo music had sent him practically screaming from the room. "Remember how you thought the Julio-Claudians would be the most interesting part of Roman history and you ended up loving the Republic most of all?"

"That was different," John said firmly. "And I wouldn't mind in the least touring Etruscan ruins or Hadrian's villa. We'd get pasta instead of okra, and wine instead of bourbon, and nobody would lynch us for sleeping in the same bed."

"I'd love to take you to Italy," Harrison said patiently, "but you know we can't afford that right now. Not until your credit cards are whittled down."

John sighed. Harrison was like his mother when it came to the

bills he'd run up on disability. What was a few thousand more in
debt if he got to see Italy for it? He was working again, it wasn't
like he couldn't manage the extra charge-card payments. But Harrison was dead set against revolving credit. And that was that. John
got off the couch. "I'm going to start getting ready."

"We don't have to be there for an hour and a half."

"Then, I'm going to take a very long shower," John replied,
to which Harrison, wisely, did not reply.

During his very long shower, John fumed, the cool water doing
little to soothe his temper. *It's like it's already settled!* he thought
to himself. *And all that remains is for him to push me into it. I
shoulda gone off with that guy Eric,* he thought darkly, before
stifling a horrified giggle at the thought. What would Harrison do
if he just didn't come home one night? He sobered at the thought;
he would be frantically calling all John's friends, hospitals, etc. . . .
no, he couldn't just go off like that.

He thought about his marriage to Harrison; nine months they'd
spent living together now. No, he hadn't been what John had fanta-
sized about when he'd dreamt about Mr. Right, but there *had* been
chemistry between them, not just the sexual kind but also the emotional and intellectual varieties. When they'd moved in together,
Harrison had seemed like a rock to him, a security blanket who'd
be there whether the pills worked forever, or not. He'd felt . . .
grateful to Harrison for taking him in, as it were. Why would
someone HIV negative, well employed, want to take on someone
with AIDS?

But since he'd gone back to work, things had changed; it seemed
to John that he was now the one doing all the work in the relationship.
*I used to worry about him cleaning up after me if I was too sick
to take care of myself, and here I am the one cleaning up after
him—he can't even remember to pick up the mail! I worried about
being underfoot because I wasn't employed, and now here it is
summer and he's going to be under my feet for three months.*

He put this aside as he dressed. "I'll talk to Helen about it," he said. "She'll know what to do."

Matt and Helen's house was over the hill in Noe Valley. John would have preferred to drive but Harrison was loath to take his car out of the garage for anything less than a trip out of town, parking in San Francisco being what it was. So they would walk the steep hill, there and back; either that, John thought, or wait for a bus that's never going to come. It was just one more thing to make him cross today. *And it's my birthday!* he thought petulantly. *I should at least not have to take the damn bus!*

Matt answered the door. "Hey, birthday boy!" He gave John a huge squeeze, giving John the usual shudder of pleasure. There would be eight people in the house tonight, seven of whom had various degrees of crushes on the eighth. Matt was tall, strong, handsome, friendly, funny, brilliant and, alas for six of the seven, straight. His black Irish good looks had made him the most popular cat doctor in San Francisco; the fact that he also had a way with animals was the nail in the coffin of many a heart. "Hey, nice tie. Let me guess."

"Do you need to?"

"I know Armani when I see it," said the best-dressed straight man John had ever known. "Everyone's here already. Let me take your coat."

"Dahling!" John's friend Stewart sailed into the room, arms extended, a cocktail in one hand and an unlit cigarette in the other. Helen forbade smoking in the house, but Stewart couldn't stand to drink without at least *feeling* that he was smoking. "Happy birthday! Jeremy and I wanted to get a go-go boy to pop out of your cake, but Helen wouldn't *hear* of an extra man at her table."

"Thank you, anyway," John said, accepting Stewart's air-kiss. "It's the thought that counts. Where's Jeremy?"

"Oh, bother. He and Adam are fussing over some pre-World War I atlas that Adam got at a garage sale." Stewart's lover Jeremy was a grad student in history and had been the one to encourage John to take classes while on disability. "Bill's in the kitchen helping Helen make tomato rosettes or some such."

Matt reappeared, having thrown their coats in the bedroom, and put an arm around Harrison's neck. "Hey, school's out, huh? Big plans for the summer?"

"Excuse me," John said, making his way to the kitchen to avoid hearing Harrison's response.

He found Helen slaving away over an appetizer tray. "No," she was insisting to Bill, *"those* radishes go at 180 degrees from the *other* radishes. Hi. John!" Helen was a perfect complement to Matt; her sunny California looks and perpetual tan against his pale skin and dark hair and eyes. John and Harrison often found themselves calling the pair Paul and Jamie, like the *Mad About You* leads. Her blond hair was pulled back in an efficient ponytail while she worked. "Can you carry this tray out to the living room?"

"Sure. Hey, Bill."

Bill took a swig of his wine and waved. "He can't talk," Helen said. "I forbade it. It was slowing him down." Bill rolled his eyes and moved on to slicing the bread. "Don't forget to do that on the *diagonal,"* Helen reminded him. He sighed; John laughed.

"Better you than me," he said, hoisting the platter and nudging the swinging door with his foot. "Antipasto," he announced. Matt cleared a place on the coffee table for the tray. "Harrison, would you round up Adam and Jeremy?"

John and Matt sat down on the couch and dug into the tray. "So, you and Harrison having a little disagreement?" Matt asked.

"How'd you know? Wait, let me guess. You asked him about our summer plans. What did he say?"

"Uh, I don't think I should say," Matt said. "In fact, I guess I probably shouldn't have mentioned it at all. Should've asked you about the weather or something."

"*That* would have been too innocuous. Would've tipped me right off."

"I guess I'm screwed either way, huh?"

John smiled and rubbed Matt's back. "Only in our dreams."

Matt laughed. "Keep dreaming. Who knows, maybe one day Helen will leave me for a Cuisinart attachment."

"It's just . . . we just . . . do you and Helen ever fight? I mean ever really fight?"

Matt blushed. "God, I don't want to sound like Ken and Barbie, but . . . no. Not really. Bicker, yes; fight, no."

"Hmm. Harrison and I don't really fight, either. But sometimes it's like . . . like Chip and Minnie," he said, naming two of Matt and Helen's five cats. "You know, how they want the same space and they kind of fight over it, but not really, but they could if one of them decided to stop being accommodating?"

"Sure."

"That's what's going on with this stupid vacation thing. But it's like Harrison is Chip and this Civil War thing is the easy chair, and he's just not going to get out of it, period. He's just going to wait for me to give up and give in, and I'm not going to! I don't want to go and I especially don't want to be bullied into it!" He stopped as Harrison brought Jeremy and Adam into the room.

"Happy birthday to you, happy birthday to you!" Adam sung gaily. Talk about opposites attracting, John thought. Bill was the strong silent type, Harrison's age, while Adam was like a happy puppy, fifteen years Bill's junior. "What did you get for your birthday?"

"Nothing yet," John said. "I've heard tell, presents are in order after dinner."

"Did you see the atlas? It's really neat! All these countries that aren't even around anymore. Jeremy was telling me what happened to all of them."

"Jeremy's an expert on things that get swallowed up," Stewart said, returning from having actually smoked the cigarette he'd been waving about. Jeremy frowned at Stewart but didn't fire back.

"Bill and I are going to Europe next month," Adam announced. "That's why I got the atlas when I saw it. Then I found out most of it was expired."

"You mean out-of-date," Harrison said, correcting him automatically. John shot him the look that meant "Don't be a professor."

"That's great," Matt said. "What about you, Stewart? Where are you and Jeremy going?"

"I need a drink," Jeremy said, taking himself off to the liquor cabinet.

"We're taking separate vacations," Stewart said. "We couldn't *agree* where to go," he shot after Jeremy, "and *someone* was too set in his ways to compromise."

An uneasy silence settled over them that only Adam didn't notice. "Bill's going to show me everything; he's been there lots of times."

"You'll have a great time," Matt said. "There's nothing like your first trip to Europe."

"I'm going to see if I can't help Helen," John said, making a break for the kitchen. "Please tell me dinner's almost ready."

"Why? What's wrong?" Ever the perfect hostess, Helen lived in fear of domestic disaster.

"Nothing, just George and Martha going at it again."

"Oh. I thought something out of the ordinary was happening. We even stocked up on scotch for Jeremy's sake."

"Next time put a little Valium in Stewart's cocktail, won't you?"

"You sound stressed out. Don't tell me you and Harrison are fighting, too."

"Ugh. It's too ridiculous. I'll tell you about it when the ladies adjourn."

added. "You find yourself reliving what it was like to be that age. Harrison, do you know what I'm talking about? You're not that much older than John, but . . ."

Harrison put down his cigar. "I don't know that I really think of John as being younger. With what we've been through, you know. When we met, he was taking classes during the periods he felt well enough, but not doing anything . . . not . . . making any plans. I guess neither of us was really prepared when we found ourselves thinking about each other more than we thought we should have. Because he had a terminal illness, I guess I thought of him in a way as *older*."

"But you ended up together, anyway," Bill said quietly, thinking of his own past.

"When we started to date, there was this unspoken thing hanging over it; this knowledge that this wasn't going to last. And yet even though we both knew we should hang back, that there was no future in it . . . I guess we got close to each other, anyway.

"He told me we shouldn't go any further, that he didn't want to do to me what so many people had done to him—he didn't want me to get close to him and have him die on me. But you can't help who you feel something for, you know? Even if you know it's going to be . . . inconvenient, at the least."

They were silent for a moment. "And then along came the cocktail," Matt said, referring to the drug combination that had wiped the virus out of John's system.

"Yeah," Harrison said, pulling himself out of his reverie. "Death is out of the picture, for a while. Suddenly we're a normal couple, doing normal things." He smiled and looked at Jeremy. "Like fighting about where to go on vacation."

Everyone laughed and Matt got up. "Let's go join the ladies. I think it's time to open some presents."

Any squabbles that might have lingered in the air before dinner were wiped out now by the excitement that accompanies the opening of multiple presents. "It's like Christmas!" John shouted, seeing the pile of gifts on the floor. "Even better, because they're all for me!" He plopped down happily on the floor and picked up the first one. "Harrison, would you hand me my champagne? Now, who is this from? God, I should have known someone would get around to making imitation Hermès wrapping paper."

"Don't rip it apart," Stewart said. "I can make it into a scarf later."

"From an anonymous donor. That would be Stewart," John guessed successfully. The paper was surgically removed to reveal a Neiman Marcus box. "Ohmigod, a cashmere scarf! Stewart, you shouldn't have!" He gave Stewart a hug and a kiss, thinking that he really shouldn't have, as John was the last person in the world to wear a scarf, especially cashmere.

"I decided you needed something queeny," Stewart said, "something as an antidote to that Timberland wardrobe of yours."

"Thank you, Elsa Klensch. Who's next?" He picked up a box and hefted it. "I know what this is."

"No, you don't," Harrison said.

"I do," John stated authoritatively, ripping off the paper. "Ohmigod," he gasped. "Harrison!"

"What is it?" Adam asked eagerly.

"I asked for a good set of kitchen knives. These are Wusthof Trident—they're the best. And they cost . . . well, I know what they cost." He gave Harrison a squeeze. "Thank you so much," he whispered.

"Happy birthday," Harrison whispered back.

"John, how old are you today?" Bill asked.

John smiled. "You really want to know?"

"Yes!" Stewart demanded.

John put down the knives. "I'm three."

"Three! You wish," Stewart said. "You're thirty-three!"

"As far as I'm concerned, I'm three," John repeated quietly, having given this subject some thought. "It was three years ago this month I got my AIDS diagnosis. But that wasn't really 'me,' not really. The person who got that diagnosis had already laid down to die. His friends were dead, his lovers were dead, and he didn't see any alternative to that for himself. His best friend died, and that was it, he was ready to check out, and check out is what he did. The problem was, this body was left without anyone to run it, and it wasn't as ready to check out as he was. So it made me, to take his place. I handled what he couldn't handle; I did what he couldn't do, i.e., go on living. I got the body on the medications he'd never gone on, I got it up and out of bed every day, even if only for a trip to the store. Then I got it to eat right and exercise.

"And in reward, it gave me this." He ran his hands down his flat torso and spread out his big strong arms with a smile. "It shed the old skin he'd lived in, and remade itself for me. By every medical standard, I'm supposed to be dead now, and in a way, I did die. But yet here I am, a new person, in my beautiful new body, just a baby, really. Just three years old this month. Everything new and shiny and just waiting for me to see and touch it."

There was complete silence for a moment. Helen and Matt were the first to get up and embrace John. "Well, happy birthday, baby," Helen said quietly. Matt and Helen were more than just good friends to John; three years ago, they had volunteered to take care of him—no, insisted they would take care of him—when the time came that he couldn't do so for himself anymore. And instead of that moment, this moment had come. Soon everyone was gathered around him.

"Oh, God," he laughed through his tears. "Now I've done it—I've inspired a group hug!" He broke up the huddle and groped for a Kleenex and his champagne. "Here," he said, lifting his glass. "A toast. To absent friends."

"And to present friends, too," Bill added.

John smiled. "I'll drink to that."

* * *

John lay next to a sleeping Harrison, his mind too active to let him sleep. As they got ready for bed they'd had a few good chuckles over Stewart and Jeremy, both of them careful not to mention the cause of their friends' quarrel, too close to the edge of their own disagreement. In bed John had squeezed Harrison with a degree of emotion that seemed to surprise them both. John had been ready and willing for sex but didn't go as far as making the official move, his subtle physical signals receiving no clear affirmation from Harrison.

So now he listened to his lover's deep breathing, wondering what had gone wrong. Their relationship had never been intensely sexual, but the sex had been good in a warm, fuzzy way. The irony was that now that he was in the best shape of his life, they were having less sex than ever . . . none actually. John tried to count the months since they'd made love and got lost in the fog of past time. He was afraid to talk to Harrison about it, either, afraid of the whole can of worms that might open up.

He looked at Harrison's sleeping face in profile. He was handsome, no doubt about it. But he was definitely letting himself slide, he thought spitefully, looking for a way to make himself feel better about the rebuff he'd just gotten.

Something's got to give, he thought. But what? A hot flush came over him at the thought of Eric, the guy at the bar. *Well, Harrison may not want me, but he's not the only fish in the sea.* He felt a pang at the thought of life without his partner—there had been so many good times. But maybe he really was a new person, he thought, really reborn as someone else . . . someone who might have to start all over.

CHAPTER
TWO

As it had every weekend for the last year, Saturday morning found John at the gym. He had eschewed the city's gay gyms when he began his body reconstitution program, choosing instead to join a "straight" gym (inasmuch as any gym in San Francisco can be called straight). He selected that game plan because his initially pathetic state would have made him the object of scorn at Muscle System or the Market Street Gym. There were a variety of people at this gym, including a disproportionate number of old men, so he could always console himself that he was never the lowest man on the food chain, which would have always been a nagging concern at a gay gym.

He found Kevin on the StairMaster. Kevin, Ethan's roommate, had not only recommended this gym to John when he'd told his friends he needed to join a gym (doctor's orders if he wanted to start steroid therapy) but had volunteered to train there with him. Kevin had inducted him into the mysteries of bodybuilding, showed him both the art—the proper form for lifting with free weights, how to isolate one muscle group a day and avoid overtraining— and the science—the power of creatine loading, the mysteries of what amino acids like HMB could do to "kick up" the muscular development process, what to eat and when to eat it.

When John had started working out with Kevin, he had thought, *I'll never look like that.* Kev was John's height, six foot one, a solid two hundred pounds of buff chiseled perfection and, all the more heartbreaking, a nice guy, to boot. "It's not genetics," Kevin swore a year ago. "We can have you looking like this, too. Hell, I did it natural and you've got steroids, your body will probably be even better than mine!" John had scoffed at the time, but now here he was, lighter than Kevin by ten pounds but still vastly different than the naysayer who'd started the program a year ago.

"What are you doing on the StairMaster?" John asked him. "Today is leg day."

"Saturday is always leg day, I thought we should mix it up. Variety, you know. Good for mind and body. Get up here," he said, indicating the machine next to his.

John sighed. "Yes, master." He hated doing cardio; it was exhausting and left him with wobbly legs, especially with Kevin on the machine next to him, constantly reaching over to turn up the speed on John's machine. Pushing the weights felt great, there was some chemical thing that happened during his third set that was like . . . great sex came to mind. Cardio was just a disagreeable chore to cut the fat before building the muscle with the weights.

"Hey, happy birthday! I got you a card, it's in my locker."

"Thanks, Ethan must have told you."

"He did. He said this total beef god hit on you at Badlands."

John laughed. "He did. I had to tell him I'm not that kind of guy, in so many words."

"You're not?" Kevin arched an eyebrow.

"No! Not yet, anyway. But I will be soon, from the looks of things."

"Oooh," Kevin said dramatically. "Have I created a monster?"

"You just might have. You tell me, you're a beef god. What did you do when you were in a relationship and someone irresistible hit on you?"

"First of all, thanks for the compliment! And the situation always depended on the relationship. I've had relationships that were open from day one; I've had relationships that were monogamous from day one. But I gotta say, I'm a pretty horny guy. The only times monogamy worked for me was when I was with someone so totally, totally hot that we were having mind-blowing sex all the time. Sex so good, you couldn't be bothered with anyone else."

"Oh."

"That doesn't sound like that helped."

"Yes and no. I just . . ." He paused, already breathing hard. "My relationship with Harrison isn't . . . never was, really, that intensely sexual. And I don't know if it's my imagination or if he's getting . . . well, he's a professor, so he was always . . . rumpled. But he seems to be getting more rumpled every day." He lowered the speed on his machine. "And I really don't know if that's him or if the contrast between us is just more pronounced."

"And you're a lot hornier than you used to be, right?"

"Hell, yes! Part of that is the steroids, but part of it is just . . . feeling sexy, feeling really sexual for the first time in my life. And being desired, you know? Having to think about the possibility for the first time because it's the first time the possibility has been there, at least on this scale. I think about what I have now, and what I could have just by reaching out my hand and *taking it.* . . ."

Kevin reached over and turned the speed back up on John's StairMaster. "Can you talk about this with Harrison?"

"And how do I broach that topic? 'Honey, you're looking old and fat lately, and I'm only getting hotter every day. And by the way, I have a waiting list of men who want to do me. Do you mind if I start whittling it down?' "

Kevin laughed. "There's got to be a more subtle way than that. So if sex wasn't what brought you together, what did—and is it enough to keep you together?"

John thought about what *had* brought them together. He had

taken the Roman history class on a lark, something to do three times a week to fill the long hours he had on his hands on disability, too sick to work but not sick enough to lay around the house all day. Harrison lectured for fifty minutes in the most galvanizing fashion; the class was full of students who were starved for a lecturer who could be both entertaining and informative. Harrison's reputation had really spread across campus. He made the Roman republic come alive, populating it with men who were often both self-sacrificing and self-serving, noble and arrogant, eloquent and catty. His lectures painted the heroes who gave their life for the glory of Rome and the aristocrats who profited from that glory. There was nothing he loved more than being interrupted by an intelligent question, and the students were full of them, driven by their desire to impress this true scholar. "That's a good question," Harrison would sometimes say after a pause, and a student would flush with pride.

John had brought the first draft of his term paper to Harrison's office for criticism and suggestions. Harrison had picked it apart ruthlessly, leaving John demoralized, but had then built him back up again, commending him for the paper's perceptive points. "I notice from the computer that you're taking the class through open enrollment," Harrison said, indicating the university's program that allowed nonregistered students to take any class offered, provided there was space.

"Yes, I am."

"Do you have a college degree already?"

John flushed. "No. I never finished. I couldn't afford to."

"I would really encourage you to enroll, and of course I'd like to see you become a history major. You really see the players as people, a lot of your observations on their characters is excellent."

"That's because you present them so well," John said, really noticing Harrison for the first time as a man. The professor had the most piercingly intelligent eyes, they seemed to look right into you.

"Oh, I shouldn't say that, you being the teacher and all, it sounds like ass-kissing . . . I mean flattery."

"No," Harrison deflected the compliment. "Your perceptions are based on the texts we're reading, you're not just parroting what I say in class. *That* would be ass-kissing," he said with a smile, and they had shared their first laugh.

Something that had felt like intimacy to John had crept into the relationship, and looking back he had to admit he'd probably slacked off on his studying near the end of the semester, thinking he'd won Harrison's approval and that an A was now automatic. He had been shocked to get his grade in the mail—a C! At first he had been hurt, but the grade had come with a note from Harrison: "I think I know your intelligence well enough, John, to be able to say with certainty that you could have done better on the final. You were excellent in your observations on how Greek culture impacted Rome, but your answer on the Catiline conspiracy was a mere gloss of facts and dates and names, not an *analysis.*"

John had gritted his teeth and shown up for the first day of the spring semester with enrollment request in hand for Harrison's Roman Empire class, the sequel to the previous semester's course. Harrison had never been so pleased to see a student return. "Come back for more?" He smiled wickedly.

"I'm ready for you this time," John said. "I even got a jump start on the reading."

Harrison laughed. "Then you should get a much better grade this semester."

"That's the plan."

He *had* worked much harder, and it had paid off on the final— an A minus. And after the final, out in the hall, Harrison had asked him if he'd planned on taking Greek history from him in the fall.

"That depends on my finances, why?"

"If you're not, then you won't be my student anymore, and I'd like to know if you would go out with me sometime."

"You mean, on a date?"

"Yes, on a date," Harrison said, not at all flustered, as if normal people asked each other out on dates without a moment's hesitation.

John had been floored, but he had said yes. After all, on the first date he would tell Harrison he had AIDS and that a romance was out of the question with anybody, and that would be that.

But that wasn't that. Harrison hadn't blinked an eye, suspecting something of the sort already. "Why else is a thirty-one-year-old gay man free three times a week during the day to take a Roman history class?" he'd asked.

Harrison had been a lifesaver in more ways than one. He was someone to talk to who was intelligent; someone who took him to plays and art films and museums and always had something perceptive to say about anything they experienced. His solicitude over John's health had been endearing, always making sure to remind him to take pills, gently chiding him for eating poorly or running up the charge cards, making heads and tails out of confusing (for John) articles on the science behind new developments in HIV therapy. Ten years John's senior, he had become a father figure to a young man who had been at sea.

But what was endearingly gentle chiding when John had been indigent and facing death was quite another thing now that he was healthy and self-sufficient. Now it felt like he was being nannied to death. He resented Harrison's lectures on the charge cards, his clucking over the cost of the bodybuilding supplements. "And," John finished explaining to Kevin, "he has totally *decided* on our vacation, and it's the last thing I want to do."

"What are you doing tonight?" Kevin asked abruptly.

"Nothing, as usual. Why do you ask?"

"We're all going out for drinks tonight, me and Ethan and a bunch of people—you know most of them. Why don't you come along? You sound like you could use a boys' night out."

John thought about it for all of a second. "You're right. You're absolutely right! I'm going to go out and have some fun and that old stick can stay at home and snuggle up with Ken Burns for all I care!''

When John returned home, Harrison was gone, as was their arrangement—John cleaned house on Saturdays and it was too difficult to clean around someone. Where Harrison might be was a mystery, what with school now officially over for the summer.

He scoured the bathroom, wishing he had the courage to talk about things with Harrison. Hell, how could he talk about extramarital sex when he still couldn't raise the issue of changing the cleaning duties? It had been one thing for him to be the housewife in the family when he had been on disability. But now that he was working full-time and trying to cram a demanding gym regimen in on top of that, it seemed only fair that Harrison pick up some of the cleaning, especially since their roles were to be reversed for the next three months. But it seemed to him that Harrison should *just know,* that he shouldn't have to *ask* him to share in the household chores. And so he hadn't brought it up, waiting for Harrison to realize what the right thing was to do.

What if I weren't married right now? he thought idly, a little chill going up his spine. *I'd probably still be in bed, with a hangover from a wild Friday night of partying. And not alone, either. I turned down two incredibly gorgeous men yesterday,* he thought incredulously. *First Tim, then that guy Eric. And for what?* he wondered bitterly. *So I could be here to clean this house!*

He turned his attention to Harrison's desk. This was usually a no-man's-land. Harrison kept a mysteriously ordered clutter that would be disrupted by any reorganization from tidier hands. John, however, was in no mood today to tiptoe around. He started shoveling bills into a pile, when he froze at the sight of an unearthed airline envelope.

He picked it up. It had already been opened. He pulled out the contents, turning red with anger as he perused them. Two plane tickets to Atlanta! In his and Harrison's name! "Goddamit!" he shouted, startling their cat, Rafsanjani, who was already edgy at the sight of the vacuum cleaner.

Unbelievable. Unbelievable! He moved to put the tickets back in their place in the pile, then thought, screw it. He threw them down on top without putting them back in the envelope.

"I need some air," he said out loud, and he made for the door.

Walking down Castro Street today was no love-in; John was scowling furiously all the way down, just like the sullen beauties he'd so resented before this year. No smiles today for interested sidelong looks or blatantly needy stares, nothing but an angry focus on a fixed point far ahead of him.

I am not going! he wanted to shout. *Especially now that he's gone around my back!* He stalked up the street, focusing on nothing but his rage until a poster caught the corner of his eye in the window of the travel agency: "BABYLON: The ultimate gay resort destination, where fantasies become reality." The poster featured a gaggle of chiseled hunks under a waterfall, laughing in black and white, the only color in the photo their Day-Glo Speedos. *Now that's my kind of vacation.* He laughed, then sobered as it hit him.

Dare I?

He went into the travel agency and asked for a brochure.

The friendly agent gave him a large glossy booklet which he took to Pasqua to peruse over coffee. "BABYLON: The name conjures a lost civilization, a lost art of luxury amid green splendor. BABYLON: An all-inclusive resort where your wish is our command. BABYLON: An all-male resort where the only limits are the limits of your imagination."

He pored over the photos of the resort, a large hotel on the Mexican Riviera, built in the style of the ancient Aztec pyramids. The brochure seduced him with a vision of a pleasure dome with constantly served buffets, open bars, a series of swimming pools connected by waterfalls and slides, windsurfing and snorkeling and sailing and, of course lots of pictures of men, men, men. They were all buff and chiseled and smiling and laughing and drinking and eating and dancing all night in the giant disco. . . . "Yeah," he said out loud. startling himself.

"At BABYLON, we know that you come to BABYLON to escape everything . . . and everyone." *Hear, hear!* John applauded. "Our packages start at just $799 per person for a week you'll never forget."

That's not so bad, John thought, even as he mentally calculated the addition of the single supplement charge. *I don't have that much cash, but I've got plenty of credit on those cards, what with Harrison making me use all my money to pay them down. . . . What the hell,* he thought angrily. *He made plans without asking me, why shouldn't I make a plan without asking him!*

For a moment he thought of sleeping on it before spending that kind of money, not to mention the fact that it would be a shot over Harrison's bow, but then he thought, to hell with it! *Harrison fired the first shot so if it was war, so be it. Besides,* he thought, *I don't want to talk myself out of this, even if it's the wrong thing to do!*

He marched back to the travel agency and sat down with the guy who'd given him the brochure. Within half an hour, he had booked a week at Babylon and a plane ticket, and all this only two weeks before the date of the event (Babylon not being an actual, permanent gay destination but more a package deal whereby a group of gay people took over an otherwise innocuous resort and did things their straight replacements a week later would never dream of). *I'm going to go, and I'm going to have fun!* he shouted to himself, smiling now on his way back up the street.

Back at home, Harrison was on the couch, looking sheepish. "Hello," John said, too happy to be upset anymore.

"I see you found the tickets."

"Yes."

"John, I wanted to surprise you. . . ."

"That you did, booking a trip that I hope you enjoy."

"You're not going."

"No, I'm not. I've made other plans."

"What do you mean?"

"I've made other plans," John said flatly. "I'm going on a trip by myself. I just went and *charged it* at the travel agency," he said, unable to resist the display of his reckless impecuniousness.

"I can change the tickets for fifty bucks," Harrison offered. "We can go to New York."

"It's too late," John said, implacably, meeting Harrison eye to eye. "I've made other plans and I'm going to stick to them."

Harrison sighed. "I am sorry, John. I made a mistake."

"Yes, you did."

"And you're not going to let me make it up to you?"

"I don't need you to make it up to me, Harrison. I'm going to do something I want to do that *you'd* never do in a million years."

He could see that his partner was dying to ask him about his plans, but he held back. "Well, I hope you enjoy yourself, too," Harrison offered, flinching at the lameness of his reply.

"I will. And now I am going to go see a very long movie and then I am going out with some friends. Don't expect me home early." And with that he grabbed his coat (like any veteran San Franciscan, he knew that 2 P.M.'s heat wave was no barrier to 10 P.M.'s freezing fog) and was out the door.

He felt an agonizing pang from his conflict with Harrison; he loved the guy but Godammit, he couldn't let him run his life. *So I went out and did it—I did it!* he thought. He couldn't say what he'd done, exactly, only that he'd broken free of something, that he had been standing at the door he'd worked so hard to reach and now that door was about to open and he would walk into a whole new world.

John went and saw a movie and arrived at Ethan and Kevin's house around nine o'clock, to find the roommates and their friends

"I can't go dressed like this," John protested.

Kevin came up behind his chair and whispered in his ear, "Well, Cinderella, I bet I have a couple things in my closet that would look mighty fine on you."

"Yeah!" Ethan chorused. "We'll be your fairy godmothers!"

"More like the mice," John muttered, but before he knew it he'd been shuttled into Kevin's room. Kevin first pulled out a wild Versace vest. "I think this, with no shirt. Everybody agree?"

"Absolutely not," John vetoed the vest. "You can get arrested for wearing Versace after you're over thirty."

"Amen!" Aaron assented, which almost immediately made John regret turning it down.

"Okay," Kevin continued, "but you only get three strikes, and then you have to wear what I say."

"I don't regret using a strike on that one. Come on, Kevin, you know me. No more Versace, okay?"

"Hmm." Kevin rummaged through his closet. "Aha!" He pulled out a black knit Calvin Klein v-neck T-shirt. "Here, try this on."

John examined the shirt—it was basically conservative, but appealing. He pulled his shirt off to try it on.

"Wow, John, nice pecs!" Ethan said admiringly. "You know, I've never seen you without your shirt. I've really been missing out!"

"I owe them all to Kevin," John replied, with a laugh. "And they're nothing next to Kev's. Remember that article in the *Times* magazine I told you about, that talked about Chelsea muscle boys with 'pecs the size of sautee pans'? That's our Kev." He smiled, the liquor loosening him up.

"Nah," Ted said, with a twinkle in his eye. "You've got better cuts on yours. No offense." He nodded to Kevin.

"None taken, but then, you're not flirting with *me*. And John does have nice pecs, doesn't he?"

John flushed and smiled. "Why, thank you, boys." He pulled the shirt on and looked in the mirror. In typical CK fashion, the short sleeves were very short, to show off all that arm work, and the waist was fitted, making his broad shoulders look even broader. "I like it," John said.

"You sound so surprised," Kevin said.

"I haven't been shopping for clothes since . . . 'It' happened. I mean, I got new jeans, but I kept all my old shirts, didn't see any reason to ditch them. So, this is the first time I've put on anything . . . revealing."

"You are a hunk," Ethan said admiringly.

John looked at himself in the mirror. *I would do me in a second,* he thought with amazement.

"You can wear those baggy jeans if you want," Kevin said. "But I have some that would fit you a whole lot better."

"No, this is fine. One toe into the water at a time, please." He laughed, and gulped. Looking like this, at a club like that—something was as likely as not to happen a whole lot sooner than his trip to Babylon. "Can I have a refill on my drink?"

"Liquid courage coming right up," Ethan said, going for the bottle. "Look out world, Johnny Eames is about to have his coming-out party!"

Before John could reconsider, they piled into a cab and headed to Club Universe. The place was already packed when they got there at ten o'clock. "There's a line," John said disconsolately.

"Don't worry," Kevin said, "it moves fast."

Looking around in line, John was relieved to see that his party wasn't the oldest there! Though, of course, it was the parties of the youngest and most beautiful who swept past the line to be admitted off the list. John noted wryly that there were plenty of people whose eyes were glittering from more than excitement.

The Stoli kept everything too blurry and blunted to scrape on his nerves, and idle chatter with his friends made the wait seem short. He was nervous and excited and was glad he'd had a few stiff ones before taking on this expedition. He consoled himself with the fact that he was here with friends, and therefore safe. Before he knew it, they were in.

The beat, audible outside, was now a force to be reckoned with in his bones. The lobby was packed with sweating boys, many of whom already had their shirts tucked into their back pockets. Unlike a bar, where eyes automatically turned to new arrivals, the chaos in the club was such that nobody noticed them.

John had picked up porn magazines, and fashion magazines, and was accustomed to seeing beauty in print and on TV, but to see so much of it in person! There was no time to obsess on any one face before it was gone, replaced with one even more magnificent. San Francisco was not a media center where beauty could be made into a career, but it was the gay mecca. As such, it drew many beautiful young men who wished only to be young and gay and to party.

"Come on." Kevin pulled him forward. "Let's warm up with a dance." John was too disoriented to protest. He let Kev lead him into the main room, where he went into complete sensory overload. Lights flashed, music pounded, and all around him were all the objects of a lifetime's desire, all packed into one night. The mix segued into an anthem everyone else seemed to know from the first note, as they sent up a scream of communal ecstasy. An unmistakably black diva began wailing out lyrics of redemption and transformation, and John was pulled into the thick of the dancing mob by Kevin.

John danced awkwardly, shuffling his feet and holding his arms in. His nervousness was broken by amusement as he watched a shirtless beef god move stiffly to the beat, not moving his feet but only swiveling at the hips, holding his arms at forty-five degree angles. All the better to keep his pecs squeezed at all times, John thought, so they look bigger! The sight of the stiff gymbot, and the laugh it gave him, loosened him up a little, and he began to move a little less stiffly himself.

He looked around some more, checking out the other dancers as he was checked out in turn. It was so different from a bar, where people would positively *glare* at you to express interest, or the street, where a look unbroken long enough was bound to turn into a smile. Here the glances were so fluid, so quickly on you and gone again. Well, he thought, there was so much to see, how could anyone concentrate on one person!

John divided the dancers into groups: the guys dancing with friends, who seemed to be the only ones laughing and smiling; the cruisers, who danced only enough to justify their place on the floor while they searched out potential partners (to be hit on later, off the floor); and the serious dancers, their eyes on heaven if not outright shut, their whole bodies absorbed in the music and the dance, oblivious to anyone around them.

John noticed one exception to the cruising rule, a guy who was looking at him from several yards away. He was tall, sandy-blond-haired, handsome, and very young-looking, with blue eyes and a nice smile. John smiled back and looked away, but when he looked back, the young man's attention was still on him. He was grinning now. John laughed and waved at him; the boy saluted smartly. "You're having fun!" Kevin said.

"I really am!" At certain points in the song an air raid siren would go off and everyone would wave their hands or their shirts over their heads. John found himself waving his arms above his head with the rest of the crowd, occasionally exchanging a grin with the blond boy.

The reason for Kevin's devotion to cardio work was obvious as John's energy flagged. "I need water," he said, and Kevin waved him off.

"Go ahead, I'll look for you."

So John made his way to the bar, separated from everyone he'd come with. After an interminable wait he ordered two bottles of water and an orange Stoli for a total cost of almost ten bucks. He quickly slammed down the first bottle of water.

"You'd think you could get free water," he grumbled to himself.

"After the bar closes they put out pitchers of ice water," a voice next to him said. John turned and found the speaker to be the very boy who had smiled at him on the dance floor. "But before that, there's too much money to be made on all the guys getting all twisted and dehydrated on X."

"Hey!" John said, laughing.

"Hey, yourself. Here, let me hold one of those for you so I can shake your hand. I'm Brian."

"Hi, I'm John."

"Nice to meet you. I haven't seen you here before."

"I've never been."

"Are you from out of town?"

John rolled his eyes. "No. I've lived here eight years, actually."

"Whoa! And you never go out?"

"Let's just say I didn't used to look like this. So, since amazingly good-looking young men weren't going to come up and talk to me like they do now, I didn't bother."

"Thanks for the compliment. But just because you couldn't get laid is no reason to stay home. Don't you like to dance?"

"I do now." John smiled. "Now that I look good doing it."

Brian laughed. "You wanna prove that?"

"Can I finish my drink first?"

"Just chug it," he said, grinning wickedly.

"It's pure vodka!" John exclaimed.

"All the better."

"You are dangerous," John said slyly.

Brian smiled. "If that's your idea of danger, you've got a lot to learn."

"And you're just the man to teach me, right?"

"Drink up."

John sighed and tipped the glass back, knocking off the Stoli in two searing gulps. "Aaargh! It burns!"

"Now you're ready, let's go." Brian took his hand and pulled him back to the dance floor. He crossed paths with Kevin, who only raised an eyebrow as he passed. John wanted to stop and explain but then realized, what would the explanation be? He laughed and let it go.

Brian moved well, fluidly swaying to the beat and showing off all his physical assets for John. He was an inch taller than John, not as muscular but well-proportioned, and boyishly handsome. "So, are you here alone?" Brian asked, leaning over to shout in John's ear.

"No, with friends," John shouted back. "Though God knows where they are. And you?"

"I usually come with friends, but I'm on my own tonight. They're all at a birthday party for someone I hate, but I don't like to miss a single weekend here, even if I have to come alone. Something fun always happens, guaranteed." He smiled at John.

"I believe it," John said. "Unless I'm just having beginner's luck."

Brian laughed. "A guy as hot as you, it ain't luck, believe me."

John flushed. "My turn to thank you for the compliment."

The tempo changed and a new song began. The crowd screamed. In a flash just about every shirt was torn off, some even thrown in the air.

"What's going on?" he asked Brian, who took off his own shirt as John spoke. He took the time to admire Brian's body—a boy's body just fleshing out into a man's, with nice definition on his smooth, lean frame.

"Take off your shirt!" Brian said.

"What?!"

"It's part of the dance that goes with this song, you have to take off your shirt!"

"But. . ."

"Listen, everyone else is naked and you are wearing a black T-shirt! If you're worried about standing out in the crowd, believe me, you will definitely stand out if you don't take off your shirt!"

Aggrieved, John sighed. Once again he was on the verge of shouting "I'm not ready!" but then the Stoli he'd knocked back kicked him in the ass and he thought, *Screw it, I'm as ready as I'll ever be.* And he pulled his shirt off.

"Wow! Nice chest!" Brian said, clearly delighted with the unwrapped package.

As the song went into the chorus, Brian placed his hands on John's shoulders, just as all around them other dancers were doing the same. John watched to see if he was supposed to put his hands on Brian's shoulders, and seeing that he was, he did just that. Then Brian flipped his hands over and ran the back of his fingers over John's chest, flipping them again to grab his waist, John following suit half a beat behind. "It's like the Macarena for gropers!" he shouted.

Brian grabbed his hand, twirled him around, and pulled John's hips against his own, with one hand on John's ass. They were flat up against each other, abs to abs, and he found himself looking into Brian's eyes, where an invitation—no, an *intent*—lay waiting for him. The other dancers parted at the end of the chorus but Brian and John stayed locked together. John parted his lips, and Brian took his cue quickly. As the other dancers swirled around them, John and Brian kissed.

The effect on John was electric. The softness of Brian's skin under his fingers, the caress of his lips as he got a kiss like no kiss he'd ever had before. Yes, the part of his brain that hadn't reverted to a primal state managed to think, *I've never been kissed like this, not ever.* A flick of motion of Brian's lips and John exploded, his hands all over Brian, hips pressed against hips, a flick of tongue between his teeth like a blasting cap, setting off a thousand fireworks.

"Do you live alone?" Brian asked.

"No," John answered, with a pained flush. *I should tell him I have a lover,* he thought, *but that would be saying no, wouldn't it?* A part of his brain asked sarcastically, *What happened to taking it one step at a time, what happened to having it out with Harrison first?* But the effect of the music and the touch of Brian's skin was activating brain centers constitutionally immune to sarcasm.

"I do," Brian offered. There was no thought in John's head other than *My God, he's so beautiful.* And Brian really was beautiful, especially when projecting the whole force of all the glamour a young man can project on the object of his desire. "Do you want to say goodbye to your friends?"

"No, one of them saw me with you. He'll know what happened."

"Cool. So you're ready to go?"

"Hell, yes," John said. "Let's go."

"Wow," Brian said outside, "it's really nice out."

He was right. It was one of those rare evenings in San Francisco where a warm day had become a pleasant evening. John's leather jacket was just right for the night; he might have been too cold without it later on, but it was just right for now. "Did you drive?" John asked.

"No, took a cab. Hey, the Bay is right down the street. What do you say we take a little walk?"

"Sure, that sounds great."

They were at the waterfront in no time. "I've never been down here at night," John said.

"You really don't get out much, do you?" Brian laughed.

"It's not that, it's . . . well, no. I guess not," he finished sheepishly. "I guess I'm just an old stick."

"It's never too late to change your ways."

"So I'm discovering." The black water of the Bay lapped in sighs against the breakfront and shimmered with reflected light from the Bay Bridge. They walked up the Embarcadero, enjoying the brisk chill off the water. "So how long have you lived here?" John asked Brian.

"Just about nine months now, since I left school."

"Where were you going to school?"

"Back East," he said vaguely, and John didn't press. In his own naive youth he'd once dated a boy who'd only say he'd gone to school "in Connecticut"; John had imagined some charming little school until he learned that Yale was in Connecticut. He'd admired the guy for not shoving his Ivy League education in people's faces.

"Why'd you leave school?"

Brian shrugged. "I was a year away from a degree in marketing and I realized that working in marketing or advertising was the last thing I wanted to do."

"Right," John said. "It's kind of . . . manipulative, if not evil."

Brian laughed. "Exactly! Messing with people's heads, preying on their insecurities, then telling them buying this or that is gonna make it all better. I did it because my dad wouldn't pay for art school, said if I wanted to be creative I should get a degree in something creative that would also pay the bills. So I said I'd go into advertising; I guess I even convinced myself I would for a while."

"Wow, art school. A visual artist, huh?"

"A cartoonist, actually. I mean, that's what I do. I draw, that's what I would've done at some advertising agency."

"Are you good?"

Brian laughed. "I'm pretty good, I had a strip in the school paper. I'll show you some of them if you want."

"I'd love to see them. I respect creativity, I wish I had some kind of gift. I do graphic design on the computer for a living, desktop publishing . . ."

"That's great."

"It's not art or even artistic. Hell, I can't draw a stick person! But at least it's not something that helps destroy the world, you know."

"Really."

"So what are you doing now?"

"Just living on some money I got from my grandma and trying to get into Academy of Art College, if I can get loans and grants for it."

"How old are you?"

Brian laughed. "Old enough to drink, smoke, and screw, and young enough to think none of it'll ever hurt me."

John chuckled. "Wise beyond your years."

"I'm twenty-one."

"Ohmigod," John said, having known from the first moment on the dance floor that Brian was obviously much younger but not . . . *that* young. "Well, I'm thirty-three," he said, as if that put the nail in the coffin.

"That's cool. I like older guys. Not so much older that they're all dried up and set in their ways, but, you know, old enough to have a clue. Most guys my age, well, they're okay for friends but they'd get on my nerves as boyfriends, you know?"

"Really, huh. I think younger guys are pretty hot, myself." Which, as of tonight, was quite true.

"Yeah? Cool."

They walked in silence for a while after that. "Are you getting tired?" Brian asked. "I thought we'd just keep walking up to Aquatic Park if that's okay with you. I live not far from there."

"Sure," John said, not feeling tired at all. "That sounds great."

They made it to Aquatic Park at Fisherman's Wharf in no time, or so it seemed. They walked down the long pier that curved out into the Bay. The fog was creeping in late tonight, just rolling in under the Golden Gate Bridge. The light from the lighthouse on

Alcatraz swept over them and across the black water. John shivered from the approaching cold, and Brian put his hand around his waist; John put his hand around Brian's shoulder. Then the cold came from inside, in the form of a sudden thought. *Shit,* he realized, *we're going to his place and I haven't mentioned the big A yet.* "You know, before we do anything, there's something I need to tell you."

"So am I," Brian cut him off.

John looked at him agape.

"You're HIV positive, right? That's what you were going to tell me."

"But you're only twenty-one!" John protested.

Brian sighed, looking out to sea. "Like I said, I like older guys. When I was a freshman in college, I met this guy. I grew up in a small town in Texas, so there wasn't a whole lot you could do without everybody knowing about it. So when I went off to school, I was ready for just about anything, I was so horny. Anyway, the long and short of it was that this guy said he was negative, and I believed him, so we did it without rubbers. Then one day I'm over at his house and I find a bottle of AZT with his name on it."

"Oh, shit."

"That's what I said. So I confronted him and he confessed."

"That's unbelievable. He lied to you all that time!"

"He was all rationalizing and shit, you know—'We used lube with nonoxynol-9 and that kills HIV, and I never came inside you; well not very many times, blah blah blah.' So I took the test and, of course, I was positive."

"Jesus."

Brian shrugged. "Shit happens. I mean, that's why I quit school, so it was a good thing. I thought, I'm gonna get this degree so I can go to work in some fucking job I hate selling detergent and then I'm gonna die? Screw that."

"Absolutely. God."

"How long have you been positive?"

"Since practically right after I moved here, like in 1989. I wasn't that cute, but, you know, when you're that young you're cute enough for some people. And so I got laid a lot for a while there. I don't know, I wasn't too careful. I guess all my friends were positive and I just figured it was inevitable."

"You've kept your health, though, obviously."

John laughed. "Looks are deceiving, believe me. No, I was pretty sick for a while. You name it, I had it. I was lucky, I was strong. There was never anything I had so bad that I had to be hospitalized for it, everything was something that could be taken care of with drugs. Then I got on a protease cocktail and everything turned around. Are you taking anything?"

Brian shrugged. "Not yet. My viral load's pretty low and I figure, better to wait until my body can't fight it as well anymore and not waste all my ammo now."

John bit his tongue, wanting to shout, "You have to hit it early and hard!" But forebearing—you couldn't dictate anyone else's health decisions. "Besides," Brian continued, "I don't have any insurance, so how would I pay for them?"

"You could get on ADAP, the AIDS drug program through the state, or you could get MRMIP, that's what I've got, the Blue Cross program that's paid for half by MediCal and half by Blue Cross. You could get a job at Starbucks, they've got health insurance for everyone, even part-timers. . . ."

Brian laughed. "You're a wealth of information. I need to get you to write all this down."

"Hey, if you're going to be HIV positive, this is the town to be in. They won't let you die, that's for sure."

"And now look at you—you look like you've never been sick a day in your life."

"Weird, huh? Now I have a good-paying job, a bitchin' bod, if I do say so myself. . . ." He laughed.

Brian moved his hand lower. "Yeah, you do. I wanna take it home and undress it."

John turned to face Brian, the intensity in Brian's eyes was a wonder to him. And Harrison was as far from his thoughts at this moment as his elderly aunt. "I already know you feel good with half your clothes off, I'm dying to see what you feel like with all of them off."

Brian smiled. "C'mon, let's go find out."

CHAPTER THREE

It was strange waking up in bed alone, John thought. He still got out of bed stealthily, out of habit, even though Harrison was gone off on his Civil War vacation and there was nobody to wake up. On his way out of the bedroom, he had to stop himself from automatically shutting the door behind him to block out the noise of the TV and the coffee grinder.

He did his crunches but no push-ups (it would be a chest workout tonight at the gym and there was no point in overdoing it), made coffee, and called Patsy.

"*Mmmmggph.*"

"It's time. Get up."

"Oooh, you are in a worse mood this morning than I am," Patsy said.

"Let's just say I am not feeling warm and fuzzy today."

"Harrison's gone, isn't he?"

"Yup. I'm surprised he didn't leave me one of those damn letters he cries over—'My dearest John, I am off to battle and may ne'er see you again, give my love to that banjo twanging in the background.'"

Patsy cackled. "No romantic foolishness for you."

"That's not true," John said, thinking not of Harrison but of Brian. "There's just a difference between romance and schmaltz."

"Schmaltz made this country great."

"It made Hallmark a going concern, that's for sure."

"Okay, I'll come in if you'll go out with me for a drink after work."

"I would, but I'm leaving early. I have a doctor's appointment."

"Anything wrong?"

"Nah, he would've called me if there was anything funky in my last blood work. This is just to get blood drawn and check in with him, go over the results from last time if there's anything to go over."

"That's good. So you won't even be there all day to brighten my vista. Definitely a good day to call in sick."

"Oh, God, don't do that. Did I tell you about the last temp we had? I don't know where they get them. She answers the phone: 'Umm . . . hello? Umm . . . Obelisk Incorporated? I don't know, I'm just a temp.' What a nightmare. She's the reason Obelisk broke down and got us the second line so we can get dialed direct now. I gave her a brochure and said, 'Call a messenger.' She looks at me and says, get this, 'I don't know how to do that.' Duh!"

Patsy laughed. "See, they don't appreciate me until I'm not there, the cheap bastards."

"Well, I appreciate you, okay? I'll stop at Eppler's and pick up something gooey if it'll motivate you."

"Oh, baby."

"Excellent. Now get your ass out of bed and get to work."

John worked diligently on a new project, a brochure designed to showcase Mr. Obelisk's latest venture, a casino in Vegas, but his mind kept wandering. He had been in complete turmoil since the episode with Brian a week earlier.

John hadn't had a lot of sex, at least not by the standards of the average urban gay man of his age, but he'd had a good measure of it. And he could think of one, maybe two instances in his past that had measured up to what he'd had with Brian that night. Though John was the older of the two, it had been Brian who had been the smooth one—pouring them each a glass of wine, putting the Chet Baker record on the stereo (which, in truth, was so smooth it made John giggle, though he quashed it before Brian could notice), settling down next to him on the couch to show John his cartoons (which were quite funny and done in a unique visual style), casually making the first move, leading the way into the bedroom.

The sex had been . . . an event. Truly great sex, he reflected, was like being underwater; you just *forgot* about everything except the amazing sensations you were feeling. The kisses took you deeper and deeper, and when you came up for air, it was only to stare at the face of your fellow swimmer, himself gasping and drugged from lack of oxygen. He had sat on Brian, looking down on his beautiful lean body, encompassing it with his strong legs, marveling at his conquest. And Brian had sat on him, John marveling at the vast expanse of his shoulders and how small his waist was in comparison.

They had gone on for hours, climaxing, nestling, talking about everything—growing up, lovers, jobs. And then, recharged, their hands had started moving again, and another round would begin. Time had no meaning and it was dawn when they fell asleep in each other's arms.

John woke up at two that Sunday afternoon in a panic. *Ohmigod, Harrison!* He could have been dead for all his partner knew. "I have to get going," he said to Brian, dressing hastily.

Brian eyed him lazily from the bed. "I thought so."

"Huh?"

"That you were married."

John sat down. "Yeah. I mean, I was. I honestly don't know anymore."

"You still live with him, though."

"Yeah. . . ."

"You're still married, then."

John sighed. "I should have told you."

"No, you didn't need to tell me that. I appreciate your being honest about the HIV. I mean, that was important. It was just a screw, you didn't have to tell me your domestic situation."

"Oh," John said sheepishly.

"So, can I have your number, or is that a no-no?"

"Sure you can. Of course." He hastily wrote his number down and took Brian's in return.

"Just a screw" rang in his head the whole way home. But it had felt like . . . it had felt like what he thought love was supposed to feel like. He loved Harrison, but this was different. This was the passionate, romantic love that pop culture had shoved down his throat all his life, making him feel bad for not having experienced it. The intensity of it!

Could this be what life was really like for *them*, he wondered, the hot guys he'd seen all these years from the other side of the glass, and finally up close last night. Did they have encounters like this every weekend? Did the earth move all night, every time? Was this incredible pleasure, so rare and precious to him, just as commonplace in this new world they took for granted? He couldn't help stabbing himself with the thought—does Brian have sex like that every time he goes out?

At home, it was his turn to be the apologetic errant partner. "Hi," he said to Harrison. "I'm sorry, I should have called."

"I paged Kevin, he called and told me you were okay," Harrison said, looking away and furtively pushing his Bruce Catton book down between the cushions.

"Oh. Good." He suddenly flushed as Harrison looked him up and down; he was still wearing the skintight black T-shirt from last night. "Uh, I need to shower and change, I'll just be a minute."

"Fine."

"Listen to the expert!" Patsy cracked.

"Hey, I've lived in this town for eight years, there ain't a pastry shop in town worth its salt whose products I don't know backward and forward. Il Fornaio for the cinnamon twist sticks, which are like ninety-five percent butter; Just Desserts for brownies; Suzanne's Muffins for, duh!, muffins, and SF Sconeworks for scones. I'm just going to put this one in the microwave for about seven seconds," he said, selecting a chocolate chip scone, "flip it over, seven more seconds, flip for seven more, and I suggest you all do the same if you want the full, gooey experience."

Soon they were all settled down with their goodies, chomping silently for the most part. "I need to work out if I'm gonna keep eating like this," Patsy complained.

"Have a cup of coffee," John suggested. "Caffeine has thermogenic properties."

"Say what?"

"It speeds up your metabolism, helps you burn fat."

"So I can eat everything I want as long as I drink coffee with it? Excellent!"

John laughed. "No, no! But it helps."

Miss Plinth practically started out of her chair, her wide eyes suddenly wider with frantic alarm. "Oh! John, you're leaving on vacation soon—did you get a temp lined up from the agency?"

"You know that girl who answered the phone when Pats was out? She s coming in." Watching Miss Plinth turn pale, he laughed. "I'm kidding you. No, MacTemps is sending in someone to hold the fort while I'm gone, though you know how Obelisk is. The temp'll sit there for two weeks doing absolutely nothing, no matter how much work comes in, and then when I come back . . ."

"He'll pile it on." She nodded. "Well, that's a sign of how much Mr. Obelisk depends on you, John."

"Hey," Annabelle asked, "where are you going on vacation?"

John smiled and stretched languorously. "Mexico, darling."

"Wow, you and the hubby, huh?"

Patsy nudged her roughly in the side. "Ixnay on the acationvay. Not to mention the ubbyhay."

"No, we're doing our own thing this year." *And maybe forever,* he thought. He finished off his scone. "Okay, kids, I'm off. Don't eat too much."

"Hell," Patsy said, "if we didn't eat too much, what would we do for fun?"

Dr. Richards had been John's doc for eight years, ever since John had been hospitalized with a mysterious fever that, looking back on it years later, he and Dr. Richards now surmised was his seroconversion experience. The doctor had been there when John had tested positive, and continued over the years as they helplessly watched his T-cells dwindle, as well as the day he'd had to tell John that the flu that wouldn't go away was pneumocystis pneumonia and that he had AIDS. The doc had been an angry man in those years; he'd lost his own partner and seemed to see his patients only so that he could tick off their decline in an orderly manner.

But so much had changed in the last year and a half. John had been one of the first patients Dr. Richards had put on protease inhibitors. He'd done a baseline viral load test the day he'd written the scrips, which had revealed a shockingly high viral load of nearly one million. "You should be dead, you know," Dr. Richards said, looking at him with black humor shining in his sharply glittering eyes. "As it is, you haven't even been hospitalized. You've got some strong constitution, I'll say that. I'm going to put you on this new drug combination and we'll see what happens. No guarantees," he'd said sharply, "but the initial news is good."

But it was a pleasure to see Dr. Richards now. Not only was John happier, so was the doc, who no longer spent as much time in the hospital by the bedsides of sick and dying patients. That was reason enough to be happier, but Richards had also found love with a younger man, Hart, who was not only his lover now but one of his nurses. Hart had come in as a temp through the registry and suddenly Dr. Richards, who'd developed a reputation at the hospital as a notoriously cruel berater of those he perceived as incompetent, was now a vastly more cheerful and tolerant man.

Seeing John come in, Hart clucked at him. "You are late. Come right in."

"He's always late, so I thought, why should I come on time and cool my heels?"

"We had two cancellations this afternoon, which has put him on time." He ushered John into an exam room and shut the door. "Let's get your vitals."

Well versed in the rituals of a doctor's visit, John lifted his tongue to accept the disposable thermometer and got on the scale. "Wow," Hart said, "one hundred ninety-five pounds. All beef, too!"

"Ass wi' the boos," John said through the thermometer, indicating his Timberlands.

"So we take off five pounds, that's still one hundred ninety. Honestly, John, you look better every time you come in here."

"T'anks."

"What dose are you doing of the testosterone?" He plucked the thermometer out of John's mouth.

"Umm, one-point-five milliliters every two weeks. And a bottle of deca every two weeks. And just about every supplement known to man. Creatine, glutamine, HMB, whatever else they've got."

"Our gym is full of queens like you, spending the gross national product of Peru every month on bodybuilding supplements."

"They're not cheap," John agreed, getting up on the table, "but if women can spend all their money on Shiseido and M.A.C., why can't I spend all my money on TwinLabs and EAS?"

"They obviously work," Hart said, taking John's blood pressure. "Are you doing your own shots?"

"Since I went back to work." Self-administering testosterone had not been an easy skill to learn; injecting yourself not just in the ass but in the right place in the ass every two weeks was a skill developed over time. Still, it had become impractical to leave work early twice a month just to get a shot, and so the skill had to be mastered. *Amazing what you can do when you have to,* John thought.

"Damn, now that your ass is so fine I don't have any reason to ask you to take down your pants." Hart winked.

"Who wanted to see it before, right?"

Consternation overtook Hart's features. "Oh, I didn't mean . . ."

John put up a hand. "Never mind. I'm just still getting used to having an ass people want to see out of pants, so forgive me for being a little cynical."

"Listen, it's not the ass, it's the man behind it. Wait, that didn't come out right!"

John laughed. "Maybe not, but that's true, too!"

They were interrupted by a knock on the door and Dr. Richards came in. "Everybody decent?"

"I haven't been decent since my eighteenth birthday," Hart cracked.

"I know all about you," the doc said with a smile. "How's the patient?"

"See for yourself." He handed Dr. Richards the chart. "One-twenty over eighty, 98.9, and one hundred ninety with the boots off, yee-haw!"

"Thank you. Begone, please," he said with an indulgent smile. "How are you feeling?" he asked after Hart left.

"Fabulous," John replied honestly. "No complaints."

The doc flipped through John's chart. "Your blood work is fine, viral load still undetectable, white count still low. Are you still doing Neupogen?"

"Half a bottle a week."

"Your testosterone levels are out of the subnormal range and into the normal range. How are you tolerating the shots?"

"Tolerating!" John said with mock shock. "Why, I don't know what I'd do without them. Seriously, they're a lifesaver," he added.

"Yes, they are. Are you still on antidepressants?"

"No, testosterone seems to be all the antidepressant I need right now."

"Yeah? 'Elevated mood,' " he wrote in the chart, speaking his notes out loud as he always did with his patients. " 'Patient responding well . . . no, fabulously to anabolic therapy. Return visit in two months.' I never see you anymore, I miss you, you're one of my favorite patients."

"Why, thank you. But isn't that a good thing that I don't have to see you all the time anymore?"

"Absolutely. You could always drop in and say hi, you know." The doc smiled at John, prompting him to think, *Is even my doctor flirting with me now?!*

He found his voice. "Unfortunately, I've gotten so much better under your care that I had to go back to work, so I don't have the leisure time I used to."

"You're looking wonderful," the doc said, shutting the chart. "Whatever you're doing, keep it up."

"Clean living and fresh air," John cracked.

"Don't underestimate the value of that," Richards replied. "See you in two months."

After that, it was off to the gym to meet Kevin, whom he found (of course) on the StairMaster.

"Can't we just do the treadmill?" John complained, punching his weight into the machine.

"That doesn't get your heart rate up as high as the StairMaster," Kevin said assuredly. "You don't want to get fat again, do you?"

"Heaven forbid. But I thought muscle burned fat on its own, so the more muscle you have . . ."

"It does, but I know you, John, you're not the rice cakes and chicken breast type."

"You got that," John admitted, thinking of the chocolate chip scone.

"So if you want to stay lean and still eat, you have to do cardio. Cardio work elevates your metabolism for . . ."

"For a full twenty-four hours after your workout. I know, I know. But it's so *boring.*"

"You could always join the step aerobics class instead."

"Oh, yes, me and a bunch of ponytailed X rays who come in wearing full makeup and never crack a sweat, let alone a smile. No, thank you."

John complained no further; he knew that Kevin's pushing had been essential to his success in the gym. At first, he'd put on muscle easily, the steroids making up for a lifetime of testosterone deficiency, but he'd hit a plateau quickly. For instance, his bench press was stuck at an embarrassingly measly fifty pounds, not because his pecs were weak but because his shoulders tended to fail before his chest did. Having injured his rotator cuff years earlier, he avoided doing exercises that would strengthen his delts because the work was too painful. It had been Kevin who had coached him through the first agonizing weeks of shoulder work, but it had been worth it when his bench press had doubled in only a few weeks. If Kevin said he would magically get fat overnight if he stopped doing cardio, he wasn't going to argue.

At long last, the grueling twenty-five minutes were over and they could move onto the weights, which John loved to do. But tonight his heart wasn't in it, he failed on his eighth rep in his second set of flies when he could usually take the weight Kevin assigned to twelve or fifteen reps. "Are you okay?" Kevin asked. "Are you coming down with something? You just don't seem to have it tonight."

John set the weights on the floor and sat up, sighing. "Can we talk?"

"Of course," Kevin said, sitting down on a neighboring bench.

"My life has just gotten really messy, really fast."

"It's that kid you met, isn't it?"

"Yes and no. He was the catalyst, but if it hadn't been him in particular, it would've been somebody else. I don't know. Everything is so different now! Not just my body, but . . ."

"I know. Hell, a year ago I was on unemployment, remember? Now we're living in a boom town—I could quit my job tomorrow for one that paid fifty percent more. We're all on the cocktail and it's like, 'HIV? Huh? Oh, I remember that.' Now we're making good money, we're healthy, and on top of that, you're a big stud now." He put a hand on John's shoulder. "It's a big adjustment, isn't it?"

John sighed. "It is. And Harrison is . . . I don't know. It's like he's someone I was married to in a previous life. I'm so different and he's the same!" he said with astonishment. "Maybe that's it! Same old job, same old income, same old body. I feel guilty about this, he took me in when I was on the rocks, and I feel like I owe him something, but do I owe him the rest of my life?"

"You owe him an explanation, at least."

"I know. But I'm still sorting it out myself, how can I explain it to him when I can't explain it to myself?"

"Well, let's start with the boy. You had a good time with him, right?"

"Ohmigod, Kevin. Unbelievable."

Kevin laughed. "Young guys are energetic lays—maybe not skillful, maybe not good to be around *after* the sex, but . . ."

"But he was!" John protested. "He's smart and clever and talented and sexy and . . ." He sighed. "I'm gushing. And the worst part is, I really don't know if it's really him or if it's just that I've been so goddamned sheltered all these years."

"There you go, one of the advantages of being in your thirties."

"Oh? What's that?"

"Perspective. If you were his age you'd be head over heels for him, hormones dictating your every move. At least at this age you can see that maybe it's not him, maybe it's you.''

''Hmm. That's a possibility. Okay, let me ask you a question, O expert one. You've had a lot of sex with a lot of hot guys, right?''

''I guess this is where I should protest that I'm not a slut . . . but I *have* been a slut. I have been with a lot of hot guys.'' Kevin laughed. ''So shoot.''

''Is it always great? If you've got a bitchin' bod, and he does, too, and you look each other in the eyes and it's *lust.* Let's say you really connect, and you screw like crazed rabbits all night . . . can you just exchange him next weekend for another one? Can you have unbelievably earth-shaking sex and just *walk away,* because there's more where that came from at Club Universe next weekend?''

Kevin laughed. ''Let me tell you something. Wait, first let me ask you something. You weren't a virgin or anything when you met Harrison, were you?''

''Gee, Kev, I was already HIV positive and I sure didn't catch it from a toilet seat. I've had some good sex, some great sex once or twice.''

''You know what? It's not any different when you're buff and chiseled. You get more sex, and you get more sex with better bodies, but nine times out of . . . no, ninety-nine times out of a hundred, he just lays there as stiff as a board, or he won't touch you except to position you, or he can't kiss worth a damn, or he cums in ten minutes and then tells you he's married and he has to go, or you get him home and he can't find his poppers and the deal's off 'cause he can't have sex without 'em, or you have to slap him while calling him a faggot. Listen, I've gotten into long-term relationships for good reasons and for bad reasons. I've moved in with some guy because I was sick and tired of going out and dealing with those situations and it was nice to come home to a hot meal and a blow job every night, even if I didn't love him. But there have been a couple times, well, just two really, where I've gotten married because I went home with someone and . . . and I never wanted to be parted from him again. When he was totally hot sex, when the conversation was so great, when we were just . . . I don't know, when our planets were aligned, I guess. And you don't get that very often in life, no matter how hot you are.''

"Brian is like that," John whispered. "He really is."

"So now you're in a quandary. Remember that old song? 'It's best to be off with the old love . . .' ''

" 'Before you get on with the new,' '' John finished. "And I don't know, I guess Harrison and I are over as lovers. . . .'' He sighed. "God knows I can't stay in a relationship that isn't sexually satisfying, not anymore anyway!''

"How you gonna keep 'em down on the farm . . .''

"When they've seen Paree. Geez, you're a font of clichés today. But the thing is, Kev, I don't know if I am to Brian what he is . . . well, could be, to me. I told him I was married the next morning, and apologized for not telling him before, and he was like, 'That's okay, it was just a screw.' So maybe that was it.''

"Or maybe he likes you as much as you like him, and he was feeling hurt, and he said something like that in self-defense.''

John perked up. "Hey! That's a possibility!'' His face fell. "That's my problem, I'm the 'Great Communicator.' I've been avoiding Brian's calls and I've been avoiding Harrison, or letting Harrison avoid talking this out with me. I imagine he's probably hurt, too, huh? Great. I've screwed it up for everyone.''

"You've got to com-mu-ni-cate," Kevin said, drawing his sylla-bles out for emphasis. "Nobody can read your mind. Hey, you laid it out for me pretty well.''

"But you're a friend, you're not one of the involved parties.''

"But it was a good rehearsal, huh?''

John smiled. "It was. And Brian did call me—so maybe it wasn't 'just a screw' after all!" He hugged his friend. "Thank you!"

Kevin squeezed him back. "Okay, let's see if we can maneuver your newfound enthusiasm into a couple sets of dumbbell presses."

His courage screwed up, John called Brian when he got home from the gym that evening.

"Hello?"

"Hey, it's John."

"Hi, how are you?"

Reasonably pleased to hear from me, John thought, *from the tone of his voice.* "Good, I'm sorry I haven't called you back, I've been really busy," he said, falling back on the universal urban excuse.

"That's okay, I've been pretty busy, too."

"Ah. So . . . you going out this weekend?"

"No, I'm going out of town Saturday."

"Oh, what a coincidence, so am I. Well, are you busy Friday?" John asked, immediately wanting to retract this desperate-sounding question. Just leave it, he thought, sign off and let him call you.

"I gotta pack for this trip, run some errands before I go, pick up cat food for the cat-sitter, all that stuff."

"Okay. Well . . ."

"How about I call you when I get back?"

"That would be great." He added, "I'll return your call a lot faster this time, I promise."

He could hear Brian smile. "Hey, I know how it is with married men. You gotta wait till hubby's not around before picking up the phone."

"No, that's not it," John said, meaning it but also aware how insincere it would sound on the other end of the line. "I just . . . I'm just really confused right now."

"Great," Ethan piped up, "you can spend all that money and travel all that way, just to see everyone you know back home. Travel—it's so broadening."

The salesboy ignored him, extending a hand to John. "I'm Troy."

Ethan rolled his eyes as John shook his hand. "Pleased to meet you."

"Are you going by yourself?"

"Yes."

Troy winked. "That's the way to do it. Keep your room available for adventure. Here, I bet you look good in green and blue, don't you?"

"Those are my favorite colors!"

"Those would both go with your eyes." He plucked a navy-blue rib knit shirt off the rack. "And here," he said, pulling out a dark-green zip-front polo shirt with short-short sleeves. "This'll look good at the cocktail hour—which is every hour at Babylon! How are you set for bathing suits?"

"Not at all, actually."

John and Ethan eventually walked out with nearly three hundred dollars' worth of clothes, which comprised only one shopping bag's worth. It was actually two sixty, because Troy had given John a discount, "because you're so cute."

" 'Because you're so cute,' " Ethan mocked outside. "It's like a friggin' conspiracy! If you're buff and good-looking you not only get the best clothes, you don't even have to pay retail!"

"Didn't everything look good on me?" John asked.

"You coulda probably put on that hideous lime-green thing he showed you and looked great in that, with your bod. I don't know why you need me along," Ethan complained.

"I'm sorry, this isn't fun for you, is it?"

Ethan sighed. "I'm just jealous, I'll admit it. God, John, I've known you for five years, and I guess I just thought . . . you know, we were in the same boat. Now it's like your boat is the friggin' *QE II.*''

"Am I a different person than I used to be? Do I treat you differently?'' he asked anxiously.

"Yes and no. Yes, you're a different person. Not to me, you're still my friend John, but when we walk down the street, it's like you're Marilyn and I'm . . . Truman Capote! I never felt so invisible as I do around you and your new body. And no, you don't treat me any differently, it's just that everyone else treats *you* differently, and I feel diminished.''

John stopped in his tracks. "Ethan, I want you to start working out with us. With me and Kevin.''

"Right! Just like those comic books with the ninety-eight-pound weakling who magically becomes Charles Atlas.''

"If you eat right, take supplements, work out. . . .''

"John, I'm a *word processor,*'' Ethan said impatiently. "I can't afford a gym membership, let alone all that stuff you and Kevin shovel down every day. And I'm not positive, so I'm not going to get the steroids from my doc the way you guys have.''

"You don't have to have the steroids. As for the supplements, well, just go into debt. I'm serious! Listen to me. You're pissed, aren't you? Because of *how men are.* Well, are you going to devote your life to trying to change them, or are you going to do what it takes to be happy?''

"If you can't beat 'em, join 'em. Great. My faith in humanity is restored.''

"Ethan, I don't want to see you miserable! Kevin gave me a leg up, now the two of us can give you a leg up. I've got some extra creatine at home, you can have it if you promise to work out. . . .''

"Look, I'm me, okay? If nobody wants me, fuck 'em. If I've got to gain fifty pounds to get noticed on the street, forget it! I'll just be single forever, or move somewhere where you don't have to literally measure up to be popular.'' He sighed. ''John, I'm sorry. I shouldn't take it out on you. You've been through a lot and you deserve to be happy. Part of me wants what you've got, but part of me says, screw those stupid queens if all they've got on their minds is muscles! Like Scarlett O'Hara said, 'I have my pride.' It may not be as good as getting Rhett, but hey.''

''I know. Believe me, I've been there! I spent my fair share of years walking down the street with guys who were . . .'' He fished for some nonoffensive way of putting it.

''Cuter than you were?'' Ethan laughed.

''And I felt invisible, too. And I swore, *I swore!* I'd never be one of those stuck-up fags who won't even be friends with someone who's not 'hot enough.' Ethan, you are my friend! I'm not trying to make you miserable. I think we should call it a day for the shopping. I don't need to drag you into another den of gymbots today.''

''Are you kidding?'' Ethan said, putting an arm around John's neck. ''I've still got to alienate the salesdrones in All American Boy. Come on!''

The days rushed by and it was soon time to depart for Babylon. Kevin picked him up, having volunteered to take him to the airport. ''You're so jumpy, you look like you need a vacation.''

''This vacation is what's making me jumpy,'' John confessed.

''What! Why?''

''All those hunks, all younger than me and cuter than me.''

''God, don't tell me you believed the brochure! Haven't you learned? Beef sells stuff to gay men! Do you really think everyone there is going to look like the guys in the poster?''

''Yes,'' John said firmly.

''And have you talked to anyone who's been?''

''Well . . . the travel agent. He said it was 'hot.' '' Kevin rolled his eyes and groaned. ''And your friend Ted, remember, who learned how to open a pair of 501s with his teeth.''

"John, I bet you'll be the best-looking man there."

"Please! You know, this is why I didn't take you clothes shopping with me—you're too supportive!"

"So what should I be, hypercritical? Would that make you happy, to have someone around to pick at all your flaws?"

"What flaws are you talking about exactly?"

"Shit. You know, I had a boyfriend like you once. Totally gorgeous, and totally insecure. He spent all his time telling me, 'I can't believe you're going out with me.' Got on my nerves, I tell ya. And when I dumped him—for being such a basket case—he said, 'I knew I wasn't good-looking enough for you!' *ARGH!*"

"I'm not that insecure," John protested. "I know I'm a hell of a lot better-looking than I used to be. It's just that, when we went to Universe, I wasn't scared because I was with friends, even though we were plunging into Hot Boy Central. But I'm going here all alone and . . ."

"And you were all alone in Universe for about a minute before you met this incredible kid Brian, right?"

"Yes."

Kevin grinned from ear to ear, ruffling John's hair. "I say no more."

"So I guess this isn't a good time to ask you for a Valium?"

"You couldn't take one anyway, you're on Crixivan, remember? You'd be stoned for three days on one Valium."

"Hmm . . ."

"John," Kevin said warningly.

"I was kidding." He sighed. "I'll be okay. I just don't know. I started all this trying to dip one toe in the water at a time, and here I am two weeks later plunging into the deep end."

"Hey, that's the way the Vikings used to teach kids to swim— throw 'em in the water and hope instinct took over."

"Every man for himself, huh?"

"John, whatever you're going for, you're going to get it. If you just want to lie in the sun for a week and exchange glances and maybe pleasantries with cute boys, well, you can do that. If you want to get drunk as a skunk every night and have sex you won't remember the next day, you can do that, too. Why don't you just go and see what feels right when you get there?''

"You're right. As always!" he said, feigning friendly irritation.

"We're here," Kevin announced, pulling up to the curb at the airport. They got out and John shouldered his backpack and duffel bag.

"Thank you, doll. I'll send you a postcard." He gave Kevin a kiss and a big squeeze.

"Have a mai tai for me. I'll pick you up in a week."

"Thanks, you got it. See ya!"

The flight was quick and uneventful. John's gaydar locked in on more than a few fellow travelers; he wondered how many of them were Babylon-bound. He fell into one of Stephanie Barron's involving Jane Austen mysteries and the time slipped past until he disembarked, blessing his ability to pack every necessity into two carry-on bags, avoiding baggage claim areas worldwide.

He followed the directions Babylon had sent and found the complimentary bus to the resort waiting. It was so warm! San Francisco had about three really lusciously warm days a year, usually in September, and it being only June now, John was delighted to feel actual full-fledged, non-fog-obscured hot *sunshine* on his face after months of Vitamin D deprivation.

A handsome young man took his bags. As the bus filled, John saw that Kevin's prediction was true—there were certainly a hefty number of hot young studs being packed into the bus but there were also a substantial number of ''normal'' people. John sighed with relief, assured that he would fall no lower than the middle of the food chain.

The bus quickly transported them through lush jungle territory to the resort. John got excited just arriving on the grounds, gaping out the window at all the men already traipsing around in their swimsuits. He checked in quickly and was led to his room. The resort's main building was a series of terraces, mimicking the local Aztec pyramids, so even John's room, the cheapest available, had a balcony overlooking the ocean and the swimming pools below. He stood out on the balcony for a while, leaning on the railing, just so relieved to be warm at last.

The ocean was so beautiful and inviting, he didn't dawdle long, unpacking hastily and selecting a well-fitting square-cut bathing suit. (Ethan had expressly forbidden him from buying bikini briefs, and John knew with his big hips that the square-cuts were more flattering, anyway.) A pair of flip-flops, an unbuttoned short-sleeve shirt (if you got it, flaunt it, he thought wickedly), a beach towel, and a pair of Ray-Bans, and he was ready.

Drinks were free from eleven in the morning until one at night, but John took only a bottle of spring water for now. No point in getting potted and drowning, at least not on your first day, he thought, feeling happier every minute.

The pools were beautiful, one leading to the next, connected by waterfalls and slides with clusters of palm trees breaking them up visually. They were also very cruisey, and a little too crowded for John's taste. The ocean was calling him, anyway. At the beach he found a cute fortyish couple who stared at him openly, especially as he got closer. He took off his sunglasses to give them the full wattage of his smile. "Excuse me, will you be here for a bit? Can I leave my things here with you?"

"Yes, oh yes!" the chunkier one said delightedly, and John thanked them, dropped his stuff, threw off his shirt, and ran into the ocean.

After so many years in San Francisco, he braced himself for a shock as he plunged in, only to find himself welcomed into a warm, almost amniotic sea. He splashed around for a while, luxuriating in the warmth of the water on his body, the sun on his face; even the sand on his feet gave him an erotic charge. *Ohmigod, I'm so horny!* he thought suddenly. It was definitely sex weather. He came out of the sea, pushing his hair back off his face and not unconscious of how good he looked, albeit a little pale from being UVA-deprived for so long.

The couple hadn't moved, and were now staring up in awe at John's muscular, dripping form. "There are some . . . showers over there, to get the salt off," one said with effort.

"Thanks, don't want to get crusty." He found the showers and quickly rinsed off the sea before rejoining the couple. This was strategic on his part—he didn't want to sit alone because he wasn't ready to get hit on yet, he didn't want to have to ask some hot stud to watch his stuff (a relic of his old, pre-gym days when to be fat and to approach a young god for any reason was to dare to presume too much), but he did want to talk to somebody. These guys were perfect.

He spread his towel out and frowned. "Damn, I forgot my sunscreen in my room."

"Here, you can use ours." The chunky one offered him a bottle of SPF-15.

Fifteen! John thought irritably. *I'll never tan with that on!* Well, it's only my first day. "Thanks," he said, taking the bottle. "I guess I should shake your hand before I'm all greasy. I'm John." He extended his free hand.

"Charlie," the chunky one said. "This is my partner Jim," he said, indicating his bald friend.

"I can speak for myself!" Jim said indignantly. "Nice to meet you. Can we help you put that on your back?" he asked impishly.

John smiled and laughed. "No, thanks, I can do it myself. I'm double jointed." He proved it to them by applying the lotion all over his own back. "So where are you guys from?"

"We're from Ohio," Charlie said. "This is our first gay resort vacation."

"Are you enjoying it?"

"Jesus," Charlie blurted, "our first day and the hottest stud in town is lying right next to us!"

"I wouldn't hazard to say you've seen the hottest stud in town if it's only your first day; there's a lot more beef on the hoof still pouring in from the airport."

"Okay," Jim said, "so flattery won't work. Maybe we can try plying you with liquor instead."

"Ah, but the drinks are free," John said, enjoying the harmless flirtation.

"Shit, and so's the food. So's everything, for that matter. Guess the suntan lotion wasn't sufficient bribery, huh?"

John smiled, changing the subject. "Are you guys going to go to the tea dance today?"

"Oh no, not our speed," Charlie said. "We'll probably hit the pool then, since all you hot young things will have freed up the lounge chairs."

"You just want to sit closer to the bar so the cocktail waiters get your drinks faster," Jim laughed.

"Do you *know* how fast a margarita turns into Kool-Aid at this temperature?" Charlie said with mock indignation. "Really, every second is crucial." He turned to John. "Are *you* going to the tea dance?"

"I think so," he said, knowing full well that he would. *Horny, horny, horny!* his libido sang as his flesh roasted deliciously. The cocktail waiter came around and this time John was ready. "Orange Stoli, please."

"Wow, the hard stuff," Jim said.

"Cures what ails ya."

"Maybe I should get one of those."

"No, you don't," Charlie said warningly. "As if the AZT hadn't already done a number on your liver."

"Don't mention the Big A around the young man, you'll scare him off."

"Oh no," John said hastily. "I'm positive, too."

"Then you shouldn't be drinking hard liquor, dear," Charlie clucked.

"And I shouldn't be roasting in the sun, and I shouldn't be eating junk food, and blah blah blah."

"Right on," Jim said. "What's the point of living if you don't enjoy it?"

"I just don't want you checking out any earlier than necessary," Charlie said to Jim, stroking his arm.

"And I don't want to live forever if it means sitting in the dark and eating nine-grain bread, am I right, John?"

"I don't want to get involved in a domestic dispute, but . . . yeah, exactly."

"There, you're outnumbered," Jim gloated. Charlie only "hmph'd" in response.

The drinks came and John sipped his, sinking deeper into the contentment that had been engulfing him since he'd arrived. He nearly passed out but was woken up by the sound of raucous laughter from a group of young men passing by. He looked up to find one of them cruising him, and he smiled in return, which provoked the little cutie-pie into not only looking back again and again to see if John was still looking (he was) but caused the rest of his group to look, as well, to see what was holding up their friend. "Okay," he heard them say, "three, two, one. . . ." And all at once they blew him kisses. He reached and caught them one after another and waved with his other hand. They laughed and moved on.

Charlie sighed. "That never happened to me when I was young."

"Me neither," John said.

"Oh, right, you being so godlike and all, everybody just ignores you."

"I didn't used to be," he said, having decided to drop the self-deprecating "if I really am" part and just accept that he was, well, *hot* now. "It took a lot of hard work. Do you work out?"

"Us? No. Jim used to, I never did."

"They have a gym here. I can show you the basics and you can go back home and join a gym and not have to worry about not knowing what to do. . . ."

"I can't. It takes too much time, I'm so busy, it leaves me so tired. . . ."

"It is a time investment, but it's worth it. Your self-esteem goes up, your health improves, and once you get going, your workout leaves you with more energy rather than less. And if you take the right supplements . . ."

"I've seen those. They're *so* expensive. And gym memberships, well! There's a rip-off for you. . . ."

John tuned him out. Since his own conversion, he had become quite the proselytizer, eager to teach every lumpy person who complimented him how he, too, could become a chiseled hunk. But he was also familiar with the litany of reasons not to change your body and your life. *That could have been me,* he thought, *sitting here telling some hunk why he's so lucky and I could never look like that* . . . he sighed. It was funny—he remembered the outrage his fellow ACT UP members had felt years ago when the Louise Hay types had nattered on about AIDS being "a blessing." It had most certainly not been a blessing, but if every black cloud had a silver lining, the silver lining to this disease, for John, had been the kick in the ass it had given him. Without it, he would have still been floppy, pudgy, drifting, aimless . . . a blessing in disguise, was maybe the way to put it, seeing how obscenely good life was right now.

As the clock approached four o'clock, he gathered up his things and said goodbye. "Will you join us for dinner?" Charlie asked.

"I'll look for you, but I don't . . . want to make any concrete plans for after the tea dance."

Jim laughed. "No, I guess you shouldn't." He winked. "Have fun."

John smiled back. "Thanks. That's exactly what I'm going to do."

John went back to his room, turning this way and that to see if he had acquired a tan yet. A shower brought out some redness but of course it was silly to think he would be tan within hours of his first day in the sun. Nevertheless, he suspected that the other attendees at the tea dance had probably cheated with everything from the Wolff bed to tan-in-a-can in order to look on their first resort day as if they had already spent a summer in the sun.

What to wear? He puzzled over his alternatives. Not tan enough for the white ribbed T-shirt; the green zip-front polo would be best saved for night wear. *Well, I may not have a tan,* he thought, *but dammit, I've got muscles!* He put on a dark-blue tank top with a deep scoop that revealed *mucho* chest, tucked it into his denim shorts, and agonized briefly over shoes before chucking fashion for comfort and putting the Timberland sandals back on again. "Sunglasses," he muttered to himself, grabbing them more for the security of anonymity amongst so many handsome strangers than to guard against the blazing sun, and then he was out the door again.

Babylon held a tea dance every afternoon, timed exquisitely not to conflict with prime tanning hours. John arrived at five, and the party was in full swing. The party was staged on one of the cliffs surrounding the resort, providing a breathtaking view of the ocean and the rest of the grounds. While it was certainly not forbidden to wear one's swimwear to the tea dance (little, in fact, was forbidden at Babylon), few did. Just as the tea dances of old allowed Edwardian ladies one more opportunity to change bright plumages to the gasps of the assembled company, this one allowed gay men to show off outfits that would never be seen again. While some of the tea dances were built around themes, the first day's event was very "come as you are."

The stud quotient was definitely higher here, he noted, but then he'd always known tea dances in San Francisco as a very "boy" event. He took a margarita from a tray of them and looked around, his sunglasses deflecting inquiries until he was looped enough to field them. Out on the dance floor he noticed a gaggle of shirtless young hunks, one of whom looked strangely familiar even from the back. A prickly sensation that wasn't just the tequila shot up his spine as he waited for the boy to turn around, and when he did, John gasped.

The boy noticed him, froze in his tracks, then burst out laughing and ran to embrace him. "Hey!"

"Brian!" John said eagerly, hugging him with his free arm.

"I can't believe you're here!"

"I can't believe it, either. That's right, you said you were leaving town today."

"And so did you!" Brian laughed.

John tore off his sunglasses and looked Brian in the eyes. He didn't wait long to be kissed. As Brian's lips grazed his again and again, he felt himself sinking back into that underwater sensation they'd shared that night. It wasn't a dream! It wasn't just a screw! This feeling, this was . . .

Some kind invisible soul took his glass out of his hand and he was free to embrace Brian wholeheartedly, and he surrendered as he had that first night to the music, the heat, the passion, and forgot everyone and everything but Brian, Brian, Brian. . . .

CHAPTER
FOUR

Their embrace was interrupted by a voice behind Brian. "Brian always was good at making new friends."

Brian and John turned around to find three smiling and shirtless young men gathered around them. One of them, a short and slender blond with Paul Newman-blue eyes, nodded wisely. "Oh yuh, uh-huh. Okay." He held out a hand to John. "My name is Scott, and I say you're *hot.*" This was obviously a familiar routine as the others, including Brian, groaned and rolled their eyes.

The next one, a muscular little bulldog, introduced himself. "Don't mind Scott, he does that to everyone. I'm Evan." John shook his hand and turned to the third of the party, very tall and lean with an intelligent twinkle in his brown eyes and an "alternative" look. He had dark brown hair buzzed short, a string of brown beads around his neck, and a pair of extremely baggy and saggy denim shorts hanging low enough to reveal several inches of his plaid boxers.

"Scott is the Mr. Blackwell of gay bodies," he said with a voice much deeper than his thin frame would have led John to think him capable. "I'm Slater."

"Like Christian Slater," Scott appended, "who even though he is getting up there is still *hot.*"

"Nice to meet you all. I'm John."

"And you've met Brian," Slater added.

"We actually know each other from back home."

"Oh," Evan said, "you're from San Francisco?"

"Hey!" Scott cried. "You're the guy he met at Universe the night the rest of us went to Rupert's birthday party!"

"That's right, I am."

"Fly a thousand miles to meet new people," Slater said, "and guess who you run into? It's like English people on tour in Italy, all running into people from home, very E. M. Forster."

John was intrigued and determined to keep up, unable to block Ethan's words on the same subject. "You think anybody will get violently murdered before our delicate eyes?" he asked Slater.

"No, and there's no field of lavender to be found around these parts, either."

"I could get ravished by some hot-eyed Italian, though, couldn't I?"

"Well," he countered, grinning, "I'm Italian, but that was another book."

John laughed. "That's right. So you guys are all from San Francisco?"

"Yep, all friends of Brian here," Evan said, giant muscles flexing as he put a hand on Brian's waist.

"So is your husband with you?" Brian asked.

"No," John said. "In fact, I'm not even sure he's my husband anymore." His own words startled him. Was he just saying it to sound like he wasn't cheating? But then, if he wasn't, why did he feel such a hot flush of shame at the thought? Hell, for that matter, why was he still thinking about Harrison at all, if it was as "over" as he told himself it was?

"Ooh!" Scott and Evan chorused.

Brian put an arm around John's waist. "So if I ring your room and leave a message, you'll call me back this time?"

"Hopefully you'll be in the room with me, and the only call we'll have to make is room service."

"Come on," Slater said to Scott and Evan. "Let's let these guys catch up. Later," he said, pulling the other two with a strength surprising in someone so slim.

"Nice guys. All friends of yours?"

"Uh-huh. I met Evan at the gym, Slater at Eros, and Scott at Universe."

"And did Scott come up to you and say . . ."

"He did. I'd heard of him before that, though. There was an article about him in *Oblivion,* so I was prepared. It's like the *Good Housekeeping* Seal of Approval when Scott says you're hot, so congratulations."

"Well, I like approval, so I'll take it."

The hand Brian had slipped around his waist moved a little lower. "Hey, we have a couple of hours before dinner. You wanna . . ."

"Take a long walk?" John laughed.

"Yeah. Let's take a long walk."

The first time had been magic, and John had wondered on the way up to his room if it had just been the excitement of that evening that had made it so. But now, lying on the bed, spent and sticking to Brian, wrapped in his arms and breathing as heavily as he was, John knew otherwise. The way they had kissed that first night, losing themselves in it only to pull back and gaze in wonder into each other's glowing, panting faces; the way Brian's lean hard body had felt wrapped around his; the way his fingers had glided over Brian's smooth, soft, twenty-one-year-old skin had all been repeated.

The beat of the tea dance in the distance had been like drums out in the jungle surrounding the resort, and the music and the heat and the sight of so many cute boys had certainly contributed to the experience, but it was *the two of them, together,* John was certain, that had been the real secret ingredient to the magic.

"Are you hungry?" Brian asked him, parting their flesh to roll over to reach a glass of water on the bedstand.

"Ravenous. I ate a bagel in the airport but I haven't eaten since."

"The food is great here."

"You've been here before?"

"Remember the guy I told you about? The one who infected me? One year when I was on spring break he took me here. I didn't get the full experience, wink wink, because I was so besotted with him that I never even noticed anyone else. Anyway, it was fun, so much fun it was a good memory even after I dumped his sorry ass. So I talked these guys into going with me."

"You're splitting rooms?"

"Me and Slater are rooming together, and Evan got stuck with Scott. I don't know if he knew what he was in for." Brian chuckled.

"Stuck, huh? Scott's not fun to be around all the time, I bet."

"He's pretty cute, and he's charming, and he's fun to party with, but I wouldn't want to room with him." He stuck his finger into his water glass to the first joint. "He's about this deep."

"Party animal, huh?"

"Boy toy from the word go."

"Slater seems pretty smart."

"He's in grad school, comparative lit or something like that. And he's a professional skateboarder."

"Wow."

Brian tried to tickle John. "You like him, don't you? He turns you on."

"Intelligence is sexy. I didn't just go home with you because you were so blond and cute, you know."

"He has a really, really big one, too."

"Really?"

"See! You are interested! You should do him."

"Ow! Stop that! I'm interested in him, but I'm *intrigued* by *you.*"

Brian stopped tickling him and propped himself up on one arm. "Really?"

"I'm sorry I didn't call you. I just . . . so much has happened in my life lately. So *much* that it feels like a whole new life. Like I'm a whole new person. And things have been happening so fast, mostly good things, but I just wanted to slow things down, or try to, and they just . . . wouldn't. And you were another thing that was happening so fast." He bit his lip, wondering to ask Brian about his "just a screw" comment, but decided not to appear too overanalytical about it. "And I came home from that wonderful night and there was my husband, whom I haven't really talked to about how I've been feeling." He sighed.

"Anyway," he finished, "I am so glad you're here. You probably want to mess around this time, since you didn't get to last time, so don't feel that just because you ran into me your first day . . ."

"Hey," Brian cut him off. "You are the hottest sex I have had in my short adult life. Believe me, I would much rather hit the jackpot with you night after night than go around this place the whole time trying to find something that might, maybe, be better." And he kissed John.

He hugged Brian impulsively, squeezing him hard. His conversation with Kevin rang in his ears; it must be something everybody has to deal with when they find a hot partner, and he was glad to hear Brian wasn't in any mood to trade him in for a better model. "Mmm. Thank you for the compliment."

"Whoa, there, stud, watch it with those big muscles of yours."

"Sorry." He let go.

"Hey, no prob. Let's take a shower and dress for dinner, huh?"

They joined Scott, Evan, and Slater downstairs and headed to the buffet, the lavishness of which bowled John over.

"Here," Slater said, "try some of these meatballs."

"No, thanks. I have to wear a swimsuit for the next week, I need to avoid anything that can come served with gravy." He watched as Slater piled his plate with meatballs and said gravy. "You gonna eat all that?"

"And come back for seconds. I've got one hell of a metabolism."

"Can I hate you, please?"

"Look at the desserts," Slater grinned, rubbing it in. "Mmm, chocolate."

"Mustn't . . . look . . . must . . . eat . . . fruit."

Brian laughed. "I bet you'd be cute with a little belly."

"Right," John said, thinking to himself, *I used to have a "little belly," and boys like you never looked at me twice!* He loaded up on exquisitely huge shrimp and a dish of cocktail sauce, watching with amazement as the younger men stocked their trays with everything in sight.

"Yuh," Scott said at the table, "you eat like a bird."

"You wait till you're thirty-three and watch what happens to your metabolism, too."

"Wow!" Scott said, blinking his electric-blue eyes. "You are old!"

"Scott!" Brian said chidingly.

"We're like thirty-three percent younger than he is."

"How old are you guys?" John asked. "I know Brian's twenty-one."

"I'm twenty-two," Slater said.

"Mmph. Twenty-three," Evan added through a mouthful of food.

"Well," Scott said, "my ID says I'm over twenty-one!" They all laughed.

"What do you do for a living?" Evan asked John.

"Desktop publishing, mostly. Some PC troubleshooting; we're a small company so we don't have enough machines to justify a full-time PC guy. Word processing when I have to, when I get raw materials for the brochures and stuff, but I try and remind them that I've worked hard to leave that behind. Unfortunately, I type about a hundred words a minute so they keep asking me when they're in a rush. How about you?''

"I manage a GNC," Evan said.

"Ohmigod! Will you be my friend? I spend half my money on EAS products. I need a lot deeper discount than Super Tuesday can offer."

"Uh-oh," Slater said, "the muscles are gonna start talking about their supplements and their workouts and . . .''

"Muscles are hot!" Scott said, nodding. "I want more!''

"Get your daddy to buy you some," Evan said. "He can afford it."

"Yuh, uh-huh, he sure can. He's rich!''

"He means sugar daddy, not family daddy," Brian clarified for John.

"Yuh! He thinks I'm hot! He buys me everything. He paid for this trip. I told him, 'You can't go, but you have to pay my way.' ''

Slater nodded. "Now that's power." He raised his glass. "Three cheers for our little Tadzio."

"Hell," John said, "all Tadzio got from Aschenbach were some wistful glances. Not even a Swatch out of the deal."

"You guys are making fun of me!" Scott said. "I don't get it."

"That's why it's fun." Slater winked at John.

"So what EAS products do you use?" Evan asked him.

"Let's see, the Phosphagen HP . . .''

"Gotta have creatine."

"HMB, CLA, I used Twin Labs' Ripped Fuel for a while but it made me too jumpy, I'm trying something with synephrine now instead of ephedrine. . . .''

"You know, there's a whole new class of natural testosterone boosters. Have you tried androstenedione or tribulis terrestris?''

"No, but I don't need any of that, not right now, anyway."

"Why's that?"

"My doc has me on steroids, so my testosterone's good."

Scott perked up. "Steroids? Really?"

"Scott," Evan said warningly. "You don't need any steroids. You need to eat lots of protein, work out, and do supplements."

"But I do work out," Scott complained, "and I'm still not muscular! It takes too long this way."

"I will kill you if you go on steroids, and I will kill whoever gives them to you," Evan said darkly.

"Yuh, yuh, okay, say no more." He turned to John. "So how come you get 'em?"

"Well, I've always had low levels of naturally occurring testosterone. And I have HIV, which can lower your levels even farther."

"Oh," Scott said sheepishly.

"The shots I do really just normalize my levels. I was on them for some time and never put on any muscle; it was only when I got serious about working out and doing supplements that I started stacking up," he said, nodding to Evan.

"See?" Evan said to Scott. "It's not like you don't have time to work out seriously, and God knows your sugar daddy can afford every EAS product there is."

"But it's so *hard!*" Scott complained.

"I'm officially declaring the subject changed," Slater announced. "If I hear one more fucking word about muscles, I will use what few I have to strangle someone."

I bet he could, John couldn't help thinking. Slater wasn't skinny like his friend Ethan, he was *wiry,* a deceptive look that often hid great physical strength. After all, he was a professional skateboarder; *I bet he's got great legs . . .* he mentally slapped himself. "So," he said, "I was thinking of signing up for the scuba lessons tomorrow. Anyone else interested?"

"Cool," Slater said. "I'll skip the lesson, I'm already certified, but when you're ready to go for real, I'd love to go."

"Nuh-uh," Scott said. "Are you kidding? Wear all that rubber all over your body during prime tanning hours? Forget that!"

"I'll pass," Evan said. "I get claustrophobic underwater."

Brian sighed. "Well, can't let you go by yourself, can I?"

"I don't want to force anybody," John said quickly. "I just thought it would be fun. Don't do it to humor me."

"Are you sure?" Brian asked.

"Absolutely. I'll be fine on my own."

Brian squeezed his knee under the table. "I don't know if I should leave you on your own, I might never see you again."

"A giant squid might get me, but barring that, believe me, you'll see me again." He smiled, squeezing Brian's thigh in return.

"Wow, shipboard romance!" Scott enthused. "That is so hot! I wanna be next. We should go to the disco tonight."

"I'm in." Slater nodded.

"Me too," Evan added.

Brian whispered in John's ear. "You know, the cliff is really beautiful at night. They have a hot tub up there, we could soak and admire the view."

John smiled and addressed the rest of the group. "Enjoy the disco. We're going to take a rain check."

The cliff at night was far different from the cliff at tea dance time. The moon was full and the light shimmered off the ocean, no pounding sound system this time to overpower the rustle of the waves. The hot tub was perched near the edge of the cliff, lit from beneath like a magic cauldron and, even more magically, there was nobody else soaking in it.

"Shit, we forgot our swimsuits," John groaned.

"No prob," Brian said, quickly stripping and getting into the tub. John took a moment to admire Brian's long legs and perky ass before shrugging and stripping to join him.

"I hope I didn't do the wrong thing, talking about HIV tonight," John said.

"What do you mean?"

"You know, young guys, they don't want to hear about that stuff, especially not on vacation."

"You think so? They know I'm positive; hell, I'm always lecturing them about safe sex and what a bitch it is to be positive."

"Amen to that. So many pills to take, I can never quit my job and freelance because I need the insurance. . . ."

"And you have to spoil the mood with everybody you go home with by telling them about it."

"You tell everyone, huh?"

"Even if it's safe sex, I just feel like, I don't know . . . what if something wonderful happens with this guy and *then* I have to tell him the awful news, and he's all freaked out *after* I've fallen for him? Screw it. I just pop it out before I go home with anyone." He nudged John's foot with his own underwater. "I was going to tell you just about the same time you told me. You beat me by about six seconds."

"Really?"

"Don't you remember? There was that awkward pause, and we both decided it was time to tell, only you beat me to it."

"Huh." He looked out to sea for a while, letting the warm jets of water massage his ass. There were so many questions he wanted to ask Brian: Are you looking for a relationship? Do you believe in monogamy? Can we have a church wedding? But he held them all back. It was too early to bombard him with prying questions with needy undercurrents that would just scare him off. Just enjoy this moment, he told himself. You're on vacation and all your problems are literally a thousand miles away.

"Penny for your thoughts," Brian said.

"That's about what they're worth." He smiled. "I'm just woolgathering. This place really is great."

"It is. A sybarite's dream. You don't mind going to that scuba class without me, do you?"

"Not at all! I don't need to keep you on a leash." He smiled.

"Cool. I just want to chill out, you know? Maybe do stuff later in the week, but right now, no schedules, no plans."

"That's fine with me. I like to keep busy, and scuba diving is just something I've always wanted to try, so . . ."

"Good, enjoy it. I'll spend my day with a clipboard, noting Scott's ratings on every man who passes by."

"Oh, God! How old is he, really?"

"We think he's nineteen, but he could be eighteen."

"Amazing. Well, I guess he's young enough to fritter away a few years being cute and doing nothing."

" 'Youth is wasted on the young,' " Brian quoted. "Oscar Wilde, according to Slater, who's always saying that."

"You know what I always wondered? If Oscar Wilde really thought that youth was wasted on the young, why did he spend so much time chasing them?"

Brian laughed. "Because we're so damn cute."

"You are. I mean, you in particular, but young men in general. Hell, when I was twenty-one, I was kind of a blob. But even so, there were plenty of guys who'd do it with me just because the bloom wasn't off the rose yet."

"I bet you were cuter than you say you were."

John snorted. "I'll show you the pictures. Believe me, I do not lie."

"It must be tough, being gay and not having the package. I'm not blind, I see guys looking at me like . . ." He shivered. "It's not even healthy lust, it's some kind of sick *need,* like if only I would touch them I could make it all better. And then there're the ones who stare at you with so much *hate.* . . ."

"I know. I remember when I moved here, my best friend was dating this guy in his late thirties, and this guy's roommates were in their thirties, and they used to stare at me and Steve with such *loathing.* I couldn't figure out what we'd done to them. We were nice as pie, it wasn't us, I know that. Then I went through a period right after I turned thirty where I found myself looking at young guys with so much resentment . . . like, how dare you replace me, how dare you make me obsolete, I'm not finished being the flavor of the month, you little bastard! All this time *I've* been what it means to be young and hip, and now you're telling me my time is past, dammit! And that was when I figured out why those guys hated me so much.''

"But you don't seem like that now, you seem to like young people.''

John smiled. "Because I am one now. I'm just a kid myself, it's all new to me all over and I get to be everything I didn't get to be the first time around.''

"Wow. You're pretty damn lucky. Lucky enough to have lived through AIDS, but to do that *and* have a real second chance . . .'' At a loss for words, he swam across and started kissing John. "God, you're such a hot man.''

"Takes one to know one,'' John whispered, looking up at the stars as Brian kissed his chest and worked his way down.

John was up and out of Brian's room early to get to the scuba class. Brian had grunted his goodbye and pulled a pillow over his head—obviously not a morning person, John thought wryly.

There weren't too many people up for it at this hour. He and the instructor traded pleasantries as the others arrived: an extremely shy boy (but cute, in a Morrissey kind of way, John thought), a pair of arrogant beauties (they frowned a lot and made sure nobody could make eye contact with them), and, to John's satisfaction, Jim who he'd met at the beach the day before, sans his partner.

"Hey, where's Charlie?''

"This isn't his thing, since it involves danger and exertion and all. As far as he's concerned, he's tempting fate enough just by getting some sun. So we saw you at the buffet last night; looks like you made some new friends pretty fast.''

"I knew one of them from back home and the rest of them kind of came with the package."

"Ah, a friend or . . . ?"

"Or . . . definitely or." John laughed. "I only saw him once before this, and we just happened to run into each other down here."

"How romantic. So what happens when you go back home? Anybody back there complicating this happy picture?"

John sighed. "There is. Not for long, though, I don't think." The thought made him queasy, but there it was—this trip was suddenly seeming less like a vacation and more like a ship that had sailed without Harrison, a ship on which John had a one-way ticket.

"Oh." Jim hesitated and then remarked, "Charlie and I have been together for fifteen years—this is actually our anniversary trip."

"My God! That's some kind of miracle. I mean, straight people don't stay together that long, let alone gay couples!"

"I'm not going to tell you it's been easy. We've had a couple fights, I mean big ones, we even had a 'trial separation' for about six months about ten years ago. But we worked through it. How long have you been with this partner you have now?"

"We've been living together for about nine months now. Which, in San Francisco, is like forever."

"Is this your first big fight?"

"How'd you know there was a fight?"

"You're married, you're here on vacation on your own, you're having a fling with someone from home. Hello, the math isn't that hard."

John flushed. "I guess not."

"So what's the problem?"

"We're . . . I'm," he corrected emphatically, "just not the same person I was when we met."

"I've heard California was famous for personal growth, but

could you really be such a different person than you were a year ago?''

John sighed, trying to come up with a good *Reader's Digest* condensed version of his story. "Imagine marrying someone when you're broke, lonely, under a death sentence, and scared, and then all of a sudden you're prosperous, popular, in remission, and eager to get on with life.''

"Ah. Another dramatic cocktail story. They're calling it 'Lazarus Syndrome' now, did you know that?''

"No, what do you mean?''

"When people who are expecting to die of AIDS suddenly get a new lease on life—like Lazarus in the Bible? Remember, Jesus brought him back from the dead.''

"Oh, right, and the jealous bastards stabbed him to death not soon afterward. Not an appealing metaphor.''

Jim laughed. "Oops, that's right. Well, I guess it's the best one we've got. Your partner—he's negative?''

"You are perceptive; how'd you know?''

"Elementary, my dear boy. You talk about changing, which implies that he hasn't. In our current boat, that implies that he hasn't had the same dramatic experience you have.''

"Yup. And he's a professor, too, tenured, so the recession didn't impact him the way it impacted me, you know? So he hasn't felt the economic change, either.''

Jim sighed. "Charlie and I got together in 1984. I told you we're from Ohio, right? Charlie's lived there all his life, but I spent a couple years in New York City, doing the scene. You ever read *Dancer From the Dance?*''

"Yes! If it's possible to be ruined by a book, that book ruined me. I read it when I was fifteen and I immediately wanted to move to the big city and be a doomed queen—dance and snort poppers and have lots of sex and swim out to sea to die after the White Party.''

"Well, I lived that. I was a pretty hot cookie back then, so I spent a lot of time at Studio 54 and Fire Island, met Halston, Bianca, Calvin, Andy, blah blah blah; I won't bore you with the details."

"Bore!? Are you kidding? I'm fascinated. I've read every Andy book, *including* the Diaries. I'm so jealous."

"Don't be. It wasn't that pretty. Anyway. That's when I got infected. I burnt out on the drugs and shit and moved back to Ohio, and by the time I met Charlie people were starting to die—not out there, but people I knew in New York. Charlie and I had unsafe sex for years, because we just didn't know.

"When the test came along, I knew I had to take it, not just for me but for Charlie. That was the worst year of my life—we hardly had sex at all, I was so afraid of infecting him. Well, he finally said he was going to take the test and if I loved him, we'd take it together. I came up positive, he was negative.

"You remember what it's like to test positive. It takes about six months for the shock to wear off, then you just kind of go on, but not like before, because the future isn't coming anymore. But we were totally safe after that, and he's still negative. We sort of built a life around waiting for the end, making sure our money wasn't ever tied up where we couldn't get at it when I got sick, that kind of thing.

"Anyway, I got into a clinical trial for Crixivan back in '95, and so my world was turned upside down long before the big media blitz about it last summer. Charlie and I had to totally reevaluate our relationship, because we'd spent thirteen years with him in the role of caretaker, of mommy, even, nagging and smothering and all that."

John nodded, thinking of his own difficulties on this front with Harrison. "We even went into counseling," Jim continued. "Death—my death—had been the linchpin of the whole relationship, and now that was gone, and so now what? Now what the hell do we do?"

"What did you do?"

"Like I said, a lot of counseling, a lot of crying. And basically we decided to stop mourning the fact that I wasn't going to die and start celebrating. So this last year we've been pretty much on permanent vacation. Charlie got someone to run his business, and I took a leave of absence and we've just been traveling, spending the money we were saving for the horrible bills to come, seeing all the places we thought we'd better not see since we'd need that money or I'd catch some weird infection from the water." He laughed jubilantly. "Europe, Africa, Asia, you name it. Oh, and here, just because we'd both seen the ads in the gay papers for so long and thought it would be fun."

"Wow," John said, feeling like he'd been given a lot to chew on. He sighed. "I wish my husband would loosen up the purse strings like that."

"The important thing is that you talk this stuff out. Frankly, we've had the best talks on these trips, because we're relaxed and happy and far away from all the day-to-day *shit* that keeps you from talking about important things because you're too tired from work or whatever."

"I know. And we haven't really talked about . . . any of this. It's all happened so fast, and we were both so busy, and now . . ." He sighed again.

Jim put a hand on his shoulder. "As soon as you get back, talk to him. Maybe even spend some time writing it out while you're here, so you have some notes to work from and you're not just free-associating and getting mad and not being able to say why, and getting caught up in the anger of the moment."

"You should be a therapist."

Jim started laughing hard. "Now you're the perceptive one!"

"You *are* a shrink!" John clapped delightedly.

"Hey, even shrinks need shrinking, you know. Okay, let's suit up and learn something new."

*   *   *

John joined Brian and company at poolside in the afternoon. As he made his way to the chaise lounge they had saved for him, despite all efforts by others to liberate it, he felt the waves and ripples all around him, few of which had anything to do with the water in the pool. Put a gaggle of gay men in a certain amount of space and the sexual tension is bound to rise as they check out the competition, the newcomers, their own reflections. Measuring, comparing and contrasting—even the object of all desire wondering if he makes the grade.

"Hey," Slater said, not lifting his silver-framed wraparound Oakleys, "how was the class?"

"Great, I get to go for a real dive tomorrow. You wanna go?"

"Cool, I'm there. You ever been windsurfing?"

"No, but I'm game."

Brian reached over and squeezed John's hand. "You're pretty adventurous, aren't you?"

"Why not? If I can survive AIDS I imagine a little water won't hurt me. A margarita, please," he asked the cocktail waiter who'd manifested next to his chaise. He sighed. "I want to live like this forever, please."

"Hear, hear," Evan chimed in. "Sun, fun, all the booze you can drink, and all the boys you can do. A Bloody Mary, please."

"Evan just got up. He was busy last night!" Scott crowed.

"Do you have to broadcast my activities?" Evan asked petulantly.

"You missed it, it was hot! He was on the dance floor and all these guys were *on him*, they tore his shirt off and everything. He went home with all of them, too."

"There were only three of them, you make it sound like an orgy."

"Three, huh?" Slater said. "Hmm, let's do the math—you've got one penis and two orifices . . . yeah, that's about right."

"Hey!" Evan laughed. "I'll have you know I was in charge the whole time."

"No wonder you just got up," Brian said. "And you'll do it again tonight, too, won't you?"

Evan shrugged and flexed as a passing pretty boy regarded him. "Maybe. Unless I can find one man to satisfy me completely, and that's not likely."

"That boy is checking you out," Scott said, noticing the young man's backward glances at Evan. "I say he is *hot!*"

"I'll make a note of that," Evan said. "Get his license plate number and I'll look him up tonight. I'm too damn tired to even flirt right now."

John kept silent but was awed—imagine, ravishing three guys and being ready for more the next night! How wonderful it must be to be really young, to have all that sexual energy.

"So are you up for the tea dance later?" Brian asked John.

"Sure. Is it themed today?"

"Yuh, uh-huh!" Scott enthused. "It's an '80s party!"

"Oh God," John groaned. "Please, I had to live through the '80s, I don't want to relive them."

"The '80s were cool," Scott declared. "Everybody had lots of money and Ronald Reagan was president."

"Ronald Reagan!" John practically fell out of his chair.

"Yuh, he was a great president."

"You are out of your mind! Ronald Reagan killed more people with AIDS than you can count! He just let it get worse and worse and did nothing, because it was just niggers and junkies and faggots and everyone else who didn't vote Republican, so let 'em die! Then when he got out of office he had the *nerve* to go on TV and say, 'Since I left office, I've learned that all kinds of people can get AIDS,' as if it was just fucking *fine* for us to get it, but once white Republicans got it, well then!"

"Please."

"I come from the East Coast, and it's just . . . different there than it is here. You walk down the street in New York, people look at you—everybody looks at everybody else, checking each other out, you know? Especially guys. Even if you're not really interested in doing it with someone, you still trade glances. Out here, guys scope you out from a block away and totally ignore you when they get close if they're not interested. Have you ever spent any time cruising on America Online?"

"No."

"Well, it's a riot. Everybody has a profile you can look up and it's like a rule. The shallowest guys, the ones who say 'I'm extremely hot and you must be, too; nobody over thirty; you must have a huge cock, blah blah blah' are the same ones who have personal quotes that say 'The journey is the reward, the more you expect the less you get, treat others as you would be treated.' All this New Age *shit,* even though they're so obviously *not* the least bit spiritual or full of love for their fellow man. And Scott is like . . . he just stares at you and comes right out and says what he thinks, you know? He's just *honest* enough to say what all these other goddamn queens are thinking but won't say because they don't want everyone to know how shallow they are! Scott doesn't pretend that he's what he isn't, you know? He's honest."

"You could really use him as a barometer, couldn't you? Ask him if you're getting fat and he'll tell you what nobody else will."

"What are you worried about, you passed his test."

"Yuh, uh-huh, I am *hot!*" John laughed.

Brian regarded John with one eye cocked. "You like Slater, don't you?"

"I do. I mean, I like him. . . ."

"You don't have to explain it to me. I met him at Eros, remember? The sex club?"

"Oh. So you've . . ."

"We had a good time, but it wasn't love or anything. We did it, it was nice and then when I saw him out at Universe he walked up to me and said hi. A lot of guys don't, you know—you do 'em and they totally ignore you the next time you see them. Hell, they're less likely to look at you if you have screwed than they would have been if you'd never even met!"

"That doesn't sound very nice."

"Which is why I think Slater is so cool. You should do it with him."

"What!"

"You should! You think he's sexy, right?"

"Well, yes."

"He digs you, he told me."

"Oh, God, I feel like I'm back in high school. What did you guys do, pass each other notes in study hall?"

"He's a really good lay."

I don't doubt it, John thought, recalling Slater's quick wit, his cockeyed smile, his tall lean bod, his allegedly giant equipment.

"I wouldn't mind," Brian said. "You wouldn't mind if I found someone hot and did him, would you? Or are you into monogamy?"

John flushed. *Yes,* he thought, *I would, though considering I'm cheating on my husband at the moment I'm hardly in a position to trumpet monogamy.* "I've lived in San Francisco long enough to know that sex is a recreational activity, not unlike, oh, windsurfing or something, so I'm not shocked or upset or anything. But I just . . ." He sighed and fortified himself with the rest of his glass, which Brian quickly refilled.

"Like I said, I'm just trying to take all this one step at a time, you know? Two weeks ago I'd never been to Club Universe, was totally faithful to my husband, and didn't have a single item of clothing that had the word 'ribbed' in its description. Now I'm at a gay pleasure dome, having a fling with a really hot guy, and almost everything I wear fits like a glove! And right now, I'm just trying to . . . hold the line. I am just not ready for sex as a recreational activity with whoever looks good, you know? I cheated on my husband because I found you, and I was just wild about you, but now I think, no offense, that Slater is really hot, so am I going to move onto him now, and then on to another and another? I'm just . . . afraid of falling into this . . . *vortex,* where it's someone new every week and my whole life starts revolving around finding some-one new and better. Am I making sense?''

''I get what you're saying.'' He grinned. ''I guess I just don't understand the concept of sexual restraint.''

John smiled. ''You're free to go off and leave me anytime you want.''

''Hey, like I said. The kind of sex we have doesn't come along that often.''

John thought of what Kevin had told him and nodded. ''No, it doesn't.''

Brian slugged back his wine. ''So am I going to see you when we get back to the city, or are you going to go back to not returning calls?''

''I'm sorry about that. I was trying to resist temptation, and think things out, all that. I think it's a little too late now to worry about resisting temptation, don't you?''

Brian waved an arm to encompass the verdant beauty around them. ''Hey, temptation is what we're here for, right?''

''It is. Once you've bitten the apple, you might as well finish it off, right?''

Brian looked at him wickedly, then placed a slice of apple in his mouth, half of it sticking out. John took his cue and bit off the offered half; they giggled as they munched and John wiped away the juice that had run down his chin. Then Brian's lips were on his again, and there was only the sky through the trees, and the shriek of parrots.

*   *   *

The week passed in a pleasant haze for John, who found himself quite tan by the following Friday night, their last at the resort. While he and Brian had so far shunned the disco for other extracurricular activities, the rest of the group had talked them into going this night.

John had to laugh at himself as he agonized over what to wear, flinging the whole of his newly acquired wardrobe around the room in search of the perfect outfit. He was finally ready for the white ribbed-knit T-shirt—he was glad of his discipline in sticking to the seafood at the buffet as it fit like a dream, and made his deep and glowing tan look even darker—and he added a pair of baggy Girbaud jeans, perfect for dancing.

Thumping club music could be heard from behind Brian's door, so he knocked extra loud. When there was no answer he turned the knob and found the door unlocked. "Hello!" he shouted, opening the door.

Slater was hunched intently over the table, sitting in his underwear. "Hey!" John repeated, and this time Slater looked up and smiled brightly.

"Hey, come on in! Brian's downstairs making sure Scott gets dressed in time. You want something to drink?" John watched him move across the room, unable to prevent himself from checking out the infamous package. It was indeed very impressive—no wonder he wore baggy swimsuits. John chuckled.

"Sure, I'm ready, tank me up." He looked on the table where Slater had been occupying himself and saw a mirror with several lines of something laid out. "Uh-oh."

"Huh?" Slater followed his eye and laughed. "Oh. Do you object?"

"What's that line from *Tales of the City?*" John asked, and he and Slater chorused it together. " 'My dear, I have no objection to anything.' " They laughed.

"Do you want some?" Slater asked.

"Umm . . . what is it?"

"Crystal. Have you ever done it?"

"Nooo."

Slater shrugged. "I don't do it too often, but this guy I know offered me a bag, and I thought, what the hell, it's our last night, we can sleep on the plane tomorrow."

Brian came in with Evan and Scott in tow; at the sight of the lines on the table Scott made a beeline. "Yuh, cool, let's party! Dude, did you have this with you all the time?"

"Right," Slater said. "I'm retarded enough to smuggle drugs into Mexico, where I can get thrown into jail for life and be raped by fat greasy corrupt prison guards. No, I just got it. And I sure wouldn't have let you know if I'd had it all this time."

"Scott would've hoovered up the whole quarter the first night," Evan said.

"What's a quarter?" John asked, and they all looked at him for a minute, surprised. He flushed, realizing it was one of those things that everyone knows but you.

"How old are you again?" Scott asked.

"Leave him alone," Slater said. "So he's not a hardened drug addict. A quarter is a quarter gram," he explained. "It's how the stuff is measured out."

Evan did a line and tilted his head back, groaning slightly with what sounded like pleasure. "The first time I ever did this," he said to John, "I was at the Endup, wired out of my mind, and these guys came up to me and said, 'Have you got a quarter?' So I said. 'Sure,' and pulled a quarter out of my pocket. I thought they wanted to make a phone call."

Slater laughed and did his line. "First time I ever did it was at the baths in the East Bay. I stayed for sixteen hours and lost count after about a dozen guys."

John wanted to ask if it made you horny but decided he'd exposed enough of his naivete for one night. Brian looked at him, plainly uneasy. "I won't do it if you don't think it's . . ."

"No, no," John cut him off, making for the table. He'd never done the stuff before, but he was damned if he was going to be the only person in the group to abstain. Hell, after all the cocktails he'd knocked back this week, what could this hurt? Besides, he knew from experience that "Just Say No" was bullshit, that whole big lie that all drugs were the same, as if pot were as bad as heroin. And hell, if they were lying about that, they were probably lying about this stuff, too.

"Here," Brian said, "watch me." Brian did half his line up one nostril, half up the other, then tilted his head back, rubbed his nose, and exhaled.

John followed his example and waited. There was a pleasant tingling in his sinuses. "Does it burn?" Brian asked him.

"No, not at all."

"That's really pure," Scott said. "Excellent."

"Okay, you know the rules," Slater said. "No changing clothes after doing your line." He whispered in John's ear. "Some guys get obsessive-compulsive on this shit, they can spend hours deciding what to wear and end up never going out because the bars close before they're happy with their outfit."

"Oh," John said, tasting something nasty and metallic in the back of his throat. He took a swig of his beer to wash it away.

"Okay, are we ready?" Slater asked.

"Yeah!" Evan said.

"Let's go!" Scott whooped. And they were out the door.

As they got closer to the disco, John felt an excitement he'd never felt before, an anticipation and something more . . . a sense of *joy and power* that was intoxicating to the extreme. The music got louder and the crowd got denser and everything was *so fucking great!* He looked at his friends, eyes aglitter and nostrils flaring like racehorses just off the track, and he thought, *We are it, we're the bomb, baby; we're what they all want to be and have.*

He downed another drink in the disco. "I'm ready to dance!" Scott shouted, his foot tapping rapidly to the music.

"Me too!" John yelled in his ear, and they bopped onto the dance floor.

As soon as he worked up a sweat, John tore his shirt off. *I am hot!* he enthused to himself. This was his kingdom and he was the king; he could strip down to his underwear and they'd love him for it. *Invincible! I can have any man I want!* he thought with insane glee.

He danced and danced, never tiring. Brian and Slater joined them on the floor, bringing him a bottle of water. "You gotta stay hydrated!" Slater said.

"I feel great!" John laughed, draining the bottle quickly.

Slater smiled. "Believe me, the first time you do that stuff is the best, it's downhill from there."

"That's hard to believe," John said, fighting a sudden urge to kiss the shirtless Slater.

"That's because you're a drug virgin."

John put his hand on Slater's chest. "Then pop my cherry."

Slater looked him in the eye and John shivered—such intensity! He felt so much passion for Slater, and Slater felt it for him! Slater put his hand behind John's head and pulled him up to kiss him.

Even through the drugs, John compared it to his kiss with Brian that not-so-long-ago night. This was different; he was swept up, but this was . . . just plain hard-ass *lust.* He had his hands on Slater's hips, his chest, all over him, lost in the fires and completely unaware of the gawking crowd around them until Scott shouted, "Go for it!" The spell was broken then. He turned to see everyone on the floor watching them, even a laughing Brian, and he flushed, separating from Slater. Evan, Scott, and Brian started to applaud and Slater bowed, and John laughed, delirious with joy, and took his bows, as well.

He rushed up to Brian and kissed him. "I'm sorry."

"Hey, I knew you guys were hot for each other; go finish the job."

"No, no, I want you!" John cried, grabbing Brian's hands.

"You sure?"

"I'll show you," he said, proceeding to kiss Brian the way Slater had just kissed him, only more languorously, the fierce drug and music-fueled passion that had slammed him and Slater together giving way to something more like animal courtship, teasing and prodding and testing. It was all tongues and lips and hands and skin and sweat and denim and everything heightened, maximized by the drugs.

"I wanna fuck you," Brian whispered, and John realized how incredibly horny he was.

"You don't wanna dance?"

"We can dance any night back home. This is our last night here and we're high and I want to take you up on the cliff and fuck the shit out of you," Brian said, his eyes as glittery-glazed and intense as John's own, and there was no saying no.

"Let's go," he whispered, without a second thought for Slater or Evan or Scott or anyone or anything but the great rushing throb in his groin.

CHAPTER
FIVE

Harrison had returned from his vacation just as John had left on his—convenient, Harrison thought grimly, since that meant they hadn't even had to sit down and plan a cat-sitter for Rafsanjani, let alone anything of importance. He knew he'd avoided John in the week before his departure, but he couldn't help himself. He'd been unspeakably angry at what seemed to him like childish behavior on John's part. Okay, he deserved it when John went and booked his own vacation, and what with John's new body, he was surprised it had taken him this long to spend a night away from home, but to do it like that, to storm out and not come home and not call. . . . Childish, he kept telling himself, trying to block out his own guilt at his willful behavior in buying the tickets without settling it with John.

He'd come back from the South in a funk. Ken Burns had indeed made the Civil War-thing sound romantic, but Harrison had realized on his expedition that "romantic" and "melancholy" were separated by a very thin line, and that what might have been romantic with a partner was very melancholy when experienced on your own.

He missed John. He'd admitted that to himself the first night in bed alone in the first motel he'd stayed at, near Gettysburg. At first he'd gloated—*my* bed, all to *myself* again! But that had lasted about five minutes before the emptiness of it threatened to swallow him. John was *supposed* to be there, taking half (or more) of the space.

Worse, he'd had to admit that John had been right: It was a miserable trip, and not just because John wasn't there. He should have known better, but he'd envisioned the solitude of vast fields, where he could reflect on the folly of war, but that was because he was a professor of ancient history, and Etruscan ruins weren't as picked over as more popular destinations. Instead he'd found souvenir shops hawking Confederate flags and Johnny Reb caps, and he'd encountered loud obnoxious families whose vehicles (trucks, mostly) sported slogans and epithets that would have gotten them run off the road in California. Even the battle reenactment he witnessed seemed a little silly when the participants took time out to answer cell-phone calls or chug a Coors Light. The only solitude he got was in a motel or in his car, driving around looking for parking spaces.

When he got back, he regretted not having signed up to teach a summer class. He really hadn't planned ahead well enough, he thought, and now he had months remaining in which to dwell on his various follies.

He sighed aloud in the empty apartment. Rafsanjani looked up at him and went back to sleep. He really loved Johnny Eames, with all his heart. He'd been so happy for John when his health had taken a dramatic turn for the belter; when John had gone on steroids they'd laughed about his imminent "bicepularity." Harrison had read up on anabolic steroids and insisted John supplement with milk thistle for his liver and saw palmetto for his prostate to counter the effects of the drugs. *Yes,* he admitted to himself, *I nagged him. But he is so reckless! Look at how he took off to Mexico, just like that, how he stayed out without calling, without a thought to consequences. . . . I had to get on him and stay on him if he was going to stay well. I had to . . .*

He still hadn't had the nerve to tell John a secret. It was one of those things he thought of as "English secrets"—something you should tell right away, but didn't because it wasn't cricket to express too much emotion, and then time passed and it was too late to ever tell it. But here it was: The first day John had been in his class, Harrison had been extremely distracted. He didn't think anyone would ever believe him if he'd said that John was just as attractive to him that first day as he was today in all his muscular splendor. But it was true. And the first time he heard John's voice, asking a question in class, he had swallowed hard and labored mightily to focus on the question and not the questioner. Harrison put a lot of stock in voices, and John had such a beautiful voice, so obviously full of smarts and so warm and . . .

He'd decided to surprise John by meeting him at the airport the day he got back from Babylon, a gesture of goodwill and reconciliation. He'd brought flowers as a peace offering and picked up a box of See's Candies, John's favorite, at the airport. He'd stood off to the side as the plane emptied, not wanting to force John to deal with him at that moment if he didn't care to. Harrison was surprised at how nervous he was each time John wasn't the next person disembarking. Then he heard a raucous crowd of handsome young men coming out of the tunnel, John amongst them, one of them despite the clear age difference between him and the rest of the boys. Harrison hid himself behind a limo driver holding a sign and watched the boys and John head for the baggage claim. He watched, refusing to feel anything, as one of them put an arm around John, a favor John returned immediately. They kissed with more than warm friendship.

He left the flowers and candy in the waiting area and went home. Then, determined not to be sitting there sulking when John arrived, he started dinner, but John never came in the door. Harrison ate by himself and went to bed early.

Now he poured himself a drink and sat down in the easy chair looking out over Twentieth Street and suddenly saw himself as he must look from out there—a middle-aged man, alone in his apartment, having a stiff one on a beautiful sunny day. He felt like a goddamn Hopper painting. He put the drink down untouched and began to pace the apartment, looking for something diverting. . . .

The phone rang and he answered it on the first ring, urging himself not to hope it was John. "Hello?"

"Hey, Harrison, it's Matt."

"Hi, Matt, how are you?"

"Great, great." He paused. "Listen, are you doing anything right now?"

"Well . . . no, to be honest."

"Great! I mean, I wondered if you were free for lunch."

"I don't see why not."

"Okay, then, how about Café Flore? It's a great day to sit outside."

"Sure."

"I'll see you there in say, half an hour?"

"Sure." As he was about to hang up he put the phone back to his ear. "Matt? You still there?"

"Still here."

"Thanks."

He could hear Matt smile. "I'll see you soon."

Harrison found Matt already waiting for him, seated at a prime outdoor table and nursing an iced coffee. "That was fast."

"I walked out the door and the twenty-four was right there," Matt explained. "So how are you?"

"Okay."

Matt pondered his next move. "How was your trip?" he asked, knowing it hadn't been a raging success. Helen had called for John a few days earlier only to discover from Harrison that he'd absconded to Babylon alone.

"Not so hot, to be honest. I think I'll stick to ancient history from now on."

"Huh." Matt stirred his drink. "Listen, Harrison, I didn't ask you here to make small talk. Helen tells me you guys had a pretty big blowout, and she asked me to talk to you, see if we couldn't help."

Harrison sighed. "I appreciate that, but I don't know that there's anything you can do."

"Why not?"

"I just don't think I'm the right person for John anymore."

"What do you mean?"

"I'm too old, too out of shape, too poor. . . ."

"Come on, man. You're in self-pity mode now."

"John's met someone," he blurted out.

"Are you sure?"

"He was with someone when he came back." He explained about the airport scene, leaving out the flowers and candy.

Matt laughed. "Shipboard romance, from the sound of it. Did you really think he would go off to a place like that and not get laid?" Then he flushed, wondering if he'd gone too far. "It's like a gay Club Med, isn't it? That's the picture I got from what Helen tells me John told her."

"That's what I gathered from the brochure."

"So he probably got it out of his system and when he comes home . . ."

"He hasn't come home, remember?" Harrison snapped. "Sorry."

"That's okay." Matt busied himself sipping his drink. "So what are you going to do about it?"

"What do you mean?"

"You think you're too old, too out of shape, and you know, maybe you are." Harrison looked up at him, startled. "I don't think being too poor has anything to do with it," Matt went on, "do you? Do you really think John is after more money?"

"No, no. I don't. But . . ." He sighed. "I know that things are different for him now than they used to be—different than they ever were. Not just because of his health, but because of . . . everything. He has money now, he never had money before, he has this incredible body that I just . . ."

"What?"

"That frightens me, I guess. I look at him and I think, I'm not good enough for him anymore, not sexually at least."

"So are you saying that you guys stopped having sex? Are you telling me that you let him get all buff and chock-full of steroids and horny as a bull, and you touched him *less* than you used to?"

"That's about right," Harrison admitted sheepishly.

"Shit, man, what did you expect? I'm sorry, but if you just . . . stand by and let him ferment, he's gonna blow."

"I just couldn't imagine that he'd want to do it with me anymore."

Matt sighed. "Okay. Let's assume you're right. Let's say John wanted hot sex and wasn't going to get it from you. What are you going to do about it?"

"What do you mean?"

"He's made a big physical turnaround, maybe it's time you did the same. You're getting a little tummy there, that hair is creeping over your ears, those glasses could use replacing with a little more updated look. . . ."

"Hey, I'm the gay man, I'm supposed to be giving *you* fashion advice." Harrison sighed. "I don't know. Things are so different now. When I was a young guy, it wasn't all about having muscles. It was the 1970s, and I looked pretty good, considering. A little on the thin side, but back then a nice face and a trim bod were enough to make you plenty popular. I just don't understand this need these young guys have today, this obsession with bulking up, with being so damn perfect. . . . Well, I do. Part of it was AIDS, a defense mechanism, get enough muscles and you can't turn into one of

those terrifying eighty-pound walking dead men, and part of it was
the 1980s in general, that whole idea that only everything was
enough. . . .''

"So are you going to sit here like grandpa and kvetch about
how things were different in your day, or are you going to do what
the times require?"

"What could I possibly do?"

"Work out, update your look, become someone who *could* com-
pete with these kids. Harrison, John's not dumb, and he's not a
kid. You really think he's going to have something to talk about
with this guy when the sex is all over?"

Harrison laughed with Matt, a little chuckle at the expense of
the younger generation. "Probably not."

"And John needs that stimulation just as much as the physical
stimulation, doesn't he? So what if you could provide him with all
that he needs? And maybe what *you* need is to get to a physical
level where you don't feel intimidated by him."

"I wouldn't know where to start. I wouldn't know what clothes
to buy, I couldn't afford a trainer to . . ."

"Look at me." Matt spread his arms, indicating his own well-
dressed self. "I know all about fashion, all about nutrition, all about
exercise. Hell, if I weren't so hot for Helen, I could be the world's
happiest gay man! So here's what I suggest: I dress you, I feed
you, you work out with me. Be my Eliza Doolittle and I'll be your
Professor Higgins."

Harrison looked him in the eye. "You're serious."

"Hell, yes. Are you serious about getting John back?"

Harrison thought for half a second about himself sitting in that
chair, about to take that drink. "Yes."

Matt put out his hand. "It's a deal. We start tomorrow."

Harrison took his friend's hand. "It's a deal. And thanks."

John had slept on the plane back home; the drugs (and Brian)
had kept him up all night. Time had really flown away. It seemed

one minute he and Brian were headed to the cliff, and the next the sun was up and it was time to get back, take a shower, pack up and check out.

Brian had nudged him awake when they were approaching San Francisco and it was time to put his seat up. John yawned and stretched, regarding an amused Brian through one open eye. "What's so funny?"

"You're cute when you sleep. All snuffling and drooling . . ."

John's hand flew to the corners of his mouth. Brian laughed at him as he realized he'd been had. "That's a fine way to wake someone up."

Scott's head popped up over the seat ahead of him, also looking none the worse for the wear. "You guys missed a *hot* party!"

"They had their own," he heard Slater say from the seat next to Scott's. John could see Slater's eye between the seats, glinting at him. "You feeling okay?"

John thought about it. "I feel great." He did, too—absolutely no hangover from the drug or the capacious alcohol he'd been able to drink without feeling woozy. He put his seat up and looked out the window. *That was the best vacation ever,* he thought. *I had more fun . . .*

They got off, laughing and needling Scott about his none-too-subtle advances toward their handsome steward, who had "forgotten" several times to charge Scott for alcoholic beverages and had been insistent on handing him the peanuts, ignoring Slater's constant offers to pass them over to save him the trouble. "He was hot!" Evan said in perfect Scott-like tones.

"Yuh, uh-huh!" Brian, Slater, and John chorused, dissolving into laughter.

"Shut up!" Scott said. "I got his phone number, ya know, so there."

"What!" Slater cried. "I didn't see that."

"You weren't supposed to," Scott gloated.

Brian put an arm around John's waist, to John's pleasant surprise. He put his free arm over Brian's shoulder, and the whole gang sailed down the walkway to baggage claim, laughing after Scott gave their steward a none-too-discreet grope as they passed him at the front of the plane.

Once everyone had their bags, John was suddenly gripped with dread. It was time to go home and face Harrison.

"So are we taking Super Shuttle?" John asked.

"Nuh-uh!" Scott said indignantly. "I've got my daddy's car, one of them anyway, in long-term parking. Come on."

John lagged behind to get Brian away from the others. "I am just not ready to go home."

Brian regarded him kindly, ruffling his hair. "You're still a little wrung-out from last night, huh?"

"I guess," John said, not feeling wrung-out at all but eager to grasp whatever straw gave him a reprieve from his confrontation with Harrison.

"Why don't you crash at my place, go home tomorrow?"

John practically sighed with relief. "Great, thanks."

Brian smiled and shook a warning finger. "Don't plan the wedding now, it's just for tonight."

John kissed him on the cheek. "Yes, dear."

John hadn't really noticed Brian's apartment that first night; he'd been concentrating on getting Brian naked and into bed, and the following morning had been about creeping out guiltily. This time he had the leisure to look around while Brian unpacked. The décor was an amalgam of student funky and budget chic; he recognized bits of Crate and Barrel around the apartment. The prints were copious and what you'd expect from an art student: Dali, O'Keefe, Hockney. He noticed that Brian had framed a magazine page, the famous LaChapelle "Baby Jane" shot with a tubby Courtney Love look-alike in the Bette Davis role and a Madonna wannabe in Joan Crawford's wheelchair.

In the bathroom, more framed magazine pages, a collection of Calvin Klein ads including Antonio Sabato, Jr., in his undies and some of the famous "grunge kiddie porn" shots. The plants were mostly of the flowering variety and a large ficus tree dominated the living room. The bay window in the living room had a pleasant view of downtown.

John flopped on the couch and waited for Brian. *It is so comfy here,* he thought; *I could move in here in a second. . . .* He caught himself. *I've only known him a week and one day total and already I'm planning the wedding!*

"I have a confession to make," John said as Brian joined him on the couch with two bottles of Snapple.

"Shoot."

"I'm in love with your apartment. Can I have its hand in marriage?"

Brian laughed. "Thanks. Just a little something I whipped up."

"Can I ask how much you pay?"

"Twelve hundred."

"What!" He thought of Ethan's apoplectic reaction to the price of a one bedroom in his building and shuddered.

"You haven't looked for a place in a while, have you?"

"No, I had my place for years and then moved in with Harrison."

"That's about the going rate these days, at least if you want a one bedroom in the city proper."

"Damn." He couldn't help but shudder again. What if he did move out? How the hell would he swing rent like that?

"So what are you going to do about your situation?" Brian asked him.

"I don't know. Harrison and I have to talk, but . . . I can't see any way that things can be the way they were."

"You're not leaving him because of me, are you? Because, I mean"—he laughed—"I am not ready to get married or anything."

"I know," John said hastily. "No, I was ready to blow, you

were just the blasting cap.'' They laughed, and John put his head in Brian's lap.

"So how did you guys get together in the first place?''

John thought about it. "It's hard to put it into a sound bite. When I met him, I was really lonely. I don't just mean lonely as in alone, I was an only child so I was used to being alone.''

"Me too, I know what you mean.''

"I had a lover who died a few years ago. I'd known Lee since . . . God, since you were a baby. He was someone I had a history with, you know? All I had to do was say a word and all the memories of that place or that time would come rushing back to both of us, I wouldn't have to explain *anything*. When he died, it just . . . scooped me out. I can't explain it any better than that, just that if you've ever had someone who was everything to you just die on you, you get . . . scooped out, like a big ice-cream scooper sweeps down and takes everything out of your soul. There's nothing left of you.'' He sat up. "The bright side, if there is one, is that if you live through that, it can never happen again. I lived through it, just barely.

"When I met Harrison, he was someone who filled Lee's role in a lot of ways. The mutual associations we had weren't personal memories, but we'd read the same books, lived through the same times. Lee hated to go out, he was practically agoraphobic, but Harrison loved to go out to dinner and to plays and movies, and we'd talk afterward, for hours sometimes, just walking the streets all excited about what we'd just seen. So we got close, you know? And the sex was good—not great, not pyrotechnic, but there was passion, definitely. Back when we used to have sex, that is,'' he finished dryly.

He sighed. "He was very protective and solicitous of my health, which was wonderful when I was sick and felt defenseless, but he's still that way, and now it just feels like . . . nannying. I don't know if he even realizes how bossy he comes off when he does it now.''

"Too parental, huh?"

"Exactly. I don't need that anymore, not physically, not mentally." He looked up at Brian. "It's weird, it's like in that way I'm not a kid anymore, and yet in another way I finally get to be a kid."

Brian laughed. "Listen, I'm starving, you want a sandwich?"

"That would be great."

Only after Brian had started busying himself in the kitchen did John realize that when he had been asked if he was leaving Harrison because of Brian, he had naturally said "no, not because of you," but had tacitly agreed that *yes,* he was leaving Harrison. The realization wasn't like a punch, more like a sudden vacancy, a *whoosh* as he watched Harrison sucked out of his life just like that. He wanted to cry.

He picked up the phone and dialed Helen. "Hello?"

"Hey, it's John."

"John! Did you just get back?"

"Sort of. I'm not home, I'm at Brian's."

"Oh." A pause. "So what's up?"

"I was wondering if I could crash at your place for a while."

"A while?"

"Like a week or so. Until I figure out . . . what I'm doing. Next."

"So you and Harrison have decided to separate?"

John squirmed. "We're separated, let's put it that way."

"John, I'm not your mom, you know? But you can't just run away from the problem."

"I know." He sighed.

"I will put you up, but first you have to talk to Harrison."

"I know. I will. I have to go home and get my clothes."

"You aren't even going to try and work it out?"

"Maybe, but I can't work it out while I'm under his roof, okay?"

Helen sighed. "All right. You can sleep on the sofa bed for a week. But that's it."

"Thank you."

"So will you be here tonight?"

"No, tomorrow. I'm here at Brian's and I'm pooped. I'm just going to rest up and I'll be over at your place tomorrow afternoon. Is that okay?"

"Sure. Just don't . . . well, we'll talk more tomorrow."

He hung up the phone as Brian brought in sandwiches. "I have a place to stay, starting tomorrow."

"Great," Brian said, clearly relieved.

"You were afraid I was going to install myself, weren't you?"

Brian laughed. "No, because I wasn't going to let you. Now we can just relax and enjoy each other's company today . . . and tonight." He winked.

John smiled and wrapped himself around Brian. "You're the best souvenir I've ever picked up on vacation, you know that?"

"I'm just like those little novelty items—pull my string and my pants fall down."

"Is your battery charged?"

"Just call me ever ready," he laughed, rolling himself and John off the couch and onto the floor.

On the bus back home the next day, John thought about what Jim, the therapist, had advised him to do—make a plan for his talk with Harrison. He'd had all of a day to do it but it was the last thing he wanted to do while in Brian's company. They'd made love, taken a nap, ordered a pizza, watched a movie, made love again, and slept in late.

John was no aesthete; he was the last person likely to be swept away by a perfect moment, but he'd found himself enraptured with the area around Brian's belly button, where just the slightest pocket of fat had its residence. The skin right there was so amazingly soft, and smooth, like silk over butter, and he found himself lazily circling his fingers across it again and again, a constant reminder of how young Brian was. Nobody over thirty could have skin that felt as velvety as that. Lying there with Brian, he couldn't help thinking back to his first sexual encounters with Harrison. On him, it had been the little patches of silver at his temples that had the power to fascinate. Funny, that on one lover it had been the signs of maturity that had tripped his trigger; while on another it had been a feature that was the sole province of youth. But now he had new triggers, since everything in his life was different. And he knew damn well that it hadn't just been the end of sex with Harrison that had been the solvent dissolving the relationship.

On the bus he tried to compose a speech: "I need some time to figure out what I want. . . ." *No, too clichéd.* "I think we've grown apart . . . I'm not the person you met . . . you're too bossy . . . I'm so horny . . ." He sighed. Maybe denial was the best way to deal with it all—just pick up his clothes and say "See ya." But that was not only immature, it was cruel. He loved Harrison, there was no doubt in his mind of that, but obviously, sometimes, love wasn't enough. He finally just gave up on planning and decided to make it up as he went along.

It felt strange to come "home." He realized as he turned the key in the lock that he was already gone mentally. Whatever was going to happen next in his life, Harrison wouldn't be a part of it.

Nobody was home. Rafsanjani greeted him with a plaintive mew that almost broke his heart. He and Harrison had inherited the cat when a friend of John's had died, and it had come with a preposterous name, Chiquita or something. They'd decided to let her real name reveal itself, and after she revealed her terroristic propensity for jumping up on the bed and running across them, claws extended, Harrison had called her "our little Rafsanjani" and the name had stuck.

"Oh, kitty, I'm sorry, but I have to go." He pulled his big suitcase out of the closet and started packing, taking only the essentials—work clothes, gym stuff, personal-care items. Everything else would have to wait until he was settled in permanently, wherever he was going to end up. In the kitchen he was filling a shopping bag with his medicines and bodybuilding supplements when the door opened. "I'm in here," he announced, so as not to surprise Harrison.

To his surprise, Harrison had a gym bag in his hand. "Hey," he said, eyeing the shopping bag.

"Hey."

"Going somewhere?" Harrison asked neutrally.

"To Helen's for a while."

"How was your trip?"

"Nice, how was yours?"

"Fine. Can we . . . can we talk? Before you go?"

John hesitated. "Sure."

Harrison waved him to the couch. "John, I know things haven't been . . . right lately. I'm sorry about the whole trip thing, I really am."

John shrugged. "That's okay. Water under the bridge."

"I don't want it to be water under the bridge, because that means . . . you tell me what it means."

"I don't know. So much has happened to me. I guess I feel like I need to start over."

Harrison smiled. "I guess this is when I accuse you of having an affair."

John looked him in the eye. "I am having an affair."

"I thought so."

"What do you mean?"

"You went off to this resort, so of course you had a fling with someone there."

John blackened. "What do you mean 'of course' I did?"

"That's what you went for, wasn't it? To punish me by being with someone else?"

John laughed disbelievingly. "To punish you! Do you really think that's what this is all about? You are just so sure I had a fling."

"You did, didn't you?"

Harrison's arrogant certainty tripped John's trigger. "I did. But you know what? It wasn't someone I met there. It was someone I'd already been with here, before that. It was the guy I met the night I didn't come home." He watched Harrison's face for his reaction, but he was curiously impassive.

"I'm not surprised. I imagine since you've gotten this new body of yours that you've had plenty of adventure."

"What!" John shouted indignantly. "How dare you! You have no idea what it's been like for me. All the opportunities I've just thrown away because I was married to you. All the guys I turned down because I didn't want to hurt you. And all that time, you thought I was screwing around anyway, didn't you?"

Harrison flushed. "I didn't mean to imply . . ."

"But you did. Yes, I'm having an affair. I'm doing it with someone—the *one man* I've gone to bed with besides you in the last two years. Though now I guess I might as well have fucked them all, huh?" He got up. "I am out of here."

"John . . ."

John held up a hand. "No. Forget it." He felt himself on the brink of tears and angrily forced them back down. "This is perfect. Wonderful. I can just leave now, and not worry about you. Now maybe I'll just go fuck all those men you thought I was fucking anyway."

He was out the door before Harrison could say anything else. He made it to the building lobby before the tears started, tears of rage and pain and confusion.

* * *

"It's not supposed to be like this," he said to Helen.

"Not supposed to be like what?" Helen asked him when he'd poured out his story.

"This is not what my life is supposed to be like!" John said angrily. "I was dead, and then I was alive, and so everything was supposed to be all better. It's not supposed to be all screwed up and awful and . . . what am I going to do now?" he cried.

"Life's a bitch and then you live," Helen said, pouring him some more tea.

He couldn't help but laugh at that. "Really, huh?"

"Getting your life back doesn't mean happily ever after, you know."

"So I'm learning."

"Let me ask you something. Do you really think you have a future with this guy Brian?"

"A future? You mean first comes love, then comes marriage? I haven't even thought about it. Why?"

"I just wonder if you should throw over everything you have with Harrison for someone who's . . . well, he's twenty-one, right? He has a lot of adventure ahead of him still. You know Louis de Bernieres? The guy who wrote *Corelli's Mandolin?*"

"That was a great book."

"Well, I'm reading one of his other books, and I just read something that made me think of you. There's a man involved with a younger woman, and he says to her something along the lines of, 'everyone I knew when I was your age is part of my history now.' "

"Meaning?"

"Meaning how many of the people you knew when you were twenty-one do you still know now?"

"None. But that's because they're all dead."

Helen flushed. "Sorry. I didn't mean to . . ."

"I know," John said, letting her off. "And I know what you're getting at. When he's thirty-three I'll be . . . forty-five! But that's not such a huge age difference . . . except I know what you mean. When you're that young, people come and go in your life. I'm not planning the wedding, Helen, but he's, well, you should meet him. I know, you hear twenty-one and you think, twitty-twerpy know-nothing.'' John thought of Scott at that moment. ''But Brian's not like that. He's got a lot on the ball, he's fun to be with . . .''

''And of course there's the sex, right?''

''Right!'' He laughed. ''Let's talk! With the steroids and all, I've got the libido of a teenager anyway, so we're pretty well matched.''

Helen laughed. ''So Harrison doesn't have a prayer, huh?''

''It's not just the sex, Helen. He's so damn . . . *professorial.* I'm not one of his students! He can't just assign some trip, you know? And that shit he pulled when I went to get my stuff. 'Oh, of course you've been screwing around.' Thanks a lot! And some of it doesn't even have anything to do with Harrison. Helen, when I went out to the club that first night, when I was down at Babylon, I was *so happy!* All my life I'd had my nose pressed to the glass, watching the popular kids, whether it was high school or Castro Street Fair, and I was never going to be one of them. Then all of a sudden I *was* one of them! All of a sudden I was having fun, doing stuff I never did before, stripping on dance floors and making out with guys in public and . . . being part of the 'in crowd.' Shallow, huh? But it's fun, dammit. It's fun to be young, and I finally get to be young!'' he finished defiantly.

Helen sighed. ''I can't argue with that. I certainly had my fun at that age, and I might not have been ready to settle down with Matt if I hadn't.''

''But it's not quite the same—Matt's pretty incredibly hot, you know.''

Helen was well aware of Matt's Eliza Doolittle plan for Harrison, and so she casually ventured, "So you mean to say that if Harrison was all chiseled and hot, things would be different?"

John considered. "I hadn't thought about that. I can't imagine!" He laughed.

"But if he was?" Helen pressed.

"I guess, maybe. But then if he'd been all chiseled, he probably wouldn't have married me in the first place, since I was such a lump!"

"Is that what it's all about for gay men, is it all just body, body, body?"

"Well ..." John laughed. "Nothing's true for all of anyone, but, for the most part, yes. If you have that body, chances are if you get married you'll get married to someone else with that body. Why should you marry someone schlubby if you don't have to?"

"Maybe because you love him."

"In which case you become best friends."

"So you think you and Harrison can be friends?"

"Sure, someday. Just not today." He laughed and added, "There's so much we have together but ... but it's just not enough right now."

Helen got up. "I don't know what to say. You've been my friend for years, John, and I think you have a relatively level head on your shoulders. All I'm going to say is that while you may be the kid in the candy store right now, just remember you can still get a sore tummy if you're not careful."

"Right," he agreed. "What's going to happen to me now? I've already got the bug."

"I'm not even talking about physically. Well, partly I am. I just don't want to see you get caught up in a world where the values are not quite ... where people are all about their bodies and looks and all that, and even though they're all gorgeous and wonderful and the top of the heap, for some reason they're also all taking some chemical to feel better about themselves."

John thought about the crystal he'd done on vacation but decided to say nothing and let Helen continue. "I'm just saying take care of yourself, and don't forget who your real friends are. Don't get caught up in that scene."

"I won't. I just want to have a little fun for a while, that's all."

"I can't argue with fun." She got up. "So what are you going to do about a place to live?"

"Find a roommate, I guess," he groaned. "God knows I can't afford my own place anymore. Too bad this didn't happen a year ago when apartments were still cheap!"

"That's because the economy is so good. Look at the bright side, if it weren't, you wouldn't have such a good-paying job."

"A good-paying job that's still not enough to get my own place in this town. Everybody talks about the rising tide lifting all boats, blah blah blah. All well and good, but what if you're one of the people who can't afford a boat?"

"John, you're in the ideal position to find a roommate situation: You're gorgeous, you're employed, and you have no pets."

He laughed. "Okay, okay. I'll take that as a hint to start looking right away."

"Take your time," Helen said. "Just don't take too much of mine," she finished with mock darkness, patting him on the head.

John went in early to work on Monday, because he knew exactly what he'd find when he got there—a huge pile of work in his in-box. To confirm his suspicion that Obelisk had basically used the temp as a chair warmer, he checked the recently opened documents on the Start menu, and wasn't the least bit surprised to find "Dear Connie," "My Resumé," "Things To Do," etc., as the most recent files. He started up AOL, and sure enough the last user was "Guest." He logged in to check his mail and found to his enormous irritation that his settings had been modified. With a feeling of dread he opened Microsoft Word to find that there, too, the temp had oblivi-ously ignored the instructions he'd left not to change anything. He wasted half an hour just making things right again before he could even look at the pile.

Naturally, as soon as he did he found something marked in red with "I need by 9 A.M. Monday!" It was already 9:15. In a panic he raced through it, dreading the manifestation of Obelisk or, more likely, his anxious emissary Miss Plinth, in his doorway, demanding to know where the report was. He raced down the hall to Miss Plinth's desk and handed it to her.

"Sorry, I had to *un*screw-up my computer from the temp. I know he wanted this half an hour ago. . . ."

"Oh, Mr. Obelisk hasn't come in yet," Miss Plinth said, looking worriedly at her watch. "I should call him in the car."

John said nothing but stomped up front to see Patsy. "Hey, sweetums!" she cried, jumping up and yanking her Starset off in her race to hug him. "I'm so glad you're back. I was late every single day last week. Which was nice, but damn, did Plinth ever ride my ass!"

"That stupid temp screwed up my machine but good."

"I'm not surprised," Patsy said. "Plinth told me all about her. She gave her a table to do, and guess what? She used the *space bar* to line up the columns, and of course it kept coming out all wrong on the page. She went to Plinth and said, 'I don't know why this isn't working, it looks right on the screen.' Plinth saw what she'd done and flipped out! Then, get this. She's doing a report and there's a quoted paragraph, indented on both sides, right? Well, she tabs and returns on every line so when Plinth gets the disk and goes to edit it, it's all screwed up. She asks the temp, 'Why didn't you indent?' And guess what the temp says!"

" 'I don't know how to do that,' " John chorused grimly along with Patsy as she roared with laughter.

"Sheesh. No wonder they left all the work for me to do. God, Patsy, I'm going to have to work late for days, and this is the worst time to have to do that because I've got to look for a place to live!"

"What! What do you mean? Are you and Harrison getting kicked out?"

"No. I'm . . . I'm not living with Harrison anymore."

"Whoa. Whoa! Wait a minute. One minute it's separate vacations, and the next you're divorced? That was fast."

John thought about that. "It was, wasn't it? Well, a whole lot happened real fast, that's all."

"My God, you and Tim are having an affair! I never should have egged you on!"

John laughed. "No. Not yet anyway, though God knows what might happen tomorrow. I did meet someone else, but . . ."

"Aha. And Harrison found out about it."

"Because I told him. It's . . . oh God, Pats, I'd tell you all about it over lunch but I don't even think I have time to take lunch today. Anyway, I'm staying with a friend but I can't stay long; I need to find a roommate situation, unless I can find a cheap apartment."

"Sure you can—in Daly City. Cottage-cheese ceilings, orange shag rug that was laid in the '70s, walls and ceilings the thickness of *People* magazine. Jesus, a roommate! You did that before, didn't you, and hated it?"

"When I first moved here. Let's not speak of it."

"That bad, huh? Is there anything I can do? Workwise?"

"Could you? That would be great. If you could just type some of this stuff up so I can get it into the brochures . . ."

"No problem. I don't do much up here besides enter contests on the radio and flirt with the FedEx guy."

"Patsy, you're a lifesaver."

"Listen, I've been through this a couple of times myself— anything to help out a fellow divorcée!"

Filling out the paperwork that evening at Community Rentals, John couldn't help thinking back to his prior roommate experiences. His first apartment had been great—a "railroad car" flat with a skylight in the living room, sliding glass doors in the kitchen leading to a big sunny deck overlooking the square block of "secret gardens" one found behind the unbroken façade of old Victorians in San Francisco.

The first problem had been the roommate, whose name he couldn't even remember now, having thought of him for so long as "Mushroom Boy." Pale, wan, and sad, Mushroom Boy was employed as a mail-room clerk downtown; he never saw the light of day at work nor at home. John's bedroom was radiantly bright, hanging right over Eighteenth Street, whereas Mushroom Boy's room received only a trickle of light from the airwell. John had initially offered to change rooms with him on a twice-yearly basis, but his roommate had told him, "No, thanks, I like the dark." He did go out on weekends, but he always came home alone and never to John's knowledge got a personal phone call or had any friends over, if he even had any friends. He spent Saturday and Sunday in his room, emerging only to go to the bathroom; John had never seen him eat.

He wasn't the least bit surprised when Mushroom Boy came home one day and told him he could have the apartment because he had joined a cult and would be giving up all his earthly possessions and dedicating his life to helping make the payments on the Rajneesha's forty-two Rolls-Royces. He'd interviewed only one potential new roommate (a big mistake), but Paul had seemed perfectly normal. He took the dark room without complaint but rarely left the house, preferring to sit up on his low-slung futon, listening to the jazz station and drinking beer with the door shut. Any time John had needed to talk to Paul, he'd knock, be granted entrance, and find him staring into space, drinking, never reading or doing much of anything else.

Paul had eventually discovered that it was more fun to drink with others than to drink alone, and started bringing tricks home at closing time on a nightly basis, with an unerring eye for the ones who made the most possible noise. The morning a bleary-eyed John found barf in the bathtub (Paul had been yakking it up into the toilet, and his new friend hadn't been able to wait his turn) was the morning he'd planned to give Paul his walking papers, only to discover he'd taken a job teaching English in Japan and would be leaving immediately.

And to this day John couldn't even *think* about "Space Girl," who didn't work and didn't worry, sure as she was that "the universe will provide." Pressed repeatedly for the rent, she had solemnly informed him that "the more you expect, the less you get." Eventually she revealed that the Ant People would soon be landing and ushering in a new era on earth, and that money would no longer be necessary. Unable to get her evicted (she was frighteningly well versed in renter's rights laws, and not at all her otherwise celestially calm self when pressed to the wall), he'd decided to simply move out into a studio apartment and never, ever again share a place with a stranger. He left Space Girl in his beautiful apartment to await the sheriff or the Ant People, whichever came for her first. That place had cost a grand total of $750 a month when he'd moved in, he thought ruefully. And even with four percent increases a year, hell, today that would be a two-bedroom apartment for around a thousand bucks—about what you had to pay now to move into a studio.

But he'd been right—there was no way he was going to get an apartment of his own in the current rapacious real estate market. As Ethan had griped, the landlords were indeed charging "what the market will bear," which was far more than John could bear. Still, while his own history had been unremittingly bleak in that department, he knew that there were happy roommate situations, like the one Ethan and Kevin shared, and he was determined to make the best of it.

He compiled a list of possibilities and went back to Helen's to start making calls to potential roommates. "I'm apartment hunting," he announced in the kitchen, dramatically flourishing his notes.

"That's nice, dear," Helen said, not to be distracted from a risotto that needed constant nannying to succeed.

In the living room, Matt was more solicitous, putting down the paper and commenting on the various possibilities. After a moment's hesitation, he asked, "So you're not thinking about moving in with Brian?"

"No, I think it's a little too early for that, don't you?"

"Probably, especially since you're not really divorced from Harrison yet."

John arched an eyebrow, wondering what Matt was up to. "I'm not?"

"I don't think so. Separated, maybe, but not divorced. It's not impossible that the two of you could get back together, is it?"

"Not impossible. Just excruciatingly improbable."

Matt sighed. "John . . ."

"Don't say it. Don't tell me how wonderful Harrison is . . . etc., etc., etc., okay?"

"That's not what I was going to say. But I do want to say something."

John bit his tongue. He was Matt and Helen's guest, and as such he supposed he was obligated to listen to the occasional lecture. "Go on."

"I think you're going through a phase right now, maybe it's a phase that was bound to come sooner or later. But I hope you don't throw away everything you had with Harrison because you've met someone a little more . . . exciting. Brian is twenty-one years old, John. He's got a lot of lovers ahead of him. I remember what it was like to be that age; you're in love with someone one day and the next, well, suddenly you're done learning from that person and you want to move on."

"Great. I feel like Mary Haines, getting advice from her wise old mother." He stopped. "But I'm not Mary Haines, am I? I'm Crystal Allen, homewrecker!"

"No, you're not. You're Steven Haines; if anybody's Crystal Allen it's your friend Brian."

John looked at Matt. "I think you spend too much time with gay men, you know that? Straight men shouldn't know so much about these things, it's not natural and probably not healthy."

Matt smiled and shrugged. "You live in Japan, you pick up some Japanese. You live in San Francisco . . ."

"Really, huh? Let me tell you something. Whatever is going on between me and Harrison, should the remote possibility of our getting back together even *exist*, which I don't concede it does, it is not going to get resolved in the one week that Helen has given me to find my own place."

Matt blinked. "A week?" He lowered his voice. "That's a little tough. But you know Helen; it's not that she doesn't love you, it's just that a houseguest is . . . messy. I don't mean trash-and-crumbs messy, it's a disruption. It's that German blood of hers—that love of order."

They laughed. "It's okay. There were plenty of listings that sounded good. I'm sure finding a place will be a piece of cake."

CHAPTER SIX

J ohn didn't get out of work until seven o'clock the following evening, and only then because he had an appointment to see an apartment. The deal sounded good in the listing at the service—a sunny two-bedroom flat with a view from the hill above Davies Medical Center. It offered a deck, a garden, a fully renovated and modern kitchen, and a walk-in closet. The tenant described himself as a forty-year-old SGWM, "proudly owned by two loving cats, fond of quiet evenings and gardening." Compared to the people John had shared with before, this guy sounded like a dream.

He took the 24 up to Davies and walked up the hill, thinking it was a pleasant neighborhood, albeit a little farther from a grocery store than he would have liked. He knocked on the door and was surprised to be greeted by a short, bald, dumpy man in a caftan who seemed equally surprised to see him. "You must be John. I'm Philip. Do come in."

John followed him down the hall and into the living room, which, to his consternation, looked like a Laura Ashley showroom. John almost laughed out loud when he saw the silk flowers; apparently every floral motif was allowable, except for the actual vegetation. He was about to sit down on the couch when Philip practically shouted, "Don't sit there!" He rushed out of the room while a bewildered John stood around, wondering where would be a safe place to sit. Philip returned with a sheet he carefully laid over the couch. "You may sit down now. It's just that you're wearing jeans, which are *very* scratchy and wear down the fabric."

"Oh," John said, suspecting that Philip would probably not approve of his sitting around in his underwear, either. He suddenly realized why there were no real, potentially messy, flowers. "So, can I see the room?"

Philip arranged himself on a love seat, his caftan presumably not made of any material that would scratch the fabric. "First I want to tell you about my ground rules. What is your taste in music?"

"Pretty eclectic. I like jazz, classical, I listen to Alice . . ."

"Alice?"

"It's a radio station. KLLC; they call it Alice. Alternative music."

"Oh. Well, I can't *stand* anything but classical myself, and by that I mean classical, not that modernist twaddle. Do you have headphones?"

"Yes . . ."

"Good. You'll need them. What are your hours?"

"I work eight to five. Then I go to the gym, so I'm not really home until seven or eight."

"No, I mean how late do you stay up?"

"On the weekends I stay up as late as I want," he said defiantly. "It's been a while since I lived with my parents so I don't really think about it."

"I'm early to bed and early to rise, *every day,* including weekends. And I'm a light sleeper. Are you in a relationship?"

"I have a boyfriend." He couldn't honestly say if Brian was his official boyfriend yet, but it was good enough for this conversation.

"I hope he has a nice place, since he can't stay over here. I really don't care for hearing other people having sex."

That's because it's been about six hundred years since you've had any, John thought, wondering how he could cut this short and get out. A brush against his leg caught his attention. "Hey, kitty," he said, bending down to pet the fluffy white Persian, who responded by hissing and scratching him. "Ow, shit!" The cat darted over to Philip and nestled in his lap, sending hateful glances at John.

"Nobody can pet Queenie but me."

John got up. "Then, maybe you should send Queenie out to get a job; sounds like she's likely to be the only compatible roommate you'll find."

Philip turned red and huffed, "There's no need to be rude. You can see yourself out. Good day!"

"He didn't want a roommate," John grumbled out on the street. "He wanted a *mummy* that will only rise from the coffin to write a rent check every month." He sucked the blood off his finger, worrying about cat-scratch fever and anything else he might get from the scratch, before thinking that, considering Philip, the house was probably pretty germ-free. "That place was a morgue anyway."

He groaned at the thought of how many more frogs he was going to have to kiss before he found—if he ever found—the roommate version of Prince Charming. "I want my own place again!" he said through gritted teeth, knowing even as he said it that it would be impossible for him to ever have that again in San Francisco barring Ed McMahon's knock on the door.

His cell phone rang and he pulled it out of his jacket. "Hello?"

"Uh, hi, is this John?"

"Yes."

"Hi, this is Bart, you left me a message about the apartment?"

John thought back. "Uh, which listing was that?"

"On the Panhandle? Two-bedroom flat, your own bathroom?"

"Right," John said as it came back to him. Having your own bathroom wasn't quite having your own place, but it was more than you could expect in most situations. "Thanks for calling me back."

"Sure. So, would you like to come see the place? Say, now?"

"Well, I just went through a pretty ugly encounter." He gave Bart a thumbnail description of Philip and his abode.

Bart laughed. "You don't have to worry about that with me. I like music, I like sex, and I like to party. And I don't have any cats!"

John laughed. "I guess I could come over now." He took down the address. "I'll be there in a bit."

"Great, see you soon."

Truth be told, John was not in the mood to do another interview, but the Panhandle was reasonably close to where he was now, and Helen's kind but firm injunction that he needed to find his own place quickly was at the front of his mind.

Bart answered the door in jeans and tank top. As they walked down the hall, John noticed that the walls were covered with posters for circuit parties from the late seventies. "This is my room," Bart said, opening a door. John found himself face-to-face with a poster of a smirking clone, presumably the spokesmodel for "Handball Express," advertised as a "no-holds-barred party at the Russian River, September 1-4, 1980" that advised attendees to "bring your own supplies." John knew the type—their happiest moments had come before AIDS and no other experience could ever equal that thoughtless reckless time in their memories.

"Come on in," Bart said, and John followed, wondering why they were going into Bart's room rather than taking a tour of the house. Bart smiled and winked. "You're a pretty hot guy." On his bedside table was a miniature rolltop desk; he opened it to reveal several fat lines of something cut out and waiting. Bart produced a straw and quickly did two of the lines, then tried to hand the straw to John. "Your turn."

"Uh, no thanks, I have to work tomorrow."

"All the more reason to party tonight." He put a hand on John's thigh, and it felt to John like an electric shock.

"Sorry, I'm really not interested."

"No? You sounded on the phone like a pretty wild guy."

"I'm not," he said firmly. "I like to have a good time but I'm not . . ." *I m not that easy,* he thought to himself, and bit his tongue. "I'm not interested," he stated again.

Bart shrugged and did the other two lines. "Guess I'll just have to party without you. Shut the door on your way out."

"Wait a minute. *That's it?* You had me come all the way over here just to try and put the make on me?"

"Hey, I think you're a little too uptight for me. I like a roommate who doesn't mind being a fuck buddy, too. Maybe that guy Philip is more the kind of roommate you need after all."

"I think there's such a thing as a happy medium," John said darkly.

"Whatever. See ya."

John screamed, to the surprise and alarm of his "host." "That is IT! I can't take any more of this! I am getting my own place if it means living in the goddamn Tenderloin! You are all *crazy!*" His cell phone rang. "What!" he shouted into it.

"Hi, you called about the apartment?"

"*AAAAGGGGHH!*" he screamed, hanging up and running for the door.

Out on the street, his cell phone rang again. "I am no longer looking for a roommate; thank you for calling."

"Oh, you found a place!" Brian said.

Warmth and relief flooded John's brain. "Thank God it's you. No, just the opposite, actually—I've given up. It's an SRO on Turk Street for me, I think."

"That bad, huh?"

"Pretty bad."

"I was just watching the tube, and those girls who did *The Rules* were on, and they said nobody should accept a date for Saturday with a man who calls after Wednesday, so since today's Tuesday and I was wondering what you were doing Friday, I thought I'd better call today just in case you'd read their book.''

John laughed. ''No, I haven't. And I'd love to do something Friday. What did you have in mind?''

''I don't know, just date-stuff I guess—dinner, movie, come back here, get naked . . .''

''Mmm.'' He smiled. ''That sounds like a great plan.''

''Are you doing anything Saturday?''

''No, why?''

''I don't know, I just thought we could get up late and go to breakfast and you could show me some of the tourist spots . . . unless you're going to be apartment hunting.'' John could hear the wicked grin behind Brian's words.

''No, but we'll have to make it your place; I think where I'm going to end up there are signs in the lobby that say 'No Visitors After Nine P.M.' ''

Brian laughed. ''Something will turn up. You just started looking, after all.''

''I know. But I also know a bad sign when I see one.''

''Oops, that's the other line, I gotta go. I'll call you Friday afternoon.''

''Great. I'm looking forward to it.''

As he hung up, John did a little dance. *A date! I have a date with Brian! I'm going out on a date with a hot boy on a Friday night!* He sailed down the street, happy as a clam. This is what it's all about, he thought, why it's great to still be alive. It wasn't supposed to be just another chance to exist, but another chance to *live,* to have fun! And like a boy, he found that his hideous evening and hellish day were washed away by a giddy joy. *Now is all that matters, now is all there is, and I'm happy now, so happy . . .*

John thought about bringing Brian flowers or candy or some such, but he quashed the impulse. He desperately wanted to perform such a romantic gesture, but he kept reminding himself to play it cool. It could come off the wrong way so easily, he thought; it could either seem corny or, worse, scare Brian off if he suddenly thought he and John were engaged in an official romance.

He showed up at Brian's place Friday night and heard the sounds of an old Cure album through the door. "It's open," Brian called after he buzzed.

John let himself in. "Hello?"

"I'm in the bathroom, make yourself at home. There's beer in the fridge . . . oh, and I got you some orange Stoli."

"My hero," John said, making for the kitchen and availing himself of the Stoli.

"Is this music okay with you?" Brian asked.

"Okay? I love it. What, did you think I listened to the smooth mellow sounds of Kenny G?"

"Like I said, I like to date older guys, and they're usually not into the same music I am."

John took his drink and leaned against the bathroom-door frame, watching a glistening Brian, clad only in a towel, as he performed his cosmetic ablutions.

"You need to see my photo album."

"Why's that?"

"When I was your age, all the other gay boys wanted to be Madonna. My friends and I wanted to be Robert Smith. And we looked the part."

"No!" Brian said delightedly, looking at John with new eyes.

"We were into goth, and punk, and new wave, and what*ever* they were calling it at the moment. This was in Reno, Nevada, where I grew up, and we used to go up and down the main drag on Saturday nights scaring the boring kids by screaming at them out of our car—'I might like you better if we slept together!' Shit like that."

"Wow . . . you were cool!"

"Blush blush," John smiled.

"A real punk rocker, huh?"

"Not exactly. The punks needed us around because the cool girls hung out with us, so if they wanted to score with the cool girls they had to hang out with us, too. Of course, they'd ask you for a blow job if nobody was watching, but that was another story. And the girls hung out with us because half of us were in beauty school—not me, but plenty of the other kids—and they could make 'em look like Siouxsie Sioux or Margaret from *Liquid Sky*."

"What's *'Liquid Sky'?*"

"Ohmigod, you've never seen it? It's one of the best movies ever! We have to rent it. It's not exactly Blockbuster video material, but I'm sure we could find it. This girl plays a lesbian punk fashion model *and* her male counterpart, and she lives with this heroin-dealing performance-artist chick, and this alien lands on her roof and starts killing the men she has sex with, who she doesn't really want to have sex with, anyway, and she thinks it's doing her a favor but really it's just killing them because it eats their brain chemicals at the point of orgasm . . . anyway, it was years ahead of its time. If they released it now, it would make a ton of money; you kids would love it."

"Freaky." Brian put his arms around John's waist. "I definitely want to see your photo album. You're so conservative-looking now I can't believe you were . . ."

"Conservative!"

"You know! You look like you go to the Alta Plaza, and the Lion Pub, and drive a BMW. . . ."

"Thanks a lot. Listen, kiddo, once you're over thirty it's usually not pretty when you start piercing your face and wearing jackets that identify you as a gas station attendant, okay? I would feel like a fool if I dressed like a kid, but that doesn't mean I go to the Ultra Plastic. Ever been there?"

"Someone took me once. It was full of snotty queens, including this one I never forgot. He looks out the window ostentatiously and says, *as loud as he can,* to his friend, 'I can't see *my* BMW from here, can you?' ''

"Oh, brother."

"Not my cup of tea, you know?"

"Not mine, either, believe me. What do you suggest I do with myself, you know, so cute young boys don't think I'm some old fossil?"

Brian put his hand on his chin. "Hmm. You could start wearing baggy retro '50s shirts, you could develop some interesting facial hair. . . ."

John laughed. "Never mind! I'll just have to hope my inner grooviness shines through."

"I think you're groovy."

"And that's what counts," John said, stroking Brian's face.

Brian pressed John's hand against his cheek. "You know, we don't have to go out. We could just stay in and watch some TV, order in some food, and . . ."

"We could do that, if you're embarrassed to be seen with me in public. . . ."

"No! Of course not. What makes you say that?"

"We stayed in last time, remember? I thought it would be nice to go out, that's all."

"You are right," Brian said firmly. "I'll get dressed."

"And you've done all your facial chores, so you might as well."

"I would have done those even if we were going to stay in, silly. Wouldn't want you to see me at anything but my best."

"Now who's the Ultra Plastic queen!"

Brian threw a hairbrush at John. "Out! Go make yourself useful and pour me one of those."

Brian and John looked at each other outside the movie theater where they'd just seen *When The Cat's Away.*

"What the hell was that all about?" Brian asked. "I'm only twenty-one, maybe that's it. So you tell me, did I miss something?"

"No. If there was something, I sure as hell missed it, too." Like many an innocent moviegoer over the years, they had been lured into a flick described by highbrow critics as "charming," only to find themselves completely perplexed at the end of it.

"Not much happened, did it?" Brian asked.

"Nope. And don't ask me what the deal was at the end, when she's running down the street."

"I think that's a tribute to some scene from some other French film we haven't seen."

"That's it! At least she found the damn cat."

Fillmore Street on a warm summer's eve was a bustling place. "So you're the native, or practically," Brian said. "Where do we eat around here?"

"Do you like spicy food? Creole, jambalaya, all that?"

"Love it, baby. Burn me up."

They waited at the Elite Café's bar for their table, their heads close together so they could hear each other over the buzz of conversation around them. "Any more developments on the apartment-hunting front?" Brian asked.

"No," John answered, sighing. "I really don't know what to do. Helen isn't going to throw me out on the street, but she could make life difficult for me if I overstay my welcome. But Matt, on the other hand. . . ." He stopped short.

"What?"

"I think Matt likes having another man around the house; some-one to help him resist Helen's endless onslaught of domestic touches," John fibbed. The truth was, he knew from a loose word from Helen that Matt and Harrison were spending time together, and while John couldn't be certain, he suspected that Matt was reporting on him to Harrison. At any rate, his ex-lover's possible inquisitiveness wasn't the kind of thing he wanted to be talking to Brian about.

"Is most of your stuff still at your old place?"

"Just about everything's still there but the essentials—work clothes, gym bag, pills"—he smiled—"nightclubbing wardrobe."

Brian laughed. "He's got all your important financial papers, huh?"

"Ha! What important financial papers?"

"You don't have an IRA or anything?"

"No. What for? By the time I was out in the work force, there it was, the Big A. I grew up having nightmares about The Bomb, and just when those went away, along came AIDS. So I guess I never saw the point of saving for a future that wasn't coming."

Brian was silent for a moment. "Do you think you'll live a long time now? With the cocktail and all?"

John wrestled with this—not whether or not he believed it, but whether or not he should be honest with Brian or tell him a candy-coated lie. He opted for the truth. "I think you'll live a long time. You caught it early, and you were drug naive so everything out there works for you, and there are so many pills coming out. It's like, every advance lets you live until the next advance, which lets you live to the next, etc. So you have a lot of future ahead of you to think about."

"And you don't?"

"I guess I never believed in the future too much, and when I got sick, my sense of time . . . telescoped. In the periods I wasn't sick I thought, I was okay today, but would I be okay tomorrow? I learned to enjoy today, you know?" He took Brian's hand. "I'm enjoying today. A lot. That's enough for me, now."

Brian squeezed back. "I'm enjoying today, too. And we've got at least two more todays ahead of us, you know. Can you see that far ahead?"

John put on a look of mock concentration. "Hmm. Gee, that's a stretch, but yeah . . . I'm seeing . . . I'm seeing . . . Sunday morning . . . breakfast in bed . . . a newspaper . . . I'm seeing . . . an early-morning erection. . . ."

Brian laughed. "You should do predictions for the *Enquirer.*"

"Am I seeing correctly?"

Brian winked. "We'll find out Sunday morning, but I'm willing to bet you're batting a thousand."

John woke up early Saturday morning. Brian was on his side, facing away from him, and John tried to get out of bed while making as little noise as possible. "You're awake," Brian said clearly.

"Did I wake you?" he asked sheepishly.

"No, I was awake." Brian rolled over, stretching lazily. "You're an early riser, aren't you?"

"Too many years of office jobs, I guess. Tell me where the stuff for coffee is and I'll make it."

"I can make it," Brian said, throwing back the covers and padding naked into the kitchen. "You can toast some crumpets or something. Turn on the TV, will you? CNN?"

"Sure." John dialed in just in time for the theme song to *Style with Elsa Klensch.*

"You ever watch this show?" Brian asked. "I love it. 'The worlds of fashion, beauty, and decorating,' " he said, imitating Elsa's plummy yet indeterminate accent. "Who knows, art school may put me there, so I guess I'd better keep up."

"I haven't seen it for a long time. Lee, my lover before Harrison, was totally into fashion. Naomi, Linda, Christy, blah blah blah— Kirsten was my favorite. You know who I mean?"

"Scary insect girl! I like her, and I like Eve—the one with the tattooed head."

"Right. The freaky ones. And I like the interior design segments, where I can drool over houses I'll never live in."

"Unless you marry the rich old queen who lives in it now."

"No, thanks, I'll take independence in a studio any day."

The aroma of coffee filled the apartment. "How do you like it?"

"Coffee candy, please."

"Ugh. Okay, it's your teeth."

"And my arteries." He sipped while Brian returned to the kitchen to toast some crumpets.

"So what's on our agenda today?" Brian asked.

"I don't know, what do you want to do?"

"I want you to show me the sights," Brian called from the kitchen. "I want to be a tourist for the day."

"I can do that. Let me think. Alcatraz?"

"No, too creepy."

"I know—Coit Tower! I've never been there myself."

"You're kidding."

"No, it's one of those things—you live here, you tell yourself, I've got plenty of time to see all that tourist stuff, but you never do unless you're escorting someone from out of town."

"So you mean to tell me we might get lost on the way?"

"Hmm, I could arrange for that if you want. We could end up in some bushes somewhere."

Brian laughed, shocked. "No, that's okay! Call me square, but I like sex that ends without my having to pull leaves out of my crack."

John laughed. "Coit Tower it is, sans leaves."

They got outside with plans to take the bus but it was such a beautiful day they decided to walk. "You know what I've noticed since I moved here?" Brian huffed at the top of Russian Hill. "Everybody has great legs, even if they don't go to the gym. It's all these hills."

"That's why the official uniform is shorts and a jacket," John added. "Shorts because it's just warm enough to show off your great legs but a jacket because it's never warm enough to go without one."

"Shit, is that Coit Tower over there?" Brian asked with dismay. From the top of Russian Hill, the tower was at eye level, which meant a steep walk downhill and another steep walk uphill.

"That be it. Too far for you?"

"Is it too far for you? Will you be okay?"

"What, I'm so old and broken down you have to check on me? You wanna take my pulse?" John laughed.

"No, no, I just thought that you might tire easily. . . ."

"Ha. I wish I could use that excuse on my workout buddy, I might be able to spend less time on the damn StairMaster. No, I'm game if you are."

It was a beautiful walk on a beautiful day, and early enough that the bane of San Francisco, the constant automotive traffic, was in a lull. They walked by the campus of the San Francisco Art Institute and encountered a handful of goth kids in black from hair to toenails. "Is that what you looked like when you were a kid?" Brian asked.

"We liked black, of course, and some goth music, but we weren't really that gloomy. We were new wavers, you know, gay kids who wanted to dance but didn't want to dance to, you know, cheesy pop tunes or old gay disco. If we'd been straight, we might have been more goth, but we were gay, so we wanted to be The Go-Go's." He nudged Brian in the side. "What about you?"

"Me? I grew up on the East Coast, out in the boonies. It was nice, you know, having all that nature and stuff."

"Far from the urban crises, huh?"

"It wasn't like we were sheltered or anything. A couple of kids died of AIDS, kids got shot, lots of drugs and shit. There isn't anywhere that isn't true, you know. Not anymore."

John sighed. "I suppose not. You all grow up even faster than we did. They used to scare us with stories about Chester the Molester abducting kids from the playground, but it never happened. All kinds of shit happened, I'm sure, but it all happened behind closed doors. Family shit, that you only find out about years later when kids you grew up with show up on *Jerry Springer*. I grew up in the typical Steven Spielberg suburb, you know? A kid could ride a bike late on a summer night and there would hardly even be any cars to avoid, let alone psychos. But it was the tail end of all that stuff, you know, even when we were kids the world was getting scary. Like, instead of scaring each other with the boogeyman we used to tell each other that 'Charles Manson escaped from jail and he's coming for you!' "

Brian laughed appreciatively. "Maybe kids are still scaring each other about Charlie; he's still alive so he *could* be coming for you."

"I hate to admit it," John said, "but I do need a rest now. Can we stop here?" They'd made it nearly to the top of the hill; the street dead-ended in a cozy forested circular drive. There were benches thoughtfully provided for weary tourists to rest on before taking the steps up the rest of the hill. The shady spot at the base of the lush green hill was an ideal resting spot.

"Did you have a lot of sex back then?" Brian asked John.

"God, no. I was such a nerd . . . and such a fool! I thought all those cute jock boys were straight, and maybe they were. But I found out later that all the cute boys in my neighborhood were boinking the hell out of each other. Nobody wanted to boink me until . . . well, hell, until about six months ago! And you?"

"I kept busy . . ." Brian trailed off.

"I bet you did!"

"I was pretty normal, I guess. I even played football for a year in high school."

"No! I'm dating a football star!"

"Just for a year. Just long enough to get what I wanted."

"What was that?"

"Into the pants of the football team!" Brian grinned.

"Did you know you were gay?"

"Sure, always. By the time I graduated, everyone else knew it, too."

"Did you take a lot of shit for it?"

Brian shrugged. "Not really. The girls just took it as a challenge, and the guys took it to mean they could get an easy blow job. Not that I *was* easy, mind you. I always liked older guys better than my classmates.''

''Did you do girls?''

''Sure, when I had to. I mean sex is sex, you know?'' he said in response to John's shocked laughter. ''In the end I just happened to like sex with guys a lot better.''

''And the older-men-thing, do you ever wonder what that's about?''

''I don't have to, really. First my dad was a screwup, and then he was gone. So, surprise! Guess who's looking for a father figure. Didn't you go through that, after all, Harrison is older.''

''He is. I never had a thing for older guys or anything, but when he came along I was pretty weak and sick and . . . dependent, I guess. Maybe I reverted; needed that protector again like I was a kid again. I don't know. Maybe that's all we had, and once I could take care of myself again. No, that's not true. I don't know,'' he finished, exasperated. ''I don't want to think about it, really.''

''Okay,'' Brian said, getting up. ''That's cool.'' He smiled and took John's hand. ''Let's go see the tower.''

The day had passed for John like a big, pleasant, fluffy dream. The operator of the rickety old elevator in the tower had filled them in on the quaint history of the tower, a gift from Lillie Coit to the city in gratitude to the fire fighters who had rescued her life, which was why the tower was shaped like the nozzle of a fire hose. Charmed, Brian had dropped a dollar in the operator's tip jar, and only when they were at the top of the tower did John fill him in about the full extent of Lillie's fondness for fire fighters, and just why she had picked the nozzle of the hose to symbolize her appreciation. ''Why wasn't that in the official spiel?'' Brian wanted to know.

''What, and shock the good people of Topeka? That would be a mighty empty tip jar if he did.''

''Didn't we look like we could handle the truth?''

"They're probably told not to guess who can and can't take it. We could be Mormon missionaries, for all they know . . . what with me looking so *conservative* and all," he needled Brian.

They'd lunched at Caffe Sport, returned to Brian's and curled up for a leisurely nap, watched a tennis match on TV and idly perused the paper, thinking about what to do for dinner and if there was another movie worth seeing. John already knew the day would be filed in his memory as one of his happiest.

When the phone rang Brian groaned. "I know who this is," he said.

"Who's that?" John asked.

Brian answered the call on speakerphone. "Hello?"

"Get off that speaker!" Slater shouted.

"Yuh, uh-uh!" Scott added, making it plain they were also on one.

"Very funny," Brian said. "John's here, and I knew it would be you guys. Say hi."

"Hi, John!" they chorused.

"Hey," John laughed. "Are we in conference?"

"We sure are," Slater said. "We need a vote. Scott votes for Universe yet again, of course."

"Slater wants to go to Hole in the Wall, and I say nuh, uh-uh!"

"That's the opposite of yuh, uh-huh," Slater added.

"Shut up!" Scott laughed. "That place isn't called 'hole' for no reason, you know. You are too sleazy, dude."

"Really," Brian added, "trying to take nice neat boys like us into that dirty dark dangerous . . . hmm, it's sounding better with every adjective. What's your vote, John?"

"Oh, God," John groaned, not much feeling like going out late but well aware that staying in and playing board games would not exactly fly as a Saturday-night option with these boys. "I don't know. What about Evan? Ask him; I abstain."

"No!" Scott shouted. "You can't! Evan's gone to Palm Springs for the weekend! You have to vote with me, otherwise we'll end up somewhere scary!''

"Okay, okay, I vote for . . . Universe.''

"Boo!'' Slater hissed. "Boo! Where's your sense of adventure?''

Tucked away for the night under my nice soft pillow, John thought. "You guys don't want to go see a movie, huh?''

"A *movie!*'' Slater and Scott both protested.

"Okay, I see that won't fly. Umm, I sign my proxy over to Brian.''

"And I vote we . . . go to the bar, then to the club!'' Brian decided.

"Yay!'' was the sign of approbation from the other end of the phone. "We'll be over in a few,'' Slater said.

"Get the cocktails ready!'' Scott said. "I'm thirsty!''

Brian laughed and hung up. He looked at John. "We don't have to go if you don't want to. We can get them drunk and throw them out.''

"No, no, it's Saturday night, we should go out. I just don't want to stay out all night or anything.''

"Oh, no. Just a couple of drinks and home to bed.''

The same evening found Harrison out, as well, although in the company of a much more sedate crowd. His friend and former colleague Neil had left the faculty several years earlier on disability when his lover had passed away, and Harrison saw far less of him than he wanted. Neil's dinner-party invitation had also come with the guarantee that there would be only two other guests—a couple who were really more Neil's late lover's friends than his own— who were in no way associated with the school, thus guaranteeing Harrison a night free of office politics. "Although,'' Neil demanded, "you will have to fill me in on the dish I've missed since I left.''

At Neil's house Harrison had a drink and made small talk with

Walter and Edward while Neil put the finishing touches on dinner. "So, Neil tells me you work for the city," Harrison said to Walter.

"Yes, I'm the liaison with JC Decaux," he said, mentioning the French firm that had introduced the self-cleaning toilets to San Francisco's streets. "It's a very rewarding job," he said defensively, obviously feeling the sting of humiliation any Henry Jamesian esthete would get from working in a field even remotely related to bodily functions. "It involves quite a lot of travel to Paris," he added, as if any sane person would *scrub* the toilets in order to get to Paris.

"We *adore* Paris," Edward said in the lofty artificial tones that used to cause John to catch Harrison's eyes in order to roll his own, as if to say, "get this queen."

"Really, it's almost *unbearable* to have to come back to the States," Edward continued, his syllables radiating superiority and dripping scorn. "So much culture to absorb, so much sophistication. . . ." He sighed helplessly. "I suppose San Francisco is the closest one can come to that in *this* country, which is why we live here."

"Why not just live in Paris full-time?" Harrison asked impishly, feeling as if he were channeling John when he asked it. He knew it was just what John would have said, avoiding Harrison's eyes as he said it to avoid cracking up.

"One *would* if one *could,*" Edward huffed, as Walter shifted uncomfortably in his seat. "But the many demands of my business force me to remain here . . . as well as Walter's career, of course," he said, patting his lover condescendingly on the arm as Walter smiled stiffly.

"What business is that?" Harrison asked, finishing off his scotch and wondering for a moment how soon he could pour another without being discussed by Walter and Edward on their way home. He decided he didn't care and poured some more. His chest was tight and sore today from yesterday's workout. Matt had promised him that as his body got used to the exercise, the soreness would become more of a pleasant indicator of progress and less a cause of painful stiffness. He well knew that hard liquor wasn't part of Matt's recommended regimen, but it did dull the pain in his chest, as well as the pain he suspected he would soon have in his head.

"I have a little antique store on Hayes, *so* demanding of my time. One hires people of course but you can't trust anybody, either they steal from you, right out of the cash register, or they have absolutely no idea what they're doing." A small "ahem" from Walter startled Edward, who smiled and concluded, "But I do *so* look forward to our trips to Paris; when Walter calls me from work in the middle of the day I always know it's good news!" He finished his speech with almost hysterical cheer.

Fortunately, dinner was soon served and the chat was general and vague. Harrison found himself watching the couple. They were about his own age, maybe a little older, had been together for ten years, and had seemed to settle into a sort of comfortable misery. He couldn't help but note the way Walter looked pointedly at Edward when he got to his third glass of wine, or how Edward got his revenge at dessert by mentioning Walter's latest cholesterol level.

The couple made their excuses early and left, though Neil insisted Harrison stay behind to catch him up on the news from school. However, as soon as the door was shut behind them, Neil brushed back his hair, heaved a sigh, and said, "Thank God!" His bright eyes glinted mischievously at Harrison. "Now we can talk. Sorry to do that to you; I have to keep up the acquaintance because of Kyle," he explained, referring to his dead lover. "But I couldn't face them alone, so you being a single man now, I used you as the sacrificial lamb!" Noting the dark cloud that passed over Harrison's face, Neil appended hastily, "I'm sorry, I didn't . . . I thought it was just your ordinary breakup, you know, not . . . I didn't mean to upset you."

"No, no, that's all right, you couldn't have known."

"Listen, it's a beautiful night and I just *happened* to save the good bottle of wine for us; let's go out on the deck, how's about it?"

They took the glasses and bottle out onto Neil's deck, overlooking an exquisite garden overrun with flowers. Gardening had been Kyle's passion, and Neil had let the beautiful backyard go for a while after that, but once he went on disability he'd resuscitated the flora.

"I guess you and I have been more out of touch than I thought, if you've had a relationship that important to you that I didn't know about."

"It was pretty important."

"Can you tell me what happened?"

Harrison shrugged. "All kinds of things. He was sick when we met, and now he's not only well, he's some kind of magnificent super-stud. And he developed interests that I couldn't exactly share with him, like returning the newfound affections of beautiful young men. And it was me, too. I was a little . . . I don't know . . . bossy, I guess. Take-charge. He liked it when he was sick, it made him feel safe and provided for, and once he wasn't sick anymore, I guess I didn't know how else to treat him"—he paused and sighed— "so he's off playing with the boys and I'm . . ." He stopped himself.

"You're here hanging out with dried-up old sticks like Edward and Walter," Neil finished for him.

"They are, aren't they?" Harrison said wonderingly. "Dried up. That's just what they are. It's like nothing's ever going to be different in their lives ever again. You can see it in their eyes. There's never going to be any more excitement, any more change, any more adventure. And they're not miserable together, but they sure as hell aren't happy, are they?"

"No, it doesn't look that way. That's something Kyle used to dread—that we'd get old and we'd be *compatible*. He used to *shudder* at the thought!'' Neil laughed. ''Because once that happens, suddenly you're not striking sparks off each other anymore, you're just 'two bumps on a log,' he would say.''

''That was always the wonderful thing about John. He was younger than I was, you know? He kept me on my toes. Now I guess he's looking for someone to keep him on his toes.''

''So that's it? It's all over? What if this is just a phase for him?''

''Well,'' Harrison said hesitantly, ''I am taking steps, of a sort.'' He shrugged. ''Working out, for starters. Then probably going into hock to create a new wardrobe, new glasses, all that. A friend and I are thinking that maybe if we can change the visuals . . .''

Neil grinned. ''And give the young buck a little competition, eh? Good idea.''

Harrison blushed but laughed. ''I know that beauty is inside and it's what's inside that counts and—''

''Yadda yadda yadda,'' Neil cut him off, refilling his glass. ''You're a gay man, Harrison, it's your sworn duty to keep up appearances. Hell, who knows? If John doesn't come back, you might find yourself with your own entourage of twenty-one-year-olds!''

Harrison laughed, then sobered. ''No, that's not what I want. I want John back,'' he said, surprising himself with his own firmness. ''That's what I want.''

Neil put a hand on his shoulder. ''And he'll be lucky to get you back, my friend.''

''I hope he feels that way, too.''

''Did I see in there what I think I saw in there?'' John asked on the way out of Hole in the Wall.

''And what do you *think* you saw?'' Slater asked mischievously.

''I thought I saw people smoking *crack,* is what I thought I saw,'' John retorted, sending Brian and Scott into paroxysms of laughter.

"A glass pipe is no guarantee they were smoking crack," Slater said, eager to play devil's advocate.

"I guess I am conservative," John conceded. "If that place is liberal . . ."

It had certainly been an eye-opening experience. Being a San Franciscan, John was practically mandated by city ordinance to smoke a bit of pot now and then, and the sight of a (pot) pipe being passed around the back of a bar south of Market was hardly cause for consternation. But the combination of the aggressive punk rock soundtrack, the half-dozen completely and inexplicably naked men lounging in the back of the bar and occasionally making the necessary foray through the crowd to the bathroom, followed by the sight of the crack pipe, had given John pause to consider the depths of his own depravity. The neat, clean, boring, tourist-packed Castro bars looked like Disney Family Fun after the Hole in the Wall.

"I love that bar," Slater announced, to nobody's surprise. It was only their place in his entourage that kept them from being glared out of the bar in their too-neat club wear. Slater schmoozed with the bartenders and d.j. and regulars while John's jaw dropped, Brian laughed, and Scott kept saying, "Oh my GAWD, did you see that?"

"Slater, you are a filthy pig," Scott issued his edict.

"Ain't it grand?" Slater said wickedly. "Are we cabbing it or walking?"

"Let's walk," Scott said. "Of course everyone in there who wasn't smoking *whatever* was ignoring the law and smoking cigarettes and now my clothes smell like smoke, yucky! I love that antismoking law, don't you?"

"Did you know what we were getting into?" John asked Brian.

"Let's just say I've never seen anybody smoking crack in there before—if it *was* crack," he said as Slater opened his mouth to protest, "and never quite so very many naked people. But you know what? A year from now it'll be just as tame as the Midnight

Sun, because the tourists are going to get wind of its reputation and the place will suddenly be jammed with Hard Rock Café sweatshirts and the whole sleazy carnival will move on somewhere else.''

"It's so much fun to take new arrivals to places like that," Slater said. "Then tell them it's a slow night and they should see it during the season!"

"I like to take them all the way to the middle of the Golden Gate Bridge and tell 'em the story about how it almost collapsed when they had the anniversary party in 1987!" Scott enthused.

"No," John said, "take them out for Thai food for the very first time and watch them try and eat the lemon grass."

Brian laughed. "So mean! I thought San Francisco was like *Tales of the City,* and everyone was so nice to new arrivals."

Slater snorted. "Dream on! This town doesn't need any more new arrivals; all they're doing now is driving up the rents. Rich computer yuppies and finance and real estate sharks, not a Mary Anne Singleton in the lot of 'em."

"You know what's so funny about that miniseries now?" John asked. "That scene where Mrs. Madrigal shows Mary Anne the apartment—it's about ten thousand square feet and she's going to live in it all by herself, on an entry-level secretarial salary!" He was fuming.

"You're awfully worked up about real estate tonight," Slater noted.

"John's looking for a place to live," Brian said.

"You'd think I was looking for a thousand-acre estate, with all the luck I'm having."

"Are you looking for your own place or a share?" Slater asked.

"Share, if I can find someone who's not too crazy to share with."

Slater grinned. "I'm pretty crazy, but my roomie is moving out at the end of the month. It's a nice room, isn't it, guys?"

"Oh, yuh," Scott said, "Slater has a great place, right off Haight."

"It'd cost ya three-fifty a month, can you swing that?"

"God, yes! How long have you been there, to get a two bedroom for seven hundred dollars?"

"Not that long. Let's just say the landlord and I take part of the rent out in trade, and you'd be the beneficiary of the savings, too." Slater laughed heartily.

"It's that great big dick of yours, yuh-huh. Dude is giving up a fortune in rent for the chance to swing on it on a regular basis." Scott nodded wisely.

"Slater!" Brian said, shocked but delighted.

"Well," John said cautiously, "we should talk about that. Talk about personal habits, stereo volume, the hours you keep, having company over and when, blah blah blah. . . ."

Slater shrugged. "Sure. I'm pretty easygoing, and most of my partying takes place outside the house. I'm a student, remember, so even I need quiet time to study now and then."

"Take it!" Scott shouted. "That would be so cool!"

"We'll talk," John said firmly, but inside he was already doing cartwheels. Slater was the greatest; John couldn't imagine him being a roommate from hell like . . . like everyone else he'd talked to so far about a place.

The night seemed blessed; when they got to Universe it turned out one of Scott's friends was working the door. Presto! They were in—not only not having to stand in line but even comped.

Slater was eager to get the business settled, and he and John headed off to an ambient room while Scott and Brian shook their booties. The picture John gathered of Slater's life was that of a young, groovy grad student, living frugally while still managing to have the good time that was his right at that age, dedicated to his studies and not prone to let weekend hijinks carry over into what Slater saw as his working week. By the end of an hour of increasingly inebriated conversation, John felt that he had acquired not just a roommate but what he'd always seen in Slater, a potentially very good friend.

"So it's settled, cool." On their way back to the main room to find the others, Slater steered John off into a dark alcove and produced what looked like a bottle of poppers. "Let's celebrate the deal, what do you say?" It wasn't poppers, John saw, since the inside of the cap had a small spoon attached; he realized with a dizzy rush of excitement that it was crystal, just like he'd had at Babylon.

John thought about it for a minute, recalling Slater's admonition that it was never as good as the first time. But it was a special occasion, just as it had been before. And there wasn't any harm in celebrating something that was not just a relief but a blessing, was there?

"Sounds good to me," John said, letting Slater steer the tiny spoon to his nostril. He did another hit in the other nostril and shook his head as a small electrical storm seemed to coalesce in his head. "Wow."

"That's the benefit of hanging with the skateboarders," Slater said, his eyes glassing over. "You always get the best drugs."

When they rejoined the others, John thought his secret was safe. But one look at him, and Slater told Brian and Scott what had transpired. "It's party time!" Scott shouted. "My turn!"

"All right, greedy, come on," Slater said, moving off with Scott.

"I'm moving in with Slater!" John shouted to Brian.

"I figured you guys decided to celebrate."

"It's pretty obvious, huh?" John asked, embarrassed.

"Let's just say you guys came back looking a little *too* happy." Brian smiled broadly.

John laughed. "Sorry."

"Don't apologize to me," Brian said hastily. "I'm no angel. Just watch it. Be careful."

"Of what?"

"Getting too fond of it. Going from a recreational user to an occupational user."

"Oh. Yeah. Really, huh? That would be pretty gross."

Brian shrugged and put his arm around John. "So I guess we're going to make a night of it tonight, huh?"

John looked at Brian, smiling warmly, almost fatherly in his indulgence, and laughed. "I just hope I can keep up with you boys."

"We won't leave you behind," Brian promised, and he gave John a long, slow, teasing kiss. In any state a kiss from Brian seemed to flick a switch in his head that turned on lights in parts of his brain he didn't know could light up. But on the drugs— Brian's kiss set off fireworks that left John gasping. *This is it,* he thought, *this is everything I want, everything I never had, all of it, right now, mine, all mine. . . .*

"Guess he's getting ready to enjoy the single life, too," John said, blocking out the wall of pain. "Well, let's get this done and get out of here."

Six weeks had passed since that day. Slater's place in the lower Haight was a funky old two-bedroom flat in a four-unit building, not unlike the layout of the apartment John had shared so many years ago with Mushroom Boy, Space Girl, et al. He'd initially been delighted when Slater had offered him the front bedroom over Fillmore Street, relieved that the dark inner bedroom was more Slater's speed. "I'm no morning person, I like my bedroom dark, so it's all yours, bud," Slater had offered.

That delight had faded the first night at 2 A.M. when the bars on lower Haight closed, and hordes of young people swarmed out onto the street. The late hour and the prodigious quantity of consumed depressants did little to dampen youthful exuberance. It amazed him how very many people lived in this town who either didn't have to get up in the morning or could do so on three hours' sleep.

Living in the Castro, John now realized, he'd been spoiled. The late-night sound of drunken giggling and shrill queeny laughter could be adjusted to and slept through, but the war whoops of testosterone-soaked boys and riot grrrrls were not to be muffled with a pillow over the head. John knew from experience that shouting "Shut up!" out the window would only make things worse; it only made them scorn your old sleeping self and add to their exuberant fires.

Slater himself was a nighthawk, coming home late from Berkeley after the university library closed and relaxing with a joint, some loud music, and usually some form of company, either social or sexual. Fortunately, the bathroom was between his and Slater's bedrooms, but nonetheless a middle-of-the-night pee run was often accompanied by an X-rated soundtrack, loudest when the parties got so carried away in the living room that they never made it to the bedroom.

John told himself he just had to adjust; if he wanted to be young again, well, this was what young people did. What was the alternative, living with someone like Philip in some kind of mausoleum? So he gritted his teeth and bore it.

Weekends seemed to pass in a blur. Work had become so hectic and stressful that Friday night was excuse enough for a big blowout. Brian would meet him at work and they'd go out for drinks, dinner, a movie, then out to a club, any club, straight or gay. They would head anywhere they could dance, because Brian loved to dance and John was damned if he was going to tell him he was too tired after a week at that friggin' job. Saturday was filled with errands that needed to be run because there had been no time during the week. And Saturday night seemed to always find Slater, Scott, and Evan chopping up lines of crystal in preparation for a night on the town. John was always relieved to see the "pick me up" by then because otherwise he would have collapsed from exhaustion.

John found himself thinking about Brian's warning about becoming an "occupational user," but he dismissed it. He was only doing it on weekends, and he felt fine so his health wasn't being impacted. What was the big deal? He didn't see Brian as much on Saturdays anymore; and each Saturday John thought he should take a pass on the drugs and partying and just spend the night with Brian. However, the lure of it was too great—the fun, the excitement, the feeling of invincibility, inexhaustibility. He and the boys would go out, and everyone would look at them, and he was *popular!* God, it was shallow, but it was also so different from the way his whole life had been up to this point that he reveled in it, just reveled in the fact that he was finally on the other side of the glass. And after an exhausting week of work, gym, errands, dancing with Brian on Friday nights, there was just no way he was going to be able to keep up without the crystal.

His workouts with Kevin were definitely suffering, though. An all-nighter on Saturday turned into a morning at the Endup, and he slept Sunday nights only with the help of a sedative. This meant he was a zombie on Mondays at work, and as often as not he cancelled his Monday night workout with Kevin. This left only Wednesdays and, technically, Saturdays, though usually he didn't have time for that, either.

This particular Wednesday he'd gotten to the gym late, with only time for a desultory workout on the StairMaster to get his blood pumping for the weights. "Hey," he said to Kevin, joining him on the adjacent machine.

"Hey," Kevin replied. "What happened?"

"Just shit at work," John said truthfully. The boom economy had made Obelisk & Associates a very busy place. However, in order to reap the maximum possible profits from that boom, the firm had decided that rather than adding labor to the force, they would simply make the existing employees work harder. Truth be told, the picture of the revamped Harrison weighed on his mind, as well. *Why!* he wanted to shout. *Why couldn't he have done that before? He's better off without me, I see that now.*

Kevin stopped climbing and the machine let him sink to the floor. "Come on, let's go talk for a minute."

John followed Kevin to the juice bar at the front of the gym. Kevin got them two protein drinks and they sat down. "John, what's up?"

"What do you mean?"

"You're always late, you've totally stopped coming on Mondays, you rush through the workout like it's some kind of awful chore. Obviously something's going on in your life that you're not telling me about."

"Maybe it's getting to feel like a chore," John said irritably.

"It shouldn't. Your workout should be where you let off steam, not build up more."

"Maybe I would let off some steam if you weren't so damn bossy," John said, looking out the window.

"I'm going to let that slide," Kevin said. "You're obviously under some kind of pressure and I'm just trying to help you."

John laughed. "Some kind of pressure! How about all kinds of pressure! How about pressure from the minute I walk into that damn job till the minute I go to bed . . . and pressure even then because I can't sleep with all the goddamn racket down on the street!"

"Is there something going on with Brian that you're not telling me about?"

"No, everything's fine," John lied. In fact, the last time Brian had joined the gang for a Saturday night out, he and John had a few words.

"How much crystal did you do tonight?" Brian had asked him.

"I don't know," John shrugged. "A few bumps."

"So now they're 'bumps.' Gee, and two months ago you didn't know what a quarter was."

"I'm a fast learner."

"I see that. You know, you'd better be careful. You see that guy over there?" Brian pointed out a man a little older than John. He was tan, chiseled, and shirtless—all that he was supposed to be in the eyes of his party brethren. Yet, it wasn't pretty; his face had a starved quality to it, as if in resisting the natural flesh deposits of middle age he had stripped his body of something elemental. The skin of his face was starting to acquire a sort of papier-mâché look to it, as if not only all the fat but all the moisture had been sucked from the dermis. His eyes were aglitter with crystal and he was grinding his jaw furiously. "Do you want to end up like that?" Brian asked. "Do you want to be some queen looking ten years older than your age because you're doing so many drugs to keep up with everyone ten years younger?"

"Do I look like that now?" John asked defiantly.

"No, but give it a few months and you will."

"I'll remember that," John had said, pulling at his beer and terminating the conversation.

But the discussion came back to him now as he and Kevin skirted around the same territory. "John, you're doing crystal, aren't you?"

"So? What if I am?"

"So? *So?*" Kevin asked disbelievingly. "So you have AIDS, if you haven't forgotten! Do you know what that stuff does to your immune system?"

"My counts are still fine."

"But for how long?"

"Great. And what do you suggest I do? Stop going out and start spending quiet evenings at home knitting scarves?"

"Do you need the drugs to go out and have a good time?"

John didn't answer. Of course he did—how the hell else could he manage to stay up all night and half the next day?

Kevin sighed. "I know what it's like here. We're all free spirits in the only libertarian city in America, and nobody's supposed to judge anybody else. I watched people go down the toilet because it wasn't my place to tell them not to. And I went down the toilet because nobody told me not to, either."

Noting that he'd finally gotten John's interest, he continued. "You didn't know? I was a speed freak for a while, when I was in my twenties. What a great time I had. Cheap drugs and free drinks and all the sex I could handle and dancing all night and that feeling. You know the one I'm talking about, when you walk into that club, that bar, that bathhouse, and you have a magic shield against any attitude any bitch queen could ever throw you. You can walk in anywhere and not worry because you're *it*." John remembered his own feelings that night at the disco at Babylon and swallowed.

"Then you start calling in sick to work on Mondays, because

you can't stop tweaking after a Saturday night at Universe and then there's the Endup on Sunday morning, and what about beer bust in the afternoon, and hey, there's Pleasuredome on Sunday night, can't miss that. Then you get to the point where the drugs aren't doing it as well for you, so you have to do more to get that feeling kicked up, and then you go out and freak out because you're so fucking paranoid from all the crystal.

"That's when you start to run to the drug dealer's house and run back home again to do the drugs all by yourself, because you've got to have the drug to feel happy. But as soon as you do it, you freak out and can't deal with anyone or anything outside your house. And you start calling phone-sex lines because you need to get screwed so bad, but you can't leave your room. And then you start spending your money on escorts, because the only people who can get it up at four in the morning who are willing to put up with your crazy tweaking self will only do so if you pay them. And then you find that you can snort a whole quarter and not feel a thing, so someone tells you to start booting it up your ass, and that works for a while, but then you destroy all the absorbent tissues in your ass the way you destroyed your sinus membranes. And you get fucked but it doesn't do it for you anymore, you need a new thrill to push the button. And so you start getting fisted, and then it's time to start shooting up and right after that, my friend, is when you become a fuckin' freakass shithead street-person loser."

John said nothing. The portrait Kevin had drawn was not only graphic, he knew it was true. He'd seen people on drugs at every one of these stages, it had just never occurred to him that the stage he was at could ever lead to the next, or the next.

"And how far down that line did you get?" John asked.

"I shot up, once. The same night I did, my best friend OD'ed. Had a heart attack and died. I took that as a sign from God to quit."

"So what did you do, join a twelve-step group?"

"No. I just quit. Some people can do it that way, most people need a group. I was lucky."

John opened his mouth, shut it again. Kevin waited patiently. Finally John said, "But I'm not . . ." He sighed. There was no use arguing. "I *have* been doing it every week," he admitted. "It's fun. It is!" he said defiantly. "We go out on it and we have a good time."

"Yes, you do. You have a great time on it, right now. And you'll keep on having a great time until you wake up one day and all of a sudden realize not only are you not having fun anymore, you're having the shittiest time of your life."

John sighed. "You're right. I need to lay off. Or scale back." He noted Kevin's frown. "Isn't scaling back better than doing nothing?"

"Depends on how long you stay scaled back for."

John tossed back his protein shake. "I'm beat. I'm going to pass on the workout tonight."

"Fine."

"I'll call you, okay?"

"John . . ." Kevin looked at him imploringly.

"I know, I know, you've got my best interests at heart. Kev, I'm going to remember what you said, and I'm going to make some changes, okay? But I'm not going to sit here and pretend I'm St. Augustine and I'm going to be all holy from now on."

"You remember what St. Augustine said, don't you? Before he was a saint?"

"No, what?"

" 'Lord, make me pure, but just not yet.' "

John laughed. "Words of wisdom." He hugged Kevin, who surprised him by hugging him back fiercely.

"Take care of yourself, okay?"

"Okay. I'll see you Saturday?"

"I hope so."

John smiled reassuringly. "You will."

John gave himself some insurance by announcing to Slater that night that he was taking a "drug vacation" for the weekend, and gave himself some more by making dinner plans for Saturday with Helen and Matt. Slater had surprised him by agreeing that it was a good idea. Since he wouldn't be around Saturday, maybe they should all, including Brian, do something wholesome Friday night. Filled in on the plan, Brian enthusiastically agreed and seemed more than usually glad to see John that Friday.

"Hey," John laughed when Brian came over and hugged him nearly as fiercely as Kevin had two days earlier, "did you miss me?"

"Yes, and I'm just glad you . . . never mind. No, not never mind. I'm glad to see you taking a weekend off from the drugs." He noticed the beer in John's hand. "Not being entirely pure, I see," he said with a smile.

" 'But not yet,' " John quoted.

"Huh?"

"Nothing. You want one?"

"Sounds great."

Slater came home shortly afterward, then Evan showed up with Scott in tow. "Wow," Scott said, "we haven't all been together in a while."

"We've gotta do something about that," Brian said.

A joint magically appeared from behind Slater's ear and was passed around. It was a warm August evening and the windows were open, the conversation was light and idle. The Cranberries were on the radio and they all squeaked along with the lead singer: "It's *yewww* and *meee* in *summertime!*" John was nestled up on one end of Slater's funky old couch with an arm around Brian and he was feeling loose and mellow. *This ought to be enough,* he thought. *Who needs that crystal frenzy when you can be just as happy like this?* But he knew—out there in the night, in the clubs, on the drugs, there was a darkness, something dangerous and obviously destructive, and yet alluring precisely because of that. He couldn't forget it, that sick rush of fear and anticipation as he was just about to do the drug . . .

"Hey, what's that?" Evan asked, looking out the window. "Turn it down!" They turned down the radio to hear what sounded like a distant riot getting closer—whoops of joy, whistles screeching, people shouting, sirens blipping on and off.

"Cool!" Slater said. "It's Critical Mass; they're coming up Fillmore!"

"What's that?" Scott asked.

"Critical Mass!" Slater repeated. "The last Friday of every month, everybody who rides a bike to work, and then some, all get together at the end of Market Street and they take over the city. They snarl car traffic on Market Street and anywhere else they feel like. It's great!"

"But what's the point?" Evan asked.

"The point is, there's a couple hours in this congested city when cars aren't in charge, man! Most of the time you ride a bike in this town you're taking your life into your own hands; people in cars would rather whack you than wait for you. But you get enough people on bikes together—a critical mass—and hey! The cars have to wait for you!"

"It motivates people in cars to take public transportation at least one night a month," John added.

"Though God knows they resent having to do even that," Slater added, jumping up and down with excitement. "This is so cool!"

"If public transportation in this town didn't *suck* so bad, maybe that would be an alternative," Evan groused.

"Right," Slater laughed. "You've got a car, don't you!"

"Sure do. And thank God we got here when we did, or we'd be screwed."

The noise was getting louder. The protest/parade/event/whatever was coming up Fillmore from Market, led by police cars clearing the road. Then there they were, bicyclists by the hundreds: men in suits with a smart pants leg rubber banded to keep it out of the gears, bicycle messengers, students, people who just wanted to participate in something big and fun and noisy and occasionally a little obnoxious.

They all crowded on the couch, leaning out the open windows to see the whole carnival. "It's like a big protest!" Evan enthused. "Wow, this must be what ACT UP demonstrations were like."

There were times with Brian that John was reminded of the age difference between himself and the boys around him, but it was rare that it struck him with such force as it did now. Certainly there were times when John would mention something to Brian that he took for granted as a common point of reference, and Brian would look at him blankly, but Evan's comment struck him on just how far removed they were from him. ACT UP had blown up, what, eight years ago? Not so long ago when you were thirty-three, but for the rest of them, it was something that had happened far away when they were in . . . *high school!* John was startled by that fact. Ancient history now, only as comprehensible to them as the hippies of Haight Ashbury were to John, as the Lincoln Brigade would have been to the hippies, images in documentaries and stories old people told. . . .

"No," he blurted. "This wasn't anything like ACT UP."

They looked at him. "You were in ACT UP?" Slater asked, amazed.

"Don't look so shocked. I was. It wasn't like this at all."

"What was it like?" Slater asked keenly. "Man, that must have been something."

"It was." He paused. John was old enough to have stories of bygone days, but still young enough to identify with how irritating it could be to be the younger person who had to listen to them. "You really want to hear this?" he asked.

"You bet!" Slater enthused.

John looked at the others, starting with Brian, who smiled. "Hey, you told me you had an interesting past, let's hear some more of it."

"Yuh," Scott said. "I've seen pictures of those ACT UP demonstrations. Some of those boys were *hot!*"

Everyone laughed. "Go on," Evan urged him.

Slater lit a fresh joint and handed it to him. "To get the words flowing."

"Babbling is more like it," John said, taking a hit. "It wasn't like that," he said, indicating the whooping throng outside. "That's about . . . traffic. ACT UP was about life and death. You guys were in *high school* back then; I don't know if you know what it was like to be an adult then—especially a gay adult. The Republicans had been in charge of the White House for . . . ever, it seemed. People were dying left and right from AIDS and"—he looked at Scott—"well, I told you what Reagan said about AIDS when he left office. Then we had George Bush, whose only response to ACT UP was that it was mighty unsportsmanlike of them to come to Kennebunkport and ruin his vacation by reminding him of how darn many people were dying horrible deaths because he was too chickenshit scared of the right wing to do anything about it.

"There was a recession on, and that made it all worse, especially in one of the, what are we now, two first world countries left without national health insurance? If you had HIV and lost your job, you'd probably also just lost your life, too. And instead of doing anything about domestic problems, they just waited until Saddam Hussein invaded Kuwait—which, by the way, they had reliable intelligence reports telling them he was going to do a goodly while beforehand, which they ignored so they could have this war and distract people from the fact that they didn't have jobs and weren't going to get jobs.''

"Bread and circuses, live on CNN," Slater interjected.

"You got it. We were in ACT UP because *we didn't have a choice*. It's not like the kids who join Queer Nation because they thought it was groovy to be radical and go to protests and dress up in leather jackets with buttons but didn't want to have to deal with that icky old AIDS that they all knew only old clones get anyway. *We were gonna die* if somebody didn't do something. ACT UP was . . . genius. No activist group since Vietnam managed to dominate the evening news for a whole week the way we did during the AIDS conference in San Francisco. These kids out here, they're getting tickets for disorderly behavior; people in ACT UP got arrested by the kind of cops who join the force because it gives them an excuse to beat the shit out of the kind of people they don't like. Yeah, in San Francisco in the 1990s, cops beating up fags!

"If you made a friend then, or took a lover, it was with the full knowledge that he could be dead in a year, and there was nothing you could do about it, no matter how much money you had, how well connected you were. We weren't out there screaming our lungs out because it was fun—we were screaming because we were angry, and we were angry because we were scared, and we were scared because we were powerless. Jesse Helms sat in Washington and wrote our death warrants and nobody cared; hell, they had their own problems thanks to the recession.''

He stopped. "Anyway, Clinton got elected and things got better. He screwed us on a lot of things, but a lot of things got better. But it wasn't anything like that, out there.''

They watched the procession outside. Twentysomething hippies in unbleached cotton and sandals danced alongside the bicyclists, whistles blew and people whooped. It was a merry festival, a thumbing of the nose to the arrogant suburban commuters.

John laughed and moved to lighten the tone. "I'll tell you one similarity, though. There was one thing ACT UP did that turned thousands of people against them, and that was blocking traffic one day on the Bay Bridge. In California there's only one cardinal sin, and that's impeding traffic! Stop the orderly flow of the suburbanites in or out of town and you've got an angry mob on your hands.'' They all laughed. They could see Haight Street where the procession was committing that very same cardinal sin and could hear the honking horns and the shouts of motorists: ''Get out of the way! I'm in a hurry! I need my car! I'm a busy person!''

''Wow,'' Scott said, at once at a loss for words.

Evan nodded. ''My dad was an aerospace engineer, lost his job in the recession. We lost our house, had to move into a shitty little apartment. No health insurance and my mom got cancer. She lived,'' he added, ''but still. It was a real shit time.''

Scott broke the quiet. ''I'm the shallow one, so I guess it's up to me to say, let's go out and forget our troubles!''

Everyone chuckled. ''Amen,'' Brian said. ''Who's up for Johnny Rockets? Burgers, fries, shakes, cheesy old music?''

''Yuh!'' Scott said. ''And then a really violent movie!''

''Excellent,'' John laughed. ''Let's go.''

John brought wine to Matt and Helen's house for dinner the next night, but not without calling Matt first to check and make sure he was bringing something that wouldn't wrinkle Helen's nose.

''It's the thought that counts,'' Matt told him.

''Have you ever noticed that it's the thoughts that count that you end up taking with you to someone else's dinner party and foisting on *them?*''

Matt laughed. ''I'll check with the sommelier and see what's acceptable.''

He produced a short list of acceptable wines, but when John took it to the store he found that Helen's taste in wine was strictly in the $20 and up range. To hell with wine when you can get good champagne for less, John thought, and he picked a bottle of Mumm's Cuvee Napa out of the fridge case.

As usual, Helen was out of sight in the kitchen and it was left to Matt to entertain company. "So how have you been? How's your new place?"

"Great, except at around two A.M."

"That's right. I logged my late hours down in the lower Haight about ten years ago. You remember Mad Dog in the Fog, is that still there?"

"Damned if I know. All the signs now are done in that rapper graffiti style, so who the hell can read them?"

Matt chuckled. "So how's your health?"

"Fine, great."

"I just wondered; you look like you've lost a little weight."

"Really?"

"Your face is a little thinner."

"Oh," John said, thinking of the night Brian had pointed out the papier-mâché man. "I've been pretty busy. Guess I'm just not eating enough. I imagine Helen will fix that tonight."

"Oh God, I haven't been allowed in the kitchen all day. She put a big bottle of spring water out for me and said, 'If you need anything, ask for it but don't come get it.' "

They laughed. "How about another drink?" John asked, since his glass was empty and Matt hadn't offered.

"Sure." Matt poured John another orange Stoli. "Have you talked to Harrison at all?"

"No," John said. "Why?"

Matt shrugged. "No reason. Just wondered."

"No, I haven't. I will eventually," he promised. "It's just not time yet. Have you?"

"I see him now and then," Matt lied smoothly.

"I saw him around," John fudged. "New glasses, new hair . . ."

"He's making an effort."

"Huh," John said noncommitally. John wanted to ask, "Is he seeing anyone?" But he didn't. *It's none of my business anymore, is it,* he thought. *Why the hell didn't he make an effort while we were still together?* He was saddened by the thought.

Dinner was soon served, another typical lavish spread from Helen. The champagne was cracked after dinner, making it the fourth bottle of wine consumed with the meal.

"Are you still seeing Brian?" Helen asked.

"Still am."

"Is it serious?"

John shrugged. "I don't know."

The way he said it made Matt's ears perk up. It was one of those "I don't knows" that sounded like surrender to confusion. "What do you mean?" he asked John.

John sighed, the wines loosening his tongue. "I don't *know*. It's really exciting and fun and everything, but . . . when we first met it was all sparks and lightning, you know? He really is smart, and funny, and wonderful. But sometimes when we're together for an extended period of time, I think, what am I doing? Take the other day. We were in the kitchen and I said, 'I'm in charge here,' and he blinked. 'Sorry,' he says, all offended, 'I didn't mean to get in the way.' And I had to explain to him all about Alexander Haig saying that when he took over the White House when Reagan got shot, and then he got the joke.

"Or take K-Tel—you guys remember K-Tel?" They groaned; of course they did. In their youth the K-Tel record label had been a ubiquitous TV advertiser, selling compilation records (this being long before CDs) of current hit songs, only they were cover versions performed by "Sessions," the name given to whichever studio musicians had been corralled into the cheesy project. "We picked up this electronica collection and took it home, and I started laughing, and he said, 'What is it?' And I pointed out the words K-Tel in tiny letters. This wasn't a set of cover versions, you know, like those old records, but still, it was K-Tel, so it was funny. And he just didn't get it; he just wasn't around for that.''

''Yeah,'' Matt remarked, ''these kids think the 1970s were so great, but that's because they don't know all the *crap* we put up with. If they did, they wouldn't be so wild about it.''

''That's the scary part''—John shuddered—''they actually *like* earth tones and cheesy striped velour shirts! I don't know; maybe they figure all fashion looks silly twenty years later so why not just accept it and look silly now? Anyway, it's one thing to mention something like K-Tel and have him not get it, you know? There's just too much pop culture *crap* accumulated in the last few decades for anybody who hasn't lived through it to catch up with it. But there are just so many times he says, 'Who's that?' after I mention someone famous from when I was a kid. Or I talk about Three Mile Island, and he tries to remember what it means, and he can't. And it's not because he's dumb, it's just that he hasn't lived through what I've lived through. So sometimes I feel like . . . like there's a gap there that just isn't going to get filled.''

''Is he in college?'' Helen asked. ''A lot of that slack will get taken up in school.''

''No, he dropped out when he tested positive. He's trying to get into art school.''

''I know what you're going through,'' Helen said. ''I used to date an older man.'' John and Matt looked at her with surprise. ''Well,'' she said defensively, ''I wasn't a *virgin* when I met Matt. Anyway, this guy was about, well, thirty-five, about your age, and I was about Brian's age. This was . . . hmm. Well, sometime in the early 1980s, shall we leave it at that?'' She smiled. ''God, I guess that means he's about fifty now. Oh well. He was a big deal in the '60s, or he told me he was. I could have cared less. He'd written a few books on politics and I thought that was very impressive, the fact that he was an author, as opposed to a writer. He was always going on about the '60s, how great it was, how basically anybody who wasn't around then will never know and will never have as much fun, blah blah *blah*. And that was the truth: I could never know, he was right. So in the end we really didn't have anything to talk about, once he'd told me the stories, because that's all they were to me: just stories."

"I know what you're saying," John said. "Believe me, I've known my share of old hippies, too, and I've gone out of my way *not* to bore Brian with 'When I was your age' stories. Though God knows, we have to admit the '80s weren't exactly chockablock with carefree days, were they? The only student protests happened when the administration tried to ban keger parties. But there really is a gulf. When you think about it, it truly is *so different* for him than it was for us."

"The irony is," Matt thought out loud, "that kids these days may have more in common with the kids in the '60s than they do with us. Kids in the '60s had marijuana, free love, straight hair, Woodstock, and the Kennedys; today they've got marijuana, free love, straight hair, Woodstock II and . . . Clinton, but still!"

"And we got crack, AIDS, Joan Collins, arena rock, and Reagan," John added. "Why do I feel so cheated?"

"We had good times, though," Matt insisted. "Some good music, anyway—Elvis Costello, the B-52s, the Pretenders . . ."

"All of whom got their start no later than 1979," John amended, "so they don't even count as '80s groups."

"Okay, okay," Matt surrendered with a laugh. "The 1980s sucked. But we made it through them, didn't we?"

"Barely," John admitted, "but we did." He yawned and stretched. "God, I'm tired."

"Tired?" Matt said, looking at his watch. "It's only nine-thirty."

"I know. But I've been running an overdraft at the sleep bank lately. Now might be a good time to make a big deposit."

Matt and Helen walked him to the door. "Thanks for dinner, you guys," John said, bidding them farewell with hugs. "It's been a nice change to have a conversation with grown-ups for once."

"Thank you for coming," Helen said. "We hardly see you anymore."

"I know. I'm resolved to do better about that. G'night."

"Night," they said, watching him depart. Helen turned to Matt. "He doesn't look good."

"I asked him if he'd lost weight, and he said he hadn't been eating lately."

"That is the *last* thing he should be doing," Helen said worriedly. "Do you think he's doing drugs?"

"What do you mean *think?* Of course he is."

"Oh God, Matt," Helen said, hugging her husband. "That plan of yours to get him back together with Harrison better start moving a little faster."

"I know," he said, stroking her hair. "But there's nothing we can do to make him want Harrison back. Still, it sounded like the pump is being primed, didn't it?"

"What do you mean?"

"Talking about Brian and how they sometimes seemed to be on different planets, how it's nice to be around grown-ups for a change. When Harrison's ready for him, I think he'll be ready for Harrison." Matt smiled, pulling back and rubbing his hands together in imitation of the emperor in *Return of the Jedi.* " 'Everything is happening exactly as I have foreseen!' "

"That's what the emperor said, and remember what happened to him," Helen said darkly.

"Don't worry," Matt said. "Everything's going to be all right."

John woke up that Monday morning to find Scott on the living room couch, snoring and drooling. John's own puritan impulses had lasted all weekend, but Slater and Scott had snuffled a few bumps on Sunday night and gone out to Pleasuredome. *"Mmmgggphhh,"* Scott grumbled as John padded past. "Mmmph?"

John had already learned that the sleep of the wired was a light sleep indeed, and any disturbance would violate it. "Sorry," he whispered.

"What time is it?"

"It's about seven-thirty."

"Oh. Do I smell coffee?"

"Yep. You want some."

"Mmmpgh. Please."

John poured two cups and delivered one to Scott. "How was it last night?"

"It was *hot,"* Scott said automatically, his usual enthusiasm dampened by exhaustion. "I gotta pee." While he was in the bathroom, John automatically gathered Scott's clothes, which were tossed about the room, into a pile. He'd picked up Scott's jacket when a small bottle fell out just as Scott came out of the can.

"I'll get it," Scott said hastily, but John beat him to it. He knew what it was on sight.

"Where'd you get this?" he asked.

"This guy at the gym sold it to me," Scott said.

John held up the vial; it was clearly labeled as testosterone but the label was awfully generic-looking. "Are you planning on doing these yourself?"

"Yuh, uh-huh. I need them!" Scott said defiantly, taking back the bottle.

"They look a little suspicious. Are you sure they're the real thing?"

"Yuh! This guy who sold 'em to me? He was *huge!* He couldn't-a gotten huge if it was fake."

John sighed. "Maybe he got huge on the real thing, which he bought from the profits from selling fake shit."

"Oh. I didn't think of that."

"You should have."

Scott frowned. "Listen, dude, I am gonna get huge and I can't do it on my own. I need 'roids! And you better not tell Evan about this."

"Do you know what steroids can do to you?"

"Yuh, yuh, screw up your liver, give you a gigantic belly, shrivel your balls. Evan told me all that."

"Okay," John retorted with a sigh. "So you're going to do them. Do you know how?"

"Yuh, you get somebody to shoot you in the ass."

"Great. Just anybody, huh?"

"Why not? It's not like I could do it myself."

"I do."

"But I'm scared of needles, and I don't like the sight of blood, so I ain't gonna do it myself."

John thought about this for a moment. "Here." He got up. "Let me show you how it has to be done, if you're going to do it." He went to his room and got his own vial of testosterone, a syringe, a paper towel, a Band-Aid and some alcohol wipes. Hopefully he could put the fear of God into Scott and scare him out of it; if not, at least he would lessen the boy's chance of harming himself.

John dropped his pants. "Hey!" Scott said.

"Watch." He ripped open an alcohol wipe. "First you have to clean the spot where you're going to inject. If it's not *very clean,* you risk pushing surface bacteria down under your skin with the needle, which can lead to an abscess. Do you know what that is?"

Scott made a face. "Yuh, our cat had one once. Disgusting boil full of pus."

"That's right." John pulled the syringe out of its sheath. "This is a new bottle I'm using so I don't have to wipe the top with an alcohol wipe, but if it's been used before, you have to wipe it before every use, same reason you wipe your skin." Scott shuddered at the sight of the needle. "Now you draw the oil into the syringe, then make sure you're not injecting any air bubbles. Air bubbles are bad." Scott swallowed.

"Now you have to mentally divide your ass into four quadrants. You want the upper right quadrant of your right cheek, or the upper left quadrant of your left cheek. You want to alternate; otherwise you get one ass cheek bigger than the other."

"Uh, gross!"

"It's important to hit the outside because of the sciatic nerve. Do you know what that is?"

"No. . ."

"It's the nerve that runs down your legs and attaches to the spinal cord. If you inject yourself in the center of your ass and you hit the sciatic nerve, you can paralyze your leg, maybe temporarily or maybe permanently." John noted with satisfaction that Scott was turning gray.

"Now you inject," he said, stabbing himself in the ass with the needle. Normally he would relax his glutes but this time he tensed them; he knew what this would cause and it was just what he wanted, this time.

"Oh God," Scott groaned.

"It's very important to pull back on the plunger at this point, because you have to make sure you haven't hit a blood vessel. If you draw back and there's blood, *don't inject,* this is oil and if you inject it into a blood vessel it will go to your heart and kill you before you have the needle out of your ass." Scott watched in horrified fascination, which was just what John wanted.

"Now you need a paper towel."

"What for?" Scott asked, just as John pulled the needle out and a stream of dark blood started running down his leg.

"Oh God! Oh shit! You hit a blood vessel!"

"No, this happens all the time," he lied; it did happen quite often, though, and served its purpose. He put the paper towel over the injection site to sop up the blood.

"Oh shit," Scott said weakly.

"Now you know how it's done." He put the syringe in his "biohazard" container, put the Band-Aid on and pulled up his pants. "Do you still want to do it?"

"No!" He threw the vial at John. "Here, get rid of this or use it yourself."

"I would never use something that didn't come straight from the pharmacy," John said, dropping the bottle of whatever it was in the trash can. "Does the hard way look a little easier now?"

"Yuh! Uh-huh!"

"Good. Listen, I do this stuff because I have AIDS, Scott; the illnesses I've had have stopped my body's natural testosterone production. Now I'm going to write down some things you can take, some natural testosterone boosters that will probably cost you a lot less than you just paid for that vial of piss. Okay?"

"Okay," a cowed Scott replied. "Jesus. That guy didn't tell me any of that! He just sold me the bottle and . . ."

"And left you to it, just like any unscrupulous drug dealer."

To John's surprise, Scott hugged him. "Thanks, dude."

"Hey. There are worse things than not having huge muscles, believe it or not."

Scott laughed. "Yuh, yuh. I know. But, sometimes . . ." He sighed.

"I know. I'm gay, too; I've been there. But you're not even fully grown yet, you're . . . how old are you, really?"

"Eighteen."

"Damn. Listen, your body is still producing huge amounts of growth hormone. Scott, you need testosterone like . . . like Richard Simmons needs bigger hair!" They laughed. "You work out a lot?"

"Yuh."

"Are you eating a lot of protein?"

"I try not to eat too much so I don't get fat."

John sighed. "Sit down, kid. I'm going to be late for work and you're about to get a biology lecture."

CHAPTER EIGHT

Warming up on the treadmill at the Y, waiting for Matt to arrive, Harrison reflected that this might just be the best thing he'd ever done. His body had taken to exercise like a duck to water, and by following Matt's prescriptions to the T, he'd actually found himself getting results. Initially he'd simply put his nose to the grindstone without expectations. His feeling was that Matt had a plan whereas he didn't, so he had nothing to lose by listening to Matt. Three times a week he'd met up with Matt at the Y, starting out with what felt to him like embarrassingly small weights—embarrassing when he looked at the lunks around him, and hell, even some of the women, hoisting two, three, five times as much weight as he was.

"Don't look," Matt said, catching him at it one day. "What's important right now is for you to learn good form, and you learn—and keep—good form by using an amount of weight you can handle. You see that guy over there?" Matt subtly cocked his head in the direction of a man doing barbell curls with a sixty-pound barbell. "See how he's moving back and forth, pushing his gut out and his shoulders back? Because he's *not strong enough* to curl sixty! He's cheating; he's recruiting his back and he's using gravity."

Harrison watched intently: the man did indeed lean back to get the weight all the way up, and when it was up he simply let it fall back down again. "You don't let the weight fall like that," Matt said, launching into a lecture on eccentric and concentric movements. "At best he's doing nothing to isolate and grow the biceps and at worst he's going to screw up his back."

He hadn't believed Matt when he'd sworn it could be done in twelve weeks. "If it only took twelve weeks," Harrison insisted, "why doesn't everybody do it?"

"Because first you have to subtract the people who don't believe in themselves. You subtract the people who are too good at rationalizing why they don't have the time or the money, or whatever. Then you subtract the people who are afraid to fail, and the ones who are afraid to succeed. Then you subtract the people who are afraid to walk in the gym for fear everyone will laugh at them. Then you subtract the people who can't turn their lives upside down like that, who can't turn on a dime and go from stopping for a burger on their way to a night at home on the couch to eating a chicken breast after their evening workout. In the end, Harrison, you're left with people like you who want it bad enough that nothing else matters."

That had been months ago. Now Harrison himself confidently curled the sixty-pound barbell—not for the twelve to fifteen reps that Matt could handle at that weight, but at six to eight, which Matt maintained was ideal for growth. He'd learned to treat the Nutrition Facts box on every item of food as his guiding light, following Matt's instructions for packing in as much protein from as many different sources as he could—soy, whey, egg, beef, poultry and fish. He joked to Matt, "If I ever lose tenure as a history professor, I can get a job in either the Human Biology or Kinesiology departments." At six foot, Harrison had gone from a floppy 160 to a lean, hard 165—no giant hunk but nonetheless he found himself the object of attention in the Castro when he walked down the street.

He was glad he'd done it because it had been good for his health and great for his ego. But there was another, and honestly more important reason why. Now he understood the process John had gone through. Now he knew what it was like to suddenly be *visible,* to suddenly be a man that other men checked out on the street. Harrison had been attractive in his youth, his youth had faded and he hadn't missed it as he'd directed his energy into teaching, the profession he loved. But now it was suddenly like he had it back— *really attractive guys* were making the kind of eye contact with him he hadn't had in . . . well, a very long time. You had to turn your inner life upside down to get here, he realized. Change the way you did everything, the way you thought about everything, all your priorities, and once you got here, your outer life turned upside down, too, and that in turn changed your inner life yet again, so that in the end you were practically spinning around. And Harrison now saw that he'd sat there, nagging John about running up charge cards and worrying about planning for future disasters, when today's successes were more shattering than any of tomorrow's potential crises.

"Penny for your thoughts," Matt said, taking the treadmill next to him.

"Just thinking. That's all."

"Care to share?"

"I think I'm beginning to realize what John started going through," he said. "Imagine going from the bottom of the heap to the top, imagine thinking—no, knowing—that you're the same person you always were and yet, suddenly everyone around you starts treating you like you've become *someone else.* It can do weird things to you."

"So you're getting the royal treatment now, huh?"

"I am, actually. It's funny. Salespeople are more helpful, people smile at you more, the world is just *nicer* to you when you're more attractive. And I had no idea what was going on in John's life; all

I saw was his body changing and I had no idea how much that in itself changes your *life.*"

"It's genetics, man: natural selection prompting us to favor people with preferable traits."

"It's more than natural selection," Harrison argued. "It's *crazy.* It's making your decisions about who's good or better based on their looks."

"What else do we have to go on? You see a bazillion people a day and do you have time to figure out who's naughty or nice? We just decide that character is evident on faces and work from there."

Harrison sighed. "I want to call John. I want to talk to him about all this. Let him know I . . . well, I don't understand entirely, because his change had more to it than mine; I didn't come back from the grave or anything."

"No, but at your age it's like taking that one foot back out of the grave," Matt kidded him.

"Ha ha."

Matt hesitated. "It's about more than just looks, though. I don't want to be an interfering old auntie, but it did seem to me that you and John had some other problems. Never mind. I shouldn't butt in."

"No, I want to hear what you have to say."

"To begin with, there was that whole vacation thing."

"That was my fault."

"I don't think it was just the vacation. I think it symbolized something to John, symbolized the tenor of your relationship. From talking to him, from hearing what he's said to Helen, it just seems like . . . your relationship before was a little more parental than it needs to be now. He was the sick victim and you were his protector, his caretaker. And he's okay now. Well, kind of."

"What do you mean?"

"He just . . . he's lost some weight and . . ."

"Oh, shit. He's getting sick?"

"No, no. Not yet anyway. But I think he's getting involved in drugs, speed, and stuff, with these young guys he's hanging out with. He's lost some weight and I know he's going out pretty much every weekend."

"Shit." Harrison clenched his fists. "Shit, shit, shit." He laughed bitterly. "Great, I'm supposed to stop treating him like a child and yet now I've got to go in and get him off drugs."

"Harrison, that's just the attitude you can't take. You can't 'go in' and rescue him. He's got to follow his own course, and we have to hope that his course leads him away from where he's at."

"And there's nothing I can do?"

"There is something you can do: Be there for him when he's ready to talk. Don't lecture him, don't boss him around, just be there for him."

They finished on the treadmills and got off. "He's got to find his own way through all this stuff. But John's a grown-up at heart, really he is. What he's doing now is making up for lost time, trying to have a reckless youth he didn't get the first time around." Matt put a hand on Harrison's shoulder. "Can you really see him doing this for years? For even the next year?"

"No," Harrison said firmly. "No, I can't. But that doesn't necessarily mean he'll want to go backward, back to me."

"You know what? You're looking great. Do you realize that?"

Harrison laughed. "Am I?"

"You are. And you've learned something about what he's gone through. You guys grew apart and maybe now you're growing back together. He's tasting what's out there and once he's got his fill, he'll be ready for someone who he can relate to, communicate with. Do you know what I'm saying?"

"Sort of . . ."

"It's going to have to be fifty-fifty from now on, though. Even if he screws up, even if you think the best way to handle things is to take over, you can't. You've got to be his equal, not his superior."

"I know." He sighed. "I really want to call him."

"Don't. Not yet. Just be available. Did you take my advice about that trip to Hawaii?" Matt had recommended that Harrison go for a number of reasons—to get away from the apartment full of memories, to take a vacation more enjoyable than the one he'd had in the South, "and to finish off your 'body project' with a nice tropical tan," Matt had added with a smile.

"I did. I'm going in two weeks."

"Excellent! It'll do you a world of good."

Harrison smiled. "My first purely sybaritic vacation. Another experience to help me relate to John!"

John's weekend of purity had been desperately needed, but the chances of a repeat performance were slim. That weekend had been followed by a week of unmitigated hell at work, and on Friday, Obelisk had dumped a huge project on John. His appeal for a temp to help out had met with a frown. "I told you once you got that new computer that you shouldn't complain about the workload. And you said the computer would help you work harder."

"Not *this* much harder!" John protested. "Jesus, this is enough work for two full-time people with state-of-the-art machines, which, by the way, was not what I bought, since you limited me on how much I could spend."

Obelisk frowned. "I don't appreciate employees getting snappy with me."

"I don't appreciate being treated like a Dumpster!" John practically shouted. "Do you think I'm just *making this up?* That it's *not* enough work for two people?"

"I don't care. Just get it done."

John threw up his hands and walked out of Obelisk's office. "Pats," he groaned at the reception area. "I'm dying here."

"Tell me," she said through gritted teeth. "He's got me doing all kinds of weird shit—bank statements! Says that Lulu," she named the acccountant, "has enough to do with billing and that

I'm 'underutilized.' Which is true, but shit! I haven't reconciled my own bank statement in years! I tried a couple times, honestly, but it never would come out.'' She shrugged. ''I just gave up and decided that whatever they told me was in my account was what I had. And now this! I keep getting it wrong. You know what? This boom economy sucks.''

There was no sympathy to be had in this quarter, so John returned to his office. ''Hey,'' a familiar voice said, and John looked up to see Tim in his doorway.

''Hey! How are you?''

''Not bad. Just here to do some network rewiring.'' He looked at John funny.

''What?'' John asked.

''Nothing. Are you okay?''

''Sure, why?''

Tim frowned. ''You've lost weight.''

''I haven't been eating like I should. So what have you been up to?''

''Not much, you?''

''Just trying to have fun.'' He smiled. ''Hey, listen, it's the weekend, what are you doing tomorrow night? Me and some friends always go to Club Universe and . . .''

''Umm, I've got plans, sorry.''

''Oh, okay,'' John said. Tim's response was the kind of vague rejection that usually indicated someone had plans for the rest of their lives and it was best not to risk further humiliation by asking about next weekend. He bent his head and went back to work.

Tim reappeared on his way out. ''I'm all through. See you later.''

John smiled as brightly as he could. ''Okay. See you soon.''

Tim didn't smile back. ''Take care of yourself, okay?''

''I will.''

''You look like you aren't getting enough sleep, you know what I mean?''

John flushed. "I'm probably not."

"Well . . . I'll see you around."

"Okay. See ya." He gnashed his teeth when Tim was gone, then he raced to the bathroom to check his face in the mirror. He didn't look so bad—he wasn't made of papier-mâché yet! But there was no arguing that his bone structure had gotten a little *too* sharp and that the wrinkles around his eyes, formerly only evident when he smiled, were now a little more prominent; his skin a bit drier and just . . . not as *glowing* as it had been when he was eating right and exercising . . . and not taking speed.

Damn. Damn! Was there anything in his life that wasn't screwed up? An inconsolable rage swept over him, followed by a dramatic dip. He found himself suddenly feeling desolate, depressed . . . screw it, he thought angrily. He shut the door and dialed the phone.

"Yuh, uh-huh?"

"Hey, Scott, it's John."

"Oh, yuh!"

"Hey, are you going shopping tonight?" He flushed with embarrassment as he realized he'd just asked for drugs in code for the first time. *My secret vice—I really am an addict!* he groaned.

"Nuh, I had to go shopping for Martin last night," he said. "You want some?"

"Definitely," John said, not knowing who Martin was, and not caring. "I need something to brighten my day. Can I come by a little later?"

"Yuh, I'll be up." Scott giggled.

"I bet you will. I'll see you later." John hung up the phone with a queasy feeling of excitement.

"Oh, shit," he remarked loudly. He had plans with Brian tonight! *I can't,* he told himself, picking up the phone and dialing Brian's number. *I don't want to eat and I don't want to talk, I want to blow my fucking brains out, just blot it all out.*

"Hello?" Brian said.

"Hey, Brian, it's John."

"Are we on for tonight?"

"That's why I called. I'm just beat, you know, I'm gonna take a rain check if that's okay."

"Sure, of course. I'm glad to hear you're starting to take care of yourself."

John flushed with shame. "Thanks."

"I'm going back East on Sunday, did I tell you?"

"Yes," John said, having completely forgotten about it. Brian had decided to go see his parents and tell them about his HIV status. At this of all times John should be there for him, to give him support before this stressful occasion, but he just couldn't do it. It felt to John like one more obligation, one more goddamn thing he had to do, and he just couldn't take it. He just wanted to get high.

"Maybe tomorrow night we can have an early dinner or something?" John asked.

"Sounds great," Brian said. "I'll talk to you then."

I'm screwing everyone, he thought. *I've screwed Harrison, I've screwed Brian . . .* The thought of the crystal was the only thing that got him through the rest of his day. *It's all going to be better, in just a few hours it's all going to be better.*

John practically raced over to Scott's house after work. He was surprised to find himself in Pacific Heights, until he remembered that Scott was currently the live-in boy toy of a rich older man. The house was the sort he'd walked past for years but had never had any cause to enter, nor any cause to think he'd ever enter. He rang the doorbell and the big oak door swung open to reveal Scott in his shorts. "Come on in." He led John down the hall, barely giving John time to register the Oriental rug on the floor, the huge spray of flowers on the table in the alcove by the door, or any of the other decorations splashed about to cover the huge amount of gratuitous *space,* so unfamiliar to a lifetime apartment dweller.

"Nice place," he said.

"Sure is," Scott said. "Martin's got beaucoup bucks. Come on in the kitchen, it's like the only room I can stand to be in." John understood why after glimpsing views through the other doors along the hallway. The place was the sort of *Architectural Digest* mausoleum that so many rich people feel the need to live in; all the rooms perfect and untouched, exquisite antique furniture that wasn't to be sat on for fear of breakage and which wouldn't have been terribly comfortable anyway. The kitchen had a cozy feel to it, a small dining table and a little TV on the counter.

"Is your friend home?"

"Martin? Yuh, he's home. He's upstairs on the bed jerking off to Falcon movies. Well, not jerkin' off cuz he can't get it up." Scott tapped his nose. "He started partying yesterday afternoon. You don't wanna meet him, do you?"

"No, that's okay."

"Good. I gave him his screw for the day and then told him I was gonna party and if he wanted any more sex, he could call the service!" Scott laughed, producing a professional-looking drug kit from a drawer—a zippered black leather case containing pockets with mirror, silver straw, and what looked like a modified Exacto knife for chopping the drugs—along with a shockingly large bag of drugs.

"My God, how much is that?"

Scott shrugged. "I guess about a gram. Martin buys bulk, you know how cheap rich people are!"

"What does he do?"

"Nothing. He inherited a bunch of money so he spends his days looking for dick online when he can't get it from me and snorting lines. I let him suck me once a day, I screw him once a week, and that's it." He waved a finger mischievously. "Gotta leave 'em wanting more!"

"Oh." John said nothing more. Originally there had been something charming about the idea of Scott as a kept boy; he'd imagined him being taken to elegant parties, the opera, whatever, anything but picking up drugs for some trust-fund wastrel and hanging around this dreary house.

Scott chopped out a few lines and John helped himself. Almost immediately after his first one, he felt a sense of *relief* as the feelings of aggravation and pressure went away. His head just seemed to *clear* as the drugs kicked in. Brian would be all right, he thought cheerily, everything would be all right.

"That's good, isn't it?" Scott said, looking up from the mirror and shaking his head as the electrical charges went off.

"Definitely."

"Martin can afford the best. So are you and Brian getting together tonight?"

"No, maybe tomorrow. Can you do me a favor? I cancelled on him tonight because I . . . well, I needed to get high and have a good time, and he's not into that and he's kind of disapproving, you know?"

Scott nodded, giving John a conspiratorial grin. "You want me to tell him I never saw you, right?"

"Yes, please."

"Sure thing. God knows I tell Martin plenty of little fibs." John didn't like the comparison between his relationship with Brian, and Scott's with Martin, but he bit his tongue. "Hey! I'm going to a really hot party tonight, you wanna come along?"

"I don't know . . ."

"Come on! It'll be fun."

"I know, I just don't like to go to parties, especially where I'm the only person I know."

"You'll know me!"

"But you'll be busy, won't you?"

Scott laughed. "Yuh! Busy in the upstairs bedrooms! Don't worry, you'll be popular, too."

"And the average age of the other guests will be . . ."

"I dunno, early twenties . . ."

"I don't think so."

Scott rolled his eyes and picked up the phone. "Slater? It's Scott. Yuh! Hey, John's here . . . yuh . . . Slater says hi . . . Hey, are you going to that party at Russell's house tonight? Yuh! Me too! I'm trying to talk John into going but he's scared . . . Slater says he'll be your date. Here"—he put on the speakerphone—"he wants to talk to you."

"Hey," Slater said. "I didn't have you pegged for the wallflower type."

"I'm just not . . . used to parties. Not the kind with lots of cute young guys, anyway."

"Come on!" Scott said.

"You don't have any problem going to Universe, or Pleasuredome," Slater said

"That's different. That's public. Anyone's allowed there."

"And you're allowed at this party, John. Don't worry. You're qualified, if that's what you're worried about."

John laughed. "It is."

"Listen, I'll make a deal with you. I'll be your date. I'll hold your hand the whole time and everybody will be jealous of you."

"Cuz they'll all know you're the one getting that big ole schlong tonight!" Scott crowed.

Slater laughed. "Maybe."

The drugs and the thought of sex with Slater dovetailed and pushed John's button. "Okay. If you'll be my date. And if you bring me some party clothes from my closet; I'm just in white tennies and jeans and a polo shirt now."

"Yay!" Scott shouted. "Get over here and let's start partying."

"You guys are doing bumps already, huh? Well, it's Friday, I guess the old books can wait. I'll be there in fifteen."

"Cool!" Scott said, hanging up. "We are going to have a *great* time."

John didn't feel so good at the thought of the upcoming party. He could never forget a party he'd gone to once, years ago, a horrible mistake. He'd been in ACT UP at the time, and a whole contingent of people from the group had talked him into going. He'd felt safe with them until they'd gotten to the party, when they'd all found friends to talk to and he'd been faced with either looking like a geek by hanging onto them or circulating. It had been a "boy" party, and while back then he'd been chronologically young enough to attend, he hadn't had the body or the wardrobe or, most crucially, the attitude. His puppyish pleading smiles at strangers had been met as often as not with either cool distant polite smiles or looks of appalled frostiness from the more genetically gifted attendees. He'd ducked out without saying goodbye to his friends, the hot breath of shame on the back of his neck. Laughter had followed him out the door and he'd felt sure they were laughing at him. He hadn't been to a party full of hot young men ever since.

Now he was going to one again, and the dread was overwhelming. It didn't matter that he now had the officially approved body and wardrobe; in his own mind he supposed he'd always feel like that other boy in situations like this. "Can I have another line?" he asked Scott.

"Help yourself. I'm gonna take a shower, you want one?"

"I'll take one in a minute." John chopped out some more lines and did the biggest one. *Just a little more chemical courage,* he thought, *and I can do this. I wonder where the booze is? A little Stoli to take the edge off the crystal, if I can get the chemical cocktail just right, everything will be okay. . . .*

They took a cab to the party. By the time they got there, John knew he was whacked out of his head. "Nervous?" Slater asked him just before they'd left.

"A little." He laughed.

"Here, this'll take the edge off." He handed John a small orange pill.

"Xanax?" John asked.

Slater smiled. "Hey, and I thought you were drug naive."

"I used to have the boss from hell; had to pop one of these every morning just to get through a day at work. She took two hundred T-cells off my count." He popped it. "Okay, let's go."

The Xanax did bring him down a little; he realized he'd done just a little too much speed trying to rev himself up for this event. Still, when they got to the house in Noe Valley, he was perspiring freely.

"Maybe I should just stay in the car," he said.

Scott and Slater looked at him, realizing what kind of shape he was in. "You're messed up," Scott said, appalled.

"Come on," Slater said, "you'll be fine."

John was overwhelmed with the sheer horror that can only overtake a person on crystal. The house was like a club, packed with cute young boys, pressed together and shouting to be heard over the stereo. John could make eye contact with nobody, anybody who caught his eye for a minute only saw a deer in the headlights who abruptly turned away. *More alcohol,* he thought, and wedged his way into the kitchen, where a card table was laid out with large bottles of cheap vodka and gin, as well as mixers. John poured some of the vodka over ice and slugged it back. "Hey," a bright-eyed boy said with a smile, "you sure you can handle your liquor?"

"No problem." John smiled nervously and darted away. *Damn! He was cute, why didn't I talk to him! It's these fucking drugs,* he realized. *I'm freaking out!* He wanted to ask someone where the bathroom was, but didn't have the courage to talk to anyone, so he just looked until he found it.

He shut the door behind him, relieved to get a second of privacy. He looked at himself in the mirror, and was appalled. His pupils were dilated, his skin was glowing with beating blood but dry and drawn from dehydration and general hard living. Little web tracings of wrinkles were showing up at the corners of his eyes, tracings he hadn't had only a few months before. He was still ''handsome,'' but in a brittle way, a sort of handsome that could cave in on itself in the smallest earthquake.

Then he heard the voices outside the door. ''How old is he?'' someone asked.

''I dunno,'' he heard Scott's distinctive voice. ''Thirty-something. Old!'' They all laughed.

''He has a nice bod, but he's getting hagged out.''

''Yuh, he was hot when I met him, but that was before he met Chrissy. Now I am sorry to say he is ... no ... longer ... hot,'' Scott concluded, snapping his fingers over his head, left, right, left, on each of the last three words. John knew what was happening because he had seen others meet the same fate at Universe, and had even laughed at their downfall in Scott's book.

''Ohh,'' they said wisely, ''he can't stop seeing Tina, huh?''

''Yuh, and he's stopped going to the gym. I saw him with his shirt off tonight and he's getting smooth,'' Scott said, referring to the gym term for a lack of dramatic muscular definition. ''He's going to be a scary Carrie pretty soon, if he doesn't watch out.''

''Wow, that's too bad. I hope I'm not like that when I'm in *my* thirties!''

''If you *live* to see your thirties!'' someone else cracked, and they all guffawed.

John could take no more. He threw open the door and startled them. ''Oh, shit!'' Scott said, putting a hand over his mouth.

''Excuse me,'' was all John said, trying to muster as much dignity as he could considering the situation.

''John, wait a minute!'' Scott said, trying to grab John's arm. John tore free and pushed his way through the crowd to the door.

Near the door, to his horror, someone was looking at him. Brian's face was set in a mask of . . . what could you call it? Disappointment, anger, hurt, maybe a cynical internal "told you so" showing on the surface.

"Brian . . ." John appealed.

"Taking it easy tonight, huh?"

"I just . . ."

"Hey"—Brian put up his hands—"if you don't want to go out with me just say so. You don't need to give me some line of *bullshit* just so you can go out and get fucked up instead." He turned to walk away and John didn't dare follow him. Then, Brian stopped and turned around, tears in his eyes. "I could have used a shoulder to cry on before this fucking trip, John. But I guess you've got a new lover now. I guess the fucking crystal does for you something I can't. I hope you'll be happy together." And with that, he turned around again and walked away.

There would be a pain in his head, John knew, a pain in his heart sharp enough to kill him, but not now. The drugs were still rampaging through his system, and the sorrow and the grief would come, doubled and redoubled, as he came down off them. But now there was only a hollow spot where Brian had been.

John suddenly realized they'd had an audience who was looking at him and spreading the word. He shoved his way out the door, heedless of manners or spilled drinks.

Out on the street he walked like a robot. It was cold and he had no jacket, but the drugs and the alcohol and the hurt kept him warm. He started walking up Church Street, knowing it was probably too late to catch a bus, anyway, and not being at all capable of standing around for an hour waiting for one.

Several blocks up, he heard a voice behind him. "John! Wait up!" It was Slater, driving up beside him. "Get in, it's freezing out there."

"I'm not going back."

"I know, man, I heard what happened. Get in the car and I'll take you home."

John didn't argue. Slater shook his head. "Don't listen to those fucking queens, John. They're always looking for someone to tear apart."

"I want to kill Scott," John said, grinding his jaw. "I want to kill myself."

"Everybody wants to kill Scott at one time or another. Those guys are full of shit," Slater said, and John realized he knew nothing of the episode with Brian.

"No, they were right. I'm a mess. I'm falling apart and I'm getting hideous."

Slater snorted. "The hell you are. You aren't looking . . . well, as fresh as you did, okay, but you've been partying pretty hard lately. I still think you're hot," he said, giving John a look that couldn't be misinterpreted.

"Really?" John asked, the blood rushing to his loins, the thought of sex with Slater overwhelming all others in a way that could only happen now, with the drugs in charge of every synapse.

"Fuck, yeah, man." He put a hand on John's thigh. "When we get home, you and me, we'll have a good time, yeah?"

"Yeah," John whispered, hormones taking over all brain functions at Slater's touch. "Yeah."

"I'm gonna fuck the shit out of you all night, you like that?"

"Yeah . . ." John whispered. "Yeah, that's what I want . . ."

"Sorry."

"That's okay."

"No, I'm really sorry. I don't know what it is," Slater said. "I can always get it up, even on drugs. I musta had too much to drink on top of it."

John wiped his mouth. "That's okay." He laughed. "This just isn't my night." He got out of bed and got a drink of water.

"Hey," Slater said, coming up behind him and running his hands along John's sides. "I got some toys we could play with, does that sound hot?"

"No, sorry. I'm just not . . . I'm not horny anymore. I'm sorry."

"No, it's my fault. Shit. Let me put a cock ring on, maybe that'll help."

"No!" John shouted. "I don't want to do it anymore!" He turned away. "Sorry, I just need to . . . I just want to go to bed."

"Sure, okay. Whatever." Slater shrugged it off. "Sleep it off."

"Right. Good night."

Slater grabbed his coat. "I'm going out. I'm horny. I'll suck some dick at Mack or something, I guess. See ya."

"Okay. Slater!" he called after his friend.

"What?"

"I'm just having a really shitty day. It's all me, okay?"

Slater shrugged and gave a little half smile. "Whatever. See ya later."

John went to bed but of course didn't sleep. He tossed and turned and as the drugs wore off, the grief and pain welled up and he found himself running the tapes over and over. *This was supposed to be my fun time, my glorious youth, and it's turned all horrible!* He watched Brian slipping away, then thought of Harrison. There had been so many good times with Harrison, cozy comfy times, holding hands at a play or a movie, walking and talking for hours afterward, discussing what they'd seen. It had been Harrison who'd told John the full story of Coit Tower that he'd in turn passed on to Brian. And now he'd watched Brian turn his back on him and walk away; no, he'd turned his back on Brian, for what?

I hate this, I hate all of this. I just want my old life back, my old boring life where I don't have to get all fucked up to go out and I don't have to worry that my six-pack is still prominent and I can have a conversation with someone about something other than going out dancing!

He got out of bed and opened his wallet, pulling out the Baggie Scott had made up for him. He took it to the bathroom, thought for all of a second, and threw it in the toilet. *I know it's just a gesture,* he thought. *I could get more in a flash if I wanted it. But sometimes you have to start with a gesture,* he thought. *Sometimes a gesture is all you have left.*

Later that week he went in for a regularly scheduled doctor's visit. Hart looked at him and said, "Are you okay?"

John was amused at this by now. "I look terrible, don't I?"

"Kind of. What . . ." He caught himself. "He'll be right with you."

Dr. Richards took one look at him and asked, "So what drugs are you doing?"

John sighed. "That obvious, huh?"

"You've lost ten pounds in two months and I don't remember you having any fat to burn. You're on speed, aren't you?"

"I was. I'm stopping."

"You're stopping? Or you've stopped?"

"I'm trying to stop. I hate it." He thought of Kevin's words about how you loved it until the day you woke up hating it. *I have to call him, we haven't talked in a while . . .*

"Are you going to go into a program?"

"No. I don't think I'm an addict. I think I could become one pretty fast but I'm not one yet."

"Well, I can't make you do anything you don't want to do. But I'll tell you about a study UCSF is running through the Haight Ashbury Free Clinic. They're putting people on large doses of an amino acid called tyrosine that seems to quell the cravings for crystal." Dr. Richards wrote down the phone number. "You might swallow your pride and give them a call."

"Thanks. I just might do that."

Richards gave him the eagle eye. "Then again, you might not."

John looked away. "I have to do something, I guess. I never thought of myself as the kind of person who'd ever have to go to the Haight Ashbury Clinic, but I suppose it beats the alternative."

"Yes, it does beat dying of AIDS because you've destroyed your immune system on crystal."

"You're right," John said, thinking that the alternative he'd had in mind was having to join a twelve-step group, but he said nothing. "It does."

Outside he saw someone who looked familiar, but he shook it off. It couldn't possibly have been . . .

"John?" the man said. John turned around. "It's Gary."

John looked at him and realized he did recognize him . . . sort of. The Gary he'd known in his HIV support group had been hale and hearty; a stack of beef who'd been the object of all desire at the Eagle at beer bust, winning as many bare-chest contests as they'd let him win. But this man was a shadow of that former person, possibly a hundred pounds lighter; only the ghost of the former idol remained to remind you who he had been.

"Gary?" John asked, not believing it.

Gary laughed darkly. "Hard to believe, isn't it? You look incredible, John. A little tired, but you still look great."

"Thanks . . ." John was at a loss for words.

"I know. I look horrible. Can we sit down? I'm a little tired."

Alarmed, John looked around frantically for a place to sit. "I guess we can sit in the lobby here," he said, indicating the medical office building he'd just come out of.

"What have you been up to?" Gary asked him. "How's Harrison?"

"We're not living together anymore."

Gary nodded, grabbing John's bicep. "New toys require new boys to play with them, eh? You being careful? Taking care of yourself?"

Noting John's flush of embarrassment, Gary nodded again. "Par-

tying hard, huh? Hanging out with the hot boys and doing bumps?''
He looked away, suddenly angry. "Lucky you. You get on protease,
you get a second chance, you get some 'roids, you get a hot bod,
and now you're throwing it all away partying your brains out with
all the other morons. Shit!''

John said nothing for a moment, suddenly realizing what had
happened to Gary. "The cocktail didn't work for you.''

"No, John, it didn't,'' he said angrily. "I got kidney stones
on Crixivan, flaming diarrhea from Ritonavir, and we all know
Saquinavir is worthless shit. No,'' he sighed, "I've got CMV in
my right eye, and lost most of the vision there, though I'm getting
Foscarnet injections directly into the eyeball to keep it at bay. I
might add, that is actually a hell of a lot better than having a central
line implanted in your chest, which they tell me is what I'll need
soon if the CMV starts to spread to my organs. I've had MAI,
though the Rifabutin is keeping that at bay right now, along with
the Biaxin, though the Rifabutin's the reason my skin is orangy-
red, and the Biaxin's the reason I'm so damn skinny, because it's
hard not to puke it up.

"Yes, John, I'm dying. And I'm pissed. And I'm pissed at you,
too. I'm pissed at all you fucking shallow queens who got a second
chance at life, and what are you doing with it? Pretending it's 1979
again and you can just fuck like bunnies and take all the drugs you
want, la la la, skipping through the woods: 'We're cured, ta da,
AIDS is over so come screw with us!' Great. Lovely.''

They were silent. "I'm trying to get off the drugs,'' John said;
it was all he could offer.

"I don't care! I really don't care! You know why? Because
when we were in the support group, you and I were in the same
boat. Now you're on the *Love Boat* and I'm on the *Titanic*. And if
all the fucking rich food is giving you indigestion, I don't give a
shit. Go on.'' He waved John away. "Get away from me. Go on
with your life, with the life I'd *kill* to have again, and that YOU

ARE THROWING AWAY!'' he shouted, prompting a sudden hush in the lobby. But it was Gary who got up and hobbled away on his cane, leaving a stunned John behind.

John's own tears startled him. He suddenly *remembered* what it was like to be here, to be sitting in this lobby waiting for an X ray to come back positive, waiting for your name to be called for a blood culture to be taken that would come back positive. Your whole day rotated around this visit to the hospital, this one event that took all your strength and left you sapped, wanting only to go back to bed. In some way he had managed to erase all that from his memory, the way nature erases the pain of childbirth from a woman's memory, a highly effective method of putting suffering away, so life, normal life now restored, could go on. And of course, he thought, with a mounting dread, *this could be me again.* There was no law that said he couldn't get sick again—hell, a few more months of drugging and drinking and it would be him again, powerful drugs or not. Salvation had made him cocky, he realized, one escape from death had at least subconsciously made him think death wasn't coming, that he had an exemption.

Gary—Gary the god they'd used to call him; how consumed with jealousy he'd been the day just six months ago when Kevin called him up and told him he'd finally scored with Gary and it had been everything any of them had imagined. Nobody would die of jealousy for Gary now, the eyes that clutched and pleaded would avert now, the hot eyes of hot men that locked with his would now be fixed on some other point farther away. All of it was gone, so quickly. . . .

No more, he thought. *It's a sign from God, or the closest I'll get to one these days. No more.*

sort of untoned,what John always thought of as a Richard Simmons body. And yet, there was definitely something appealing about him, John thought. He was handsome in a sort of quiet way, from the right angles, with a nice wide mouth and obviously intelligent blue eyes.

"So you're the famous John Eames," Martin said with a smile, surprising John with the deep sexy timbre of his voice.

John looked at Ethan. "The famous, eh?"

Ethan laughed. "I haven't told him anything bad, just the amazing story of your transformation and your fabulous new life as a party animal."

John smiled weakly. "That's me." He moved to change the subject as quickly as possible. "How did you guys meet?"

Ethan and Martin exchanged glances in a manner that almost broke John's heart. It was so intimate so immediately, each checking to see if the other wanted to tell it, and both smiling at the other's consideration. "You go," Martin insisted.

"Okay," Ethan said happily, clearly relishing the opportunity. "I was looking in the paper, and I saw this listing for a one-bedroom apartment for, get this, seven-fifty! So I call and get a recording saying show up at such and such a time, at such and such an address. I get there, and guess where it is?"

"Umm, Jones and Ellis," John said, naming one of the worst intersections in the Tenderloin.

"Close," Martin laughed.

"Guerrero, right next to the projects," Ethan said. "There were *bullet holes* in the door! So I'm waiting around for the guy on the tape to show up to show the place and"—he smiled and looked at Martin—"Martin shows up. So I say, 'Hi, I'm here to see the place.' And he says, 'So am I.' So we get to chatting, and like half an hour later the guy shows up." He grinned at Martin again. "The time flew by so fast I hardly noticed.

"So this seedy old guy shows up, in *checked polyester pants* and this filthy shirt. and lets us in, and starts talking about what a great deal it is . . ."

"And it's a *pit,*" Martin interjected. "He's going on about the spacious bedroom and it's about the size of a walk-in closet, even while we're looking at it . . ."

". . . And how light and airy it is, and there's like one window in the bedroom that looks into someone else's bathroom . . ."

". . . And he shows us the kitchen, which, he insists, is 'fully refurbished,' but there's like a hot plate, a half sink and one of those mini fridges . . ."

". . . So we're looking at each other and *laughing out loud,* and this guy is getting all embarrassed, but he *keeps on.* He's got this speech canned and he's going to give it. . . ." They dissolved into laughter, leaning into each other's shoulders and letting hands fall recklessly across each other's bodies.

"So we leave," Ethan continued, "and we're talking, and it's lunchtime, so we go get lunch, and we're talking, so we leave there and go get coffee, and then . . ." Martin put a hand over Ethan's mouth, and out of spite, Ethan raised both his hands to show two pairs of fingers walking, then climbing steps, then he slid his right index finger violently back and forth through the hole he made with his left index finger and thumb.

"Pervert," Martin laughed.

John laughed, too. "Congratulations, to both of you. Ethan is a treasure, believe me," he said, blocking out his own misery and resolving to be happy for his friend.

Martin squeezed Ethan's hand. "Latte call, you want another?"

"Sure, here, let me give you some money. . . ." Ethan reached for his wallet.

"No, I'm treating today," Martin insisted. "Yesterday was pay-day and I feel like a big spender."

"In that case, get me a scone, too," Ethan called after the

retreating Martin, who gave him a "yeah, yeah, yeah" wave. Ethan turned to John and sighed theatrically. "Isn't he a dream?"

"He's nice. And kinda cute, too."

"Kinda! He's gorgeous!"

"Okay, okay, if you say so, lovebird. What does he do?"

Ethan flushed with embarrassment. "He's a Silicon Implant."

John burst into laughter. "What! After all that ranting and raving you did about computer yuppies driving up the rents, what did you go and do but fall in love with one of them! It's too rich!"

"He's not like that," Ethan insisted. "He's really active in rent-control activism, and he doesn't flash his wad around—okay, he's buying me a latte, but still—and he's *so smart,* John, you wouldn't believe it. We sit there and watch *Jeopardy!* and he knows all the answers to everything—not just the nerdy science-geek stuff, but history and literature and languages. . . ."

"And the sex is . . . ?"

Ethan rolled his eyes and fanned himself. "It's something else. Something else. I've never . . . I don't know how to describe it. We went home that first day and it had been a really nice day, you know? I knew we were going to be friends at least, and when he invited me up to his place—his old place, with these crazy room-mates, which is why he's trying to find his own place, but that's another story—anyway, we go up to his place and I'm thinking, okay, I haven't messed around with anyone in a while, it's a nice warm day and a tumble would be a good thing, and, my God! He starts to kiss me and, I don't know, there must have been some chemical on his lips that my body had been waiting for all its life, because from the moment he kissed me, it was like the top of my head blew off and stayed off for hours. . . ." Ethan sighed. "Am I glowing? People at work have been asking me if I've started using alpha hydroxy."

"You are glowing. It's called love, in conjunction with what's called 'gittin' it good.' "

"This is a first for me—love. Am I crazy? I haven't known him that long, just a few weeks, but . . . I know it! Am I crazy?"

"Maybe," John answered, smiling. "Then again, maybe your number's finally come up."

"So we're both in love! And how is your little boy toy?"

John's smile faded. "He's out of town."

"Uh-oh. Trouble in paradise?"

"If you could call it paradise," John said grimly. "It's my fault," he added hastily. "I blew it. Started doing drugs," he said breezily, "spending more time with the drugs than with Brian, etc."

"John! You can't afford to do drugs. We're not talking pot here, are we?"

"No."

Ethan nodded. "Crystal, right? Every gay man's dream drug. Turns every wallflower into a social butterfly and every sexually timid boy into the town pump."

"I know, I already got the lecture from Kevin. It's over, though, no more drugs for me."

"No? Did you join a twelve-step group or something?"

"No, I wasn't an addict—not yet, anyway. I just had . . . a series of experiences I'd rather not relate that I took as a message from God to lay off, or face the severe consequences."

"As long as you're back on track."

John shrugged. "I don't know about that, but at least I'm not flying off the rails into the ditch."

Martin came back with two lattes. "Here you go, baby."

"Thanks, darlin'. You're so good to me."

General smooching ensued and John looked at his watch. "Guys, I gotta go." He indicated his gym bag. "Been a long time since I've worked out and Kevin's waiting for me."

"Tell him I said hi," Ethan said, "and I'll be home . . . oh, one of these days."

Martin shook John's hand. "Nice to meet you. I'm glad Ethan's got a good friend like you."

John looked away, embarrassed at the praise, for he hadn't exactly been the best of friends to Ethan lately. "And I'm glad he's got you, too." He smiled and meant it as he said, "Enjoy yourselves."

John left the lovebirds with a heavy heart. The sun was shining, it was a beautiful day, the leaves of the trees lining Noe Street rustled in the breeze, which kept the heat from being oppressive. It was a day for lovers, a day for the virtuous to go out and laugh and play while people of the night drew their shades against the sun and waited for nightfall. John felt that he'd made a narrow escape from a life that would include hiding from the light. He was happy for Ethan but nonetheless sad for himself. If only it weren't for those stupid drugs, it could have been Brian and him meeting Ethan and Martin on this beautiful day. Maybe they'd even saunter out to the park to throw Frisbees, or just loll about, watching young studs frolic with their dogs.

He knew part of his depression had to do with the drugs, the way they stripped the brain of its ability to make "happy" chemicals, but his regrets ran deeper than that. It wasn't just Brian he was missing today, but Harrison, as well. What would he and Harrison have done on a day like this? Not much, he sighed; Harrison wasn't exactly into going to the park and throwing a Frisbee around, was he? *But then,* he thought, *I never asked him, did I?*

John's color was coming back, his drawn look fading, and men were starting to look at him again, but it didn't mean what it had meant before. He couldn't help noticing the irony. Here he was, proud possessor of the gay ideal, the bitchin' bod, and yet he was alone and sad on this gorgeous day, while skinny Ethan and floppy Martin were rapturously happy and having pyrotechnic sex. All the value that he'd placed in The Body before, was drained out of it.

Now he was merely glad to have had enough extra lean muscle mass to lose to get him through his dark drug-soaked time without getting seriously ill.

He met Kevin at the gym, which was pretty empty, it being a beautiful afternoon. "If I'd known it was going to be this gorgeous out," Kevin said, "I never would have made plans to spend several hours inside the gym."

"San Francisco," John stated with a shrug. "You never know what you're going to get weather-wise until you're getting it. Funny, I was just fantasizing about going to the park and throwing a Frisbee around."

Kevin looked at him. "You know what? That's an excellent idea. Let's get out of here."

"What? What happened to stern discipline, all that?" When John had asked Kevin if they could resume their workouts, Kevin had laid down the law—no cancellations. no showing up late, no complaining.

"Variety is the spice of life, remember? The reason I keep changing your workout is to keep you from getting stale." He leaned over and stage-whispered to John, "And frankly, another session on the StairMaster to nowhere is going to make me *scream.*"

John laughed. "To the park, then!"

They stopped at Kevin's house for a ghetto-blaster and a Frisbee, and made their way out to Golden Gate Park. John's mood lightened as they staked out a patch of lawn, popped Kevin's old Smiths CD, *Louder Than Bombs,* into the blaster, and started tossing the Frisbee around, occasionally losing it to eager dogs when it flew over one of their heads.

"God, I remember when I moved here," John said. "It was the late 1980s, the drought was in full swing—you had to put a brick in your toilet and take a two-minute shower, but you know what? It was warm, like this warm, all the time, from March to November. And I used to play this record all the time; I always associate it with happy summer days, back when I was young and everything was possible.''

''You're thirty-three, John,'' Kevin said, taking off his shirt to impress a skater with whom he'd been making eye contact for a few minutes. ''You're still young, and everything's still possible.''

''I guess so. Right now everything just seems so . . . like I've screwed it all up and there's no fixing it.''

''Hey, you've still got your friends, right?''

''Thank God, but I didn't exactly make a lot of effort to keep those friendships up for a while there, did I?''

''And you've got your health, despite your best efforts to the contrary.'' Kevin flipped the Frisbee backhanded to John.

''Somebody up there loves me,'' John said, catching the Frisbee and deliberately aiming it toward the rollerblader. ''Oops.''

Kevin laughed. ''Can't put anything over on you, can I?''

While Kevin made flirty small talk with Rollerboy, John took a swig of water and looked around. *I am lucky,* he thought. *I couldn't appreciate any of this until I'd nearly lost it all. . . .*

''Heads-up!'' Kevin shouted as the Frisbee struck a distracted John in the forehead. ''Oh, no, are you okay?'' Kevin asked, half concerned and half amused.

''Help, help,'' John said, collapsing dramatically onto the ground. ''So,'' he said when Kevin flopped next to him, ''did you make a date?''

''No, actually.''

''What? That's most unlike you.''

''Well . . . you know Fred? The trainer at the gym?''

''Of course; you're always flirting with him.''

''He and I have been going out lately, actually . . .''

''No! Everyone's in love but me!'' he groaned.

''What do you mean? What about Brian?''

John sighed and spilled the beans. ''So,'' he concluded. ''I blew that pretty good. Chased my boyfriend out of town, had inconclusive drug-soaked sex with my roommate, a situation which I have to get out of now, by the way, seeing as how it's not exactly going to be fun staying off drugs while watching everyone around you do them.''

"Do you want to stay with us?'' Kevin asked. "There's the couch and . . .''

John laughed. "It's not so bad, I can deal with it for a while. I've just been pretty much barricading myself in my bedroom lately to avoid the goings-on.'' It had been gruesome, really, since that night of the party. He and Slater had been civil to each other, but both had been embarrassed and both had gone out of the way to avoid meeting in the kitchen or living room or anywhere else, for that matter. Scott had been over this last Friday night and knocked on John's door, but John hadn't answered, pretending to be asleep. He'd slipped a poorly spelled note under the door apologizing and hoping that "we can party again sometime.'' Then he and Slater had gone out and hadn't been seen since.

"We'll get you out of there tonight,'' Kevin said decisively. "I'll borrow Fred's truck and we can get it all done in one load.''

"Thanks,'' John said, not protesting further and relieved at the thought of cutting his last tie to his former compatriots. "That's not the only change I'm going to make, though. I'm going to quit my job.''

"What! John, you said it was a great job, and I know it pays well.''

"It *was* a great job, until Obelisk got greedy. I guess it's just the times, nobody can resist the opportunity to make a huge pile, no matter how many people you have to screw. It's just too stressful, Kev. They've got me doing work that they should have at least two people doing. I can't stay off the drugs if I'm so stressed that I need a dramatic escape-valve every weekend.''

Kevin nodded. "Your health has to come first.'' He laughed.

"And if Ethan moves in with Martin, there'll be a vacant bedroom in my place!"

"Two vacant bedrooms soon, from the sound of it."

"Are you kidding? Listen, I have no plans to marry anybody! Fred's fun, maybe something will happen, but cohabitation is a long way away."

John smiled. "So you think you could stand me as a roomie?"

Kevin ruffled John's hair. "It would make it easier for me to keep an eye on you, kid."

John smiled. "I've never told you how much I appreciate you, have I? You're like a big brother to me, Kev. It's like there's nothing I can't tell you, ask you, nothing you wouldn't do for me." He started to tear up. "I almost threw all that away."

"Hey, hey," Kevin said softly, wiping John's tear away. "You don't think I don't know what you've been through? You don't think I've dropped off the radar for a while in my time? What's important is that you come back in one piece."

"More like back in one piece, but with a few chunks missing." John smiled wanly.

"Are you going to talk to everyone you left behind?" Kevin asked. "Meaning, are you going to call Harrison?"

John wiped his own tears this time. "Yes, I am. I have something to tell him."

John had moved his things out of Slater's apartment and into Kevin and Ethan's that night. Slater had come home during the exodus, exchanging a nod with Kevin as Kev humped boxes down the stairs.

"Hey, this is it, huh?"

"This is it," John said, straightening up from the last of his packing. "I'm sorry to leave you in the lurch like this, but . . ."

"No problem, I'll just have to get two blow jobs from the landlord this month." Slater grinned. "Listen, I'm sorry it didn't work out. All of it. Brian, and Scott and his big mouth, and when you and I tried to screw around . . .''

"It's not your fault, Slater. I screwed up my own life.''

"I don't know. I feel guilty. I was the one who got you hooked on crystal in the first place.''

John smiled ruefully. "Like I wasn't going to find it sooner or later?''

Slater sighed. "There's a lot of it around. I'm thinking of laying off the stuff myself.'' He shifted uncomfortably. "Last weekend Scott and I went to the baths, over in Berkeley, and we did a little too much. Started getting really paranoid. We ended up holed up in my room, with the lights off and the door open, but nobody would come in because they couldn't see us. But we were too nervous to turn on the lights, or leave the room. So I spent like forty bucks on sixteen hours at the baths, wired out of my head, and didn't even get laid.'' He shook his head and laughed. "A sign from God, you, know?''

John smiled. "I do.'' He extended a hand. "I'm sorry we met like this. I really like you, Slater. More than just 'like.' Under different circumstances . . . well, who knows.''

Slater took his hand, but only to pull him in for a hug. "I know. Jesus, John, you're a bright guy, you're handsome, you're a real catch. I hope things can work out for you and Brian somehow.''

"Thanks. Best of luck to you, too.''

"Thanks.'' Slater smiled regretfully. "If I'm going to change my wicked ways, I'll need it.''

Calling Harrison direct was not something for which John was prepared. While he knew nothing of Matt's Henry Higgins plan for Harrison, he did know that Matt and Harrison were friends and had been in communication on a regular basis. John decided that Matt would be a good sounding board to discover whether reopening diplomatic relations with Harrison was even possible. And truth be told, he put this off for a few days, dreading the response he might get.

"Hey, John," Matt said, "how are you?"

"Good. Fine. Listen, Matt, I wanted to ask you a question."

"Shoot."

"I know that you and Harrison see each other, and, well, I'd just like to talk to him. But first I wanted to ask you a few questions."

"Sure," Matt said calmly, jumping up and down in the kitchen and waving frantically at Helen.

"First of all, how's he been?"

"He's been okay. Lonely, I think. He misses you."

"What's that noise?"

"Nothing," Matt said, having finally gotten Helen's attention by banging a serving spoon on the countertop.

"Is he dating anybody?"

"Dating? No, he's not dating anyone, John. It's a little . . ." Matt bit his tongue.

"A little too soon after our breakup to date someone else?" John smiled. "It's all right, you can say it."

"No, no, I . . . oh, shit. Sorry."

"Never mind."

"How's Brian?"

"Brian? He's out of town. I think I've blown that pretty good, anyway, so I think it's pretty much over."

"That's too bad," Matt said, stabbing his fist in the air and mouthing a silent *yes!*

"I just wanted to give you a call first, check and see if . . . well, if you thought it would be safe for me to call him."

"He'd love to hear from you, John."

"Great. Well, okay, I better go. I'll talk to you later, okay?"

"Sure. Great. Call me and keep me posted, okay?"

"Will do."

Matt hung up and whooped. "John's going to call Harrison . . . why aren't you smiling?"

"Don't you remember?" Helen asked impatiently. "Harrison is in *Hawaii.*"

"Oh. Uh-oh. Oh, no!" He dialed John's number. "No answer."

"Try the cell phone."

"I don't have the number!" Matt said frantically.

Helen took the phone and dialed for him. "It's busy," Matt moaned. "He must be trying to call Harrison, who isn't there, and he's going to leave a message, and Harrison can't call him back because he isn't there and John will think . . ."

"Calm down," Helen said, taking the phone and hanging it up. "You can leave him a message, and he'll get it when he gets home."

"Will you call him?"

Helen laughed. "No way, baby. This is your project, you do the dirty work."

Matt sighed and dialed. "From now on, I'll leave the projects to you, Martha."

John's heart hammered as he dialed. The phone was picked up on the first ring.

"Hello?" a strange voice said.

"I'm sorry, I must have a wrong number."

"Are you calling Harrison Page?"

"I . . . yes, I am."

"Would this be John?"

"Yes, and you are . . . ?"

"Sorry! I'm Neil, I'm house-sitting . . . cat-sitting, actually."

"Where's Harrison?"

Neil paused. "He's on vacation right now. Alone," he added hastily. "Did you need to get a hold of him right away?"

"No, not really," John sighed, the air let out of his tires. "It can wait. Thanks."

"Wait!" Neil said impulsively. "He's at the Hotel Comonaya-wanaleia; I have the number here . . ."

"No, really. I'm not going to bother him there, but thanks . . ."

"John . . ."

"Yes?"

"Harrison really misses you," Neil blurted. "I suppose I'm being an interfering old woman, but I know that . . . well, that he'd really like to talk to you."

"Thanks," John said, feeling sad and relieved at the same time. "I'll call him when he gets back."

"Okay," Neil said, sounding deflated.

"How's Rafsanjani?" John couldn't help asking.

Neil laughed. "She misses you, too. Here, I'll put her on. Kitty! Hey, kitty. *Brrrroww! Mrrrup, brrrup, brrow!*"

"You speak kitty very well," John laughed.

"Your little girl here is a big talker, she's taught me quite a few kitty words. Hmm, I can't get her to talk into the phone."

"Are you sitting down?"

"Yes."

"It's one of those weird kitty social things. You have to stand up and look down at her, look her in the eye and say something. Then she won't shut up."

"Let me try that. Hey, cat."

John and Neil were rewarded with a series of *"brrows"* from Rafsanjani.

"There you go!" Neil laughed.

"Thank you," John said, suddenly feeling very weepy. "It's good to hear her voice. Okay, I gotta go. Thank you again . . . I forgot your name."

"Neil. If you want to talk again, I'll be here."

"Thanks. I just might."

Brian called him on the cell phone later that week. "Hey, I tried you at Slater's and he said you moved out."

"I thought it was best. If I was going to dry out and all."

"That's true." He paused. "Are you doing anything tonight?"

John gulped. "No, no plans."

"We should talk."

"We should."

"Dinner? Somewhere where we can hear ourselves?"

"Sure. Sounds good."

He hung up dreading the meeting. Brian had sounded so business-like, but then, their last encounter hadn't been pretty.

He was early to the restaurant and nervously went through two glasses of iced tea while waiting. Brian sat down across from him in the booth and John sighed inwardly; Brian was without a doubt the best-looking man he'd ever been with, so sunny and always smiling . . . but not tonight.

"Thanks for meeting me."

"Sure. How was your trip?"

"That's what I wanted to tell you about. I went back to see my parents, tell them about my HIV status."

"How did that go?"

Brian shrugged. "Pretty good. Really good, actually. They're going to pay my way through school."

"Wow! That's great. Congratulations."

"Thanks. So I'm starting in a week, my dad pulled some strings with some connections he has."

"Where are you going?"

"Rhode Island School of Design."

"Oh . . ." John said, as it sunk in what that meant. "Congratulations, anyway."

"I'm sorry to drop this on you, but . . ." Brian sighed. "I don't know. To be honest with you, those same connections probably could've gotten me into Academy of Art, or CCAC, or the Art Institute."

"But you wanted to move back east . . ."

"I wanted to get away from the scene out here, actually. There's just . . . it's not the same out here. Back home, you get on AOL and you can meet people and talk to them and maybe even make friends. Out here you get on and talk to people and within minutes everyone wants to suck your dick, or they're asking you if you 'like to party.' I mean, I never got really into the drugs, but I saw it happen to Slater, and Scott"—he finally looked John in the eye—"and you. I couldn't help but think, why not me next?"

"I'm off the speed," John blurted, his mouth racing ahead of his brain. "I moved out of Slater's place, I'm staying with Kevin and Ethan, I mean, if that's why you're leaving. . . ."

"No, John, it's not you. If it was just you I would've just broken up with you and stayed here. I'm homesick, you know? The town I grew up in, it's in the middle of nowhere, and it's beautiful, all the trees and changing seasons—you don't get fall out here, or winter. And people back there, they're used to winter; if you put on a couple extra pounds it's not the end of the world, but out here it's like there's no excuse, so everybody's so damn body-con, sometimes I think half of them are on the crystal just to stay thin." He stopped himself. "I shouldn't trash the place. I wasn't here long enough. But I'm ready to go."

John sighed. "I wish things had been different."

Brian smiled. "You got a little taste of the pie and you wanted the whole thing—it happens."

"I didn't just think of you as a piece of pie, Brian."

"I know, I know. But you threw me over for the pie, didn't you?" he asked kindly.

"Yes," John had to admit. "I did."

Brian hesitated. "You remember the conversation we had that night? About HIV? About what it does to your life?"

"Yes, of course."

"And you said that you were living for today. I thought about that a lot, especially after . . . well, after that night at the party. And maybe it's none of my business now, but . . ."

"Go on."

"I don't think you've been living like you're going to live. I think you've been living like you're going to die."

A cold finger laid itself on the back of John's brain. "What does that mean?" he asked, subconsciously aware that with a little thought he could answer that question himself.

"The drugs, the partying—if you're my age and you do it, it's because you think you're indestructible. If you're your age and do it, it's because you think it doesn't matter. I mean, you're not stupid, you know what you were doing to your system. I'm just saying that maybe deep down you don't yet really believe that you're going to survive, that you've done all this because you think it's your last hour and you don't have time to do anything important, so why not just have fun?"

John swallowed. "Maybe I don't. Believe that I'm going to live, I mean. Not deep down. Maybe I've seen too many people get sick and say, 'I'm going to beat this thing,' and they never did. So why should I be any different. Hell, maybe it's survivor's guilt, too—knowing what a useless piece of shit I am, and why the hell am I alive when all those virtuous community activists and brilliant artists are dead?"

"You're not a useless piece of shit, John," Brian chided him, putting his hand over John's. "But you can't answer a question like why you're alive when they're not. Nobody in a situation like that has ever been able to answer it. People blow their brains out trying to answer it."

John shook his head. "How come you're so smart so young, and I'm so stupid so old?"

Brian smiled. "You're not stupid, John. You just got handed a second chance and didn't know what to do with it, that's all."

in the mirror. He didn't look good, he knew—the drawn look had
subsided since he'd laid off the drugs, but he now had bags under
his eyes that indisputably set him on the wrong side of thirty, at
least in this place. He'd chosen the same bicep-revealing shirt he'd
worn that first night, but while the muscle was still there, it wasn't
quite as plump and full, and the definition was not as dramatic. *No
wonder those cute young things won't look at me,* he thought. *I
guess I look like papier-mâché at last.*

He'd found himself seated next to someone who, he could see
out of the corner of his eye, was giving him the eye. His old, pre-club
self would have given the man a polite smile, but the emotionally
exhausted John could only ignore him and hope he'd go away. He
wasn't bad-looking—a little short, not too old; well, a few years
older than John, balding but with his hair cropped short so it was
okay; not a bad body, slim, but not great, either. Finally, he was
caught in one of his exams when the man made eye contact.

"Evening."

"Hi," John said, smiling and looking away.

"Good luck," the man said warmly.

"What?"

"I'm not your type, so good luck tonight."

"Thanks," John laughed. "Sorry about that. I'm not . . . well,
I didn't used to be so curt. It's been a bad day."

"Stand up," the man said.

"Huh?"

"Stand up and face away from me."

"What for?" John asked warily.

"You need a massage. No strings," he added hastily.

John shrugged and got up. The man put his hands on John's
upper back and shoulders and started kneading, yielding an involun-
tary groan of pleasure from John almost immediately.

"You're tense. Very nice muscles, by the way."

"Thanks." John said little more, just closing his eyes and enjoying the rub. Finally he got a pat on the back to inform him the massage was at an end.

"I'm Mike."

"John. Thanks again."

"Glad to do it. You ready for another beer?"

"Sure," John said, flattered by the attention, especially after his rebuffs by the cuter, younger set. Mike brought back their beers and sat down.

"You're very handsome, you know that, don't you?"

John laughed. "Thanks."

"I won't keep you if you want to look around and have some fun."

"No, no, I'm fine."

Mike smiled and put a hand on John's thigh. "I'm glad to hear it."

Several beers later, he and Mike were making out. Mike was nice, he was friendly, bending over backward to keep John in liquor, and soon enough he was drunk and horny, and Mike was a warm firm body with no notable deficiencies that he could list in his current state of mind to prevent him from going home with the guy. That was what it was all about, anyway, right? A few beers, a friendly conversation, some sex, a warm body, somebody ...

They went to Mike's place, where John didn't have his coat off before Mike was all over him. "Hold on, let me get my shoes off." He tried to get out of his shoes without untying them, stumbled and fell on the bed.

The sex was a blur. The room was spinning and John had no desire to get up, so he let Mike undress him in pieces, first unbuckling his belt and unzipping him for oral sex that John supposed was probably giving him an erection, if he could have felt anything below his neck. He felt sick and only wanted to roll over on his side, but just turning his head to the side made him ready to vomit.

Mike ran his hands up under John's shirt, whispering, "You're so hot, you're so hot," over and over like a mantra.

A trophy, John suddenly thought, *I'm just a* trophy *to him.* In a flash the other man went from a nice guy, adequate for a drunken fuck, into a vampire, sucking the life out of him.

"You're so beautiful," Mike said. "Do you have a boyfriend?"

"No," John practically sobbed as a scroll unfolded before him— years of nights like this, going out alone and getting drunk with some man who still thought he was cute, each year's dissolutions bringing him just a little further down the food chain until he was going home with men he wouldn't give the time of day to today, just to hear them tell him he still had it . . . years of wondering if maybe this time he'd meet somebody who . . .

"I'd love to be your boyfriend," Mike said. "Why don't you stay the night and I'll make you breakfast?"

John lurched up, grabbing his pants with one hand and holding his shirt in the other.

"What's wrong?"

"I have to go."

"I did something wrong, didn't I?" Mike slumped. "I did it again, didn't I? I'm chasing you away. I shouldn't have moved so fast, huh? I always do that . . ."

John was in no mood to stop and offer consolation; escape was his only goal now. "I'm sorry. I have to go."

"You've got an appointment, right?" Mike asked, his voice suddenly slurred and bitter.

A light went on in John's head. For a moment he just stood there, shirt in hand and pants undone, marveling at his discovery. *I can just do it, I can just go,* he thought, and the thought brought a flood of relief, which washed away every fear, every care.

"I do have an appointment."

"And where are you going at two A.M., may I ask?"

"Hawaii."

CHAPTER TEN

Harrison had never been to Hawaii before and wasn't prepared for it when he got off the plane. Sure, he'd grasped the abstract concept from the pictures he'd seen over a lifetime—sunshine, beaches, palm trees—but then, he'd seen all that in Los Angeles and just subconsciously assumed it was the same.

So when he'd stepped off the plane in the dusk of late evening and walked into an air like . . . like perfume, like soft biscuits, humid but not oppressive, the overwhelming scent of *flowers, everywhere,* he hadn't been prepared. Walking through the open-air terminal had been a shock, too—a place where they didn't have to seal the airport hermetically against the elements! He'd hardly noticed the kitschy-ness of the lei automatically placed around his neck by someone trying to sign him up for a tour group. *My God,* he thought, *I'm forty-two years old and it's taken me this long to feel this . . .*

The Hotel Comonayawanaleia was a mid-price hotel on Waikiki, which is to say the room was nice, faced the ocean, but wasn't on the beach—no matter, as the beach was only a few minutes' walk. In no mood to go out and eat in a restaurant alone, Harrison ambled into the Burger King and ambled right out again after realizing a fast-food meal that would cost him five bucks at home would be about twice that here. At first he was indignant, but it soon dawned on him how much it must cost to transport even the buns all the thousands of miles he'd just flown. He'd had a window seat on the flight and as the plane had chased the setting sun he'd marveled as he looked out to see nothing but water, for the hundreds of miles he could see before the earth curved away, just one tremendously gigantic droplet of water. *I'm so far from home. . . .*

Instead, he went into a local grocery store and found that the economics worked in reverse—fruit was as obscenely cheap as everything else was obscenely expensive. Several dollars got him a few bags of ready-sliced pineapple, mango, and kiwi, and a loaf of the sweet Hawaiian bread. Back in his hotel room, he set up his dinner on a paper plate and sat out on the balcony to enjoy the warm evening, in itself a luxury available only a few days a year in San Francisco.

He ate his meal in silence, just listening to the ocean. He cleaned up and turned on the TV to find some news, and instead found himself watching a Japanese-language channel featuring a movie with a sword-wielding, ass-kicking geisha girl beating the crap out of about a hundred ninjas. At the end of this entertaining experience, he took a spin around the dial but found that while the hotel's internal cable system featured free HBO (he took a pass on the latest Pauly Shore vehicle), it didn't carry CNN, so off went the TV.

Back on the balcony, he realized he ought to go to bed, ten o'clock Hawaii time was 1 A.M. at home, but he wasn't tired. He thought about the books in his suitcase—Christian Meier's biography of Caesar, which he hadn't had time to read during the school year, H. D. F. Kitto's *The Greeks,* an old favorite of his for Kitto's pithy writing style, and a volume of Trollope. *The Small House at Allington* was the one he thought he'd plucked off the shelf. But actually he found his mind turning to the book Matt had

planted in his carry-on at the airport—*Ferrari's Places of Interest,*
one of the gay guidebooks.

"Matt, I don't need this," Harrison protested.

"Sure you do," Matt insisted. "You're telling me you're going
to spend a week in Hawaii and you're never going to want to talk
to another homosexual?"

"You mean never going to want to get laid?"

"What if you do? The sun, the heat, all those tropical flowers
blooming, blooming, blooming, whispering in the air, 'reproduce,
reproduce.' How can you resist their siren song?"

Harrison laughed. "Fine, I'll take the book."

Truth be told, he *was* horny. He'd asked Matt about it during
one of their workouts. "So I'm adding lean muscle mass," he said
casually. "Does that mean I'm going to produce more testosterone?"

Matt grinned. "Do you *feel* like you're producing more testosterone?"

Harrison blushed. "If you mean, am I thinking about sex more
than I used to, yes, I am. But how much of that is the fact that
it seems to have become more available, and how much is my
biochemistry?"

Matt was still grinning. "Does it matter?"

Harrison sighed. "Never mind."

Whatever it was, there was no doubt that right now, he was as
horny as a pit bull. He pulled out the Ferrari guide and looked up
Hawaii; there was a bar not three blocks away.

He dressed for the occasion in the wardrobe he and Matt had
picked out—*that* had been an experience. Matt had taken him to
Wilkes Bashford, where the entire sales force seemed to be on a
first-name basis with Matt. After the third salesman greeted him
by name, Harrison turned to him. "Come here often?"

"Veterinary medicine can be a lucrative profession," Matt
admitted, "and I admit it, shopping for clothes is my hobby."

Harrison had flinched at the prices—$150 for a pair of linen slacks!—but Matt had been firm. "These aren't indulgences, Harrison, they're *investments.*"

"No," Harrison replied, "investments return dividends. This," he whispered to avoid getting disdainful looks from the salesmen, "is money down the drain."

"It all depends on how you measure your dividends," Matt countered. "Do you want to keep your money in the bank and shamble around town in rags, maybe break down and spend it on the complete OED, or do you want to spend a little of it and look sharp? I know a certain person who'd be surprised and probably pleased to see you looking sharp," Matt concluded, grinning.

Harrison sighed. "Fine. You're right." He raised his hands for easier crucifixion. "I am in your hands."

Matt and the salespeople had pooled their expertise and for just under a thousand bucks had equipped Harrison with everything he'd need for his trip to Hawaii, a few pairs of sharp slacks, some Egyptian cotton shirts, and a pair of high-class shoes. He'd drawn the line when they'd tried to interest him in an expensive suit— "I'm a professor, not a stockbroker." Nonetheless, his wardrobe had been dramatically altered; in fact, when he'd gotten home and hung up his purchases in the closet, he'd been dismayed to see how tatty his old things looked next to the new ones. "I see how this can become an addiction," he admitted to himself.

Now he was glad of it, he put on the cream linen pants ("Don't sit down," Matt had warned him), a peach button-down shirt, and, in open defiance of Matt and Wilkes Bashford, a pair of Timberland sandals with no socks. He smiled as he sealed the Velcro straps, thinking of the day John had given him a lecture on the differences between straight fashion and gay fashion. "No gay man," John had insisted, "ever wears socks with sandals. Every gay man knows it looks ridiculous. If you need socks, you should be wearing shoes;

the whole point of sandals is to let your feet free.'' His feet free, Harrison checked himself out in the bathroom mirror one last time.

"I have an ass," he murmured aloud, amazed at how good it looked in the drapey linen pants. To his consternation, he found himself getting an erection. Something is going to happen tonight, he thought.

The bar was about as tasteful as he expected, done in circa-1955 Tiki Lounge; Harrison couldn't tell if it was a camp statement, if they'd done it to fulfill tourist expectations, or if they just didn't know better. The place was deserted, even though it was a Saturday night. He ordered a beer and asked the bartender, "Am I early or is it just slow on weekends?"

"Oh, no, it's not slow—everybody's out back." He pointed Harrison toward the patio.

Inside, Harrison hadn't been able to hear the hum of conversation over the disco mix thumping over the speakers, but the place was by no means slow. Everyone was indeed out in the back, a pleasant scene with patio furniture around the tables on the deck, and a decent-sized garden with a small fountain splashing in the middle, the fountain lit from within with colored lights and the rest of the garden dimly lit with tiki torches.

Harrison decided to investigate the garden, bending over to smell the prolific narcissus. A voice behind him warned, "You'd better not bend over too long around here, not with that ass."

He started up and turned around, embarrassed. The speaker was a lean, handsome man, around thirty, with dark brown hair and eyes, a deep tan and an inviting smile. Harrison laughed. "Thanks for the warning."

"No problem. Where you from?"

Harrison thought of John again, how he'd told Harrison that was the first question people asked you in bars in a tourist town like

San Francisco, it was obviously just as true in all tourist towns. "San Francisco, and you?"

"I live here. How long are you here for?"

"A week, I just got here today."

"Your first visit?"

"Yes."

"Welcome."

"Thanks."

"I'm Nick."

"Harrison." He shook Nick's hand.

"You here alone?"

"I am."

"That's unusual."

"Is it?"

"Most people come with a lover, or a friend. Almost nobody comes to Hawaii alone."

"Well, here I am," Harrison said, finishing off his beer.

"Sorry, didn't mean to pry."

"No problem."

"Can I get you another drink? You won't even owe me a kiss." He winked as he spoke. "I'm a bartender here, so all my drinks are free."

"I'd still have to tip you." Harrison smiled.

Nick smiled back and put a hand on Harrison's forearm. "Preferably in a way I won't have to report to the IRS. Be right back."

Harrison swallowed hard. *I can have this if I want to,* he thought. God, it was so easy—you just walk out there, and there it is. He thought of John's angry insistence that he'd turned down offer after offer before going off with that young man he'd seen him with at the airport . . . he was telling the truth, he thought with a little mortification at his treatment of John. Once you've got the body it just falls into your lap.

Nick returned with two beers and they made casual conversation for a while. Finally, Nick looked at his watch. "Well, what do you say?"

"Huh?"

"You ready to go?"

"Uh, sure."

"I have a roommate, so we should go to your place."

"Sure, sure." Harrison was amazed at the casual nature of it. Had he not been paying attention when it had been decided they would have sex? He didn't recall deciding that would be the outcome. As far as he was concerned they'd been flirting and talking, but did that automatically mean sex? He sighed, he was horny and Nick was cute and friendly, so why not?

Back at the hotel, Harrison thought he should offer Nick a drink, but after he let the beer drain out of him and came out of the bathroom, Nick was already naked on the bed, hands behind his head. "What are you into?" he asked Harrison.

"Well, I . . . I don't really have a laundry list."

"Suck, get sucked, fuck, get fucked?"

"I don't know, I guess I just start in with someone and whatever feels right . . ."

"Sure, okay."

Harrison stood there for a minute before realizing it was his turn to get undressed. Now also naked, he made for the bed. "Nice package," Nick said. "Lie down."

Harrison did as he was bid and Nick's mouth started working on him. He touched his partner's shoulders, his head, tried to pull the man up to him for a kiss, but Nick steadfastly bobbed up and down on him, one hand bracing himself and the other furiously stroking his own cock. Not much later, Nick said, "Are you gonna come, because I am."

"Go ahead," Harrison said, relieved that it was over.

Nick groaned, sighed, and rolled over. "Thanks," he said, getting up and padding into the bathroom.

Harrison was left alone on the bed, naked. Was that it? he thought. You come home with someone and that's what you do? He thought back to his own randy youth in the city, and was hard-pressed to think of a situation like the one he'd just been in. No kisses tonight, no tenderness, and if Nick were to come out, get dressed and take off without a second thought, he wouldn't be surprised. In fact, that was just what Nick did.

"Thanks, Henry," Nick said. "Enjoy your visit. See you later."

"Thanks, see you." Harrison shut the door behind Nick and leaned against it. He thought about what lovemaking had been like with John, back when they had made love. It had been cozy, he thought, not passionate but warm; the great joy of it had just been being in each other's arms. Holding John had given him more emotional and, yes, physical satisfaction than most of the sex he'd ever had. Now that was gone, and was this what was left? Pickups in bars that led to unsatisfying, impersonal, and even inconclusive sex? *No,* he thought, *not for me. If I don't get back with John, if I don't ever meet anyone else, I'll beat off for the rest of my life before I let that happen.*

Naked, he went back out on the balcony. He wanted John here, standing next to him. No strings—not back by his side forever, not in his bed tonight, just here, now, next to him, so that he wouldn't feel as horribly alone as he felt right now.

John quit work by phoning Patsy as soon as he'd gotten home from his abortive "date."

He'd called her at 3 A.M. that Sunday morning, wondering how hard it would be to rouse her at this hour, when to his surprise she answered the phone, perfectly alert.

"Patsy?"

"John! What the hell are you doing up at this hour?"

"I'm going to Hawaii."

"So you're giving me my Monday wake-up call now, is that it? Should I just file it away until I need it? What do you mean,

Hawaii? You have to be at work on Monday, you told me Obelisk has this huge new project. . . ."

"Obelisk can go stuff himself," John retorted. "I quit, as of right now. You can tell them for me, if and when you manage to go in on Monday."

"No!" Patsy wailed. "You can't quit! I will be SO BORED if you quit! You're the only fun person in that entire office, John. Don't do it!" She paused to light a cigarette. "Oh, go ahead. I should quit, too. I'm a receptionist, not a bookkeeper; the cheap bastards can get someone else to do double duty."

John laughed. "That's the spirit. Will you do me a favor? Clean out my desk before you tell them I'm not coming in, so they don't do that thing they did with Dan and have a security guard watch him pack. Just take my stuff home Monday and tell them Tuesday I quit, okay?"

"God, you don't even want to tell the old man yourself?"

"Hell, no. I'm in no mood for him right now. If I talked to him at all, he'd set me off and I'd *really* be in trouble!"

"What the hell are you going to Hawaii for? You just went to Mexico."

"Harrison's there. I'm going to . . . I'm going to . . . I don't know what. I'm going to see him, at any rate."

Patsy let out a whoop. "I love it! It's just like the movies! You go, girl!"

John smiled. "I will go, dear, and I'll tell you all about it when I get back."

"Good luck, kid. Hoist a piña colada for me, would ya?"

"Sure thing, Pats. Thanks again."

"My pleasure. I can't wait to see the look on Obelisk's face!"

Next he dialed Neil at the apartment. After apologizing for waking him up, he asked for the name of Harrison's hotel, which Neil mumbled into the phone, plainly doing so in his sleep. John wrote it down and thanked him, but he'd already hung up.

He left a note for his roommates: "Hey Kev, hey Ethan, if you ever come back from Martin's house, I'm off to Hawaii to see Harrison. If they call from work tell 'em I joined the Peace Corps and will be building bridges in Botswana or something. I'm probably crazy but here I go. Wish me luck!"

John knew well that trying to book a ticket at this point would be nightmarishly expensive, so he packed a carry-on and headed straight to the airport, hoping to get on more cheaply as a standby passenger.

August was typically not a boom time for Hawaii; most people craving warmth in that month could get it at home. But for San Franciscans, summer was a brief spurt in October, and so the plane was packed with those citizens who could take cold, gray, moist, foggy summer days no longer.

"Sorry, coach is completely full. We do have some seats in first class, however," the ticket agent said.

"How much would that cost?" John asked.

"Let's see . . . nine-seventy-five."

"Ohmigod!"

"John?" A voice behind him asked. He turned around to see Jim and Charlie, the couple he'd met his first day at Babylon.

"Hi," John said, too distracted and upset to be effusive.

"Going on another vacation so soon?" Jim asked with a smile, at which John burst into tears.

"Uh-oh," Charlie said, taking over. "Come on, sit down." He steered John over to a seat. "What's wrong?"

"Oh, God, everything . . . I . . ." He looked at Jim. "Remember Harrison? The guy I left behind for fun in the sun?"

"Your partner, sure, I remember."

"Well, he's in Hawaii and I wanted to just . . . go, just see him and tell him . . . my friend Stewart went off to Amsterdam by himself and then his lover Jeremy followed him there and so everything was all right ..." He blew his nose on the Kleenex Charlie offered him.

"Rushing to his beloved's side." Charlie sighed. "It's like a movie."

"That's the general consensus." John laughed through his tears. "And the plane's all booked up. Well, the seats I can afford are booked up, anyway."

Charlie looked at Jim, who read his mind. "We're on this flight. Would you like to come with us?"

"I can't!" John protested. "I can't take your money. I just quit my stupid job. Well, I told Patsy to tell them I wasn't coming back—and I could never repay you."

"Money, hell," Jim dismissed with a laugh. "We've been traveling nonstop for ... how long?"

Charlie shrugged. "I have no idea; I feel like Auntie Mame. What time is it, anyway?"

"Late. Or early. Who knows anymore? Anyway, we've been traveling long enough to accumulate about six-bazillion frequent-flyer miles." Jim extended his hand to John. "Come on, we're going to put you on this flight."

John had never flown first class in his life, and it proved to be a welcome distraction from his aggravation. He was seated behind the couple, who would occasionally turn around to ask how he was doing.

"Great," he said truthfully, more comfortable and pampered than he'd ever been on a plane in his life. Leg room! Ass room! Only one seat between him and the aisle, and the seat was empty! Real food on real plates! A movie without having to shell out four bucks for the headphones!

Charlie went to stretch his legs and Jim said, "John, come up here and talk to me for a minute."

John complied, taking the seat next to Jim. "So here you are," Jim encouraged, with a smile.

John sighed. "Here I am. Off I go, into the wild blue yonder."

"Does Harrison know you're coming?"

"No, he has no idea. See, what I was blubbering about in the airport was, my friend Stewart and his lover Jeremy had a fight, and Stewart went off on vacation by himself to Europe, and Jeremy showed up unannounced, and ever since they've been like couple of the century. I'm not saying Harrison and I are going to fall into each other's arms," John said hastily, "but I want to make a gesture—a *great big* gesture, you know what I mean?"

"Sure. And Harrison is there . . . by himself?"

"Oh, yeah!" John laughed. "I wouldn't have gone otherwise."

"I've never met Harrison, so I can't tell you if it's a good idea or not. But as a therapist, I'd warn you not to expect too much, though it sounds like you're already warning yourself on that account."

"Definitely," John replied, nodding. "I know he might not even be glad to see me. But . . . I . . . well." He sighed. "This is just the last thing. Either I can get back something of what we had, or it's over, the way . . . well, the life I left him for is over, and if it's *all* over, then I can just start with a clean slate. No regrets that there was something I could have, should have done."

"You sound like you have some well-thought-out reasons for your impulsive action."

John laughed. "I guess so."

"Have you thought about where you're going to stay?"

John flushed. "There's a bathhouse on Waikiki, I can stay there."

"Right," Jim said with a twinkle in his eye. "You're going to leave a message: 'Harrison, I want you, please call me, I'm staying at the Club Baths.' "

John groaned. "Maybe there's a Y where I can get a room."

He looked at Jim. "I'm not staying with you guys and ruining your trip!"

"Actually, we're not staying in Hawaii. We're on our way to Australia; Hawaii is just the refueling stop."

John swallowed. "Oh."

Jim patted his arm. "Don't worry, we got you an open-ended round-trip ticket with our miles. You can come back in a week, or you can come back the same night if . . . things don't work out."

John nodded. "Thanks. I've still got charge cards with *some* credit on them, I'll find a cheap room if I have to."

Back in his seat, he looked out at the moonlit ocean, unable to avoid schmaltzy thoughts like, *Harrison was looking out this window only days ago, what was he thinking when he saw this gigantic teardrop?* He was afraid. This was the craziest thing he'd ever done . . . no, doing speed was the craziest thing he'd ever done. But while he'd been doing it, he'd been able to deny its craziness. There was no denying the craziness of this. Quitting his job, hopping on a plane to see a man he'd walked out on after one big fight so he could screw cute boys and snort crystal. . . . *Yeah, I'm real mature and levelheaded, aren't I? Harrison would be crazy to want me back. . . .*

Harrison's phone rang before dawn. *John,* he thought automatically. "Hello?"

"Harrison?"

"Neil? Is everything okay?"

"Everything's fine, nothing's burned down, the cat is fat and happy. Are you asleep?"

"Mmm-hmm."

"God, it's three hours earlier there, isn't it?"

"Mmm-hmm."

"Well, I'm just calling you because . . . well, I think John is coming to Hawaii."

"What?"

"Actually, now I know he is. He called here in the middle of the night, I didn't even remember the call until I was making coffee and saw the brochure for your hotel. He just asked me for the name of your hotel, that was it. Right after that I call him at his friend Kevin's house and Kevin says, 'John's gone out of town.' So I can only presume . . ."

Harrison was awake now. "He's coming," he whispered.

"I can't be sure . . ." Neil said hesitantly.

The sun was just dawning and for just this minute the grin on Harrison's face was brighter. "He's coming." He laughed jubilantly.

John bid farewell to Jim and Charlie as the plane crawled toward the terminal. "Thank you," he said, tears welling.

Charlie dabbed away his own tear. "Good luck, dear."

Jim gave him a surprisingly strong hug. "Call us, let us know how it turns out."

"I will."

The air of Hawaii had startled John as it had startled Harrison, as it must surely startle most everybody on their first arrival. Outside, he found a shuttle provided by the Comonayawanaleia for its guests, and swallowing hard, he got on it.

At the hotel he picked up a white courtesy phone and asked to be connected to Mr. Page's room. "Is this Mr. Eames?" the operator asked.

"Yes," a startled John replied.

"Thank you, sir. Could you please go to the front desk and identify yourself? They have something for you there."

John did as he was told. "I'm John Eames, I wanted to . . ."

The clerk beamed, in on a joke that John himself was not yet aware of. "Mr. Eames, welcome to the Comonayawanaleia." He signaled for a bellboy. "Your bags?"

"I'm not staying here, I just . . ."

"Your room is ready, Mr. Eames," the clerk insisted with a grin. "The bellboy will show you."

Befuddled, John let the bellboy lead him to a room. To his amazement, it was a suite, with an ocean view and an enormous gift basket on the table. He fumbled for his wallet, and the bellboy put up a hand. "That's already been taken care of, sir."

"Okay. Thank you." The bellboy left and John examined the gift basket, which was heaped high with fruit and flowers and, of course, macadamia nuts. He opened the card:

Sleep tight today after your long flight. Meet me in the Tiki Room at 7:30 tonight. I'm glad you came. Love, H.

Love! The card said love! A dam burst, and a flood rushed through his heart, awash wih relief and gratitude and exhaustion. *I want to see him now,* he thought, *now!* He thought about the last twenty-four hours; they'd seemed like a thousand days—the park with Kevin, the lonely hours in the apartment, going home with that guy from the bar, his long flight over thousands of miles of water, and tears, tears, tears on so many occasions. He would call Harrison, but first he'd just flop out on the bed for a minute, just to rest . . .

The next thing he knew, it was 4:30 in the afternoon; he'd slept the day away. He ordered coffee from room service and munched on some of the food in the basket. He was so excited he hardly needed the coffee, but it sure helped clear the cobwebs.

Harrison! He's glad to see me! How the hell did he find out I was coming? John wondered, but no matter now. He perused his wardrobe; he hadn't been in the best frame of mind when packing, but he'd had the presence of mind to pack for the weather, and now it was time to pick an outfit. He realized as he'd packed that he hadn't packed any of the most revealing clothes he'd bought—

no rib-knit T-shirts, or the like—but he had put in a few polo shirts with shorter than usual sleeves that would show off his arms without being too blatant. He wanted to look good for Harrison, but not . . . well, slutty.

He took a long shower, dressed with care, fixed his hair, and looked at the clock—6 P.M. *Well, I can go down and get a drink—just one, just to take the edge off—and wait down there in case he's early.* He turned on the TV and took a spin around the dial, looking at his watch every five minutes and wondering why Hawaii time was so slow.

Finally, it was time to go down. The Tiki Room was just what you'd expect, wooden idols and torches and lots of bamboo. The advantage was that it was dark, and therefore the worst of the last few months' hard living would be erased from his face. At the last minute he decided against alcohol and elected for tonic with a twist. This was gone quickly, as was his refill, and he could feel the quinine stimulating the acid production in his already butterfly-filled stomach.

He had chosen one of the big cane chairs that faced the door so that there would be no missing Harrison when he came in, but when a man who looked like Harrison actually came in, John thought, *But it's not him, he's too . . . ohmigod . . .*

For it was Harrison, in khakis and, yes, a black short-sleeve rib-knit mock turtleneck, showing the tan and tendon and muscle and vascularity of his startlingly fit arms. His hair was the same short cut John had seen outside the apartment building, the smart glasses were in place, and Harrison's very face seemed different, not just the tan but the jawline, no longer soft and jowly, but firm and . . . ohmigod . . .

John stood up as he approached. "Harrison?"

Harrison smiled. "See what happens when you leave me alone?"

John steadfastly refused to burst into tears. *No, then he'll move to hug me, hold me, and I don't deserve that now, I'm not here for his pity.* "You look great."

"Thanks." A moment's pause. "Let's sit down."

"Sure."

"How have you been?"

"I've been better. Though I'm good now," he amended. "Thanks for the basket. The room, too."

"I was so glad to hear you were coming."

"How'd you find out?"

"You asked Neil for the hotel name, he gave it to you in his sleep, when he woke up he called Kevin who told him you'd gone out of town."

"And you did the math."

"I did the math."

"And now here I am."

Harrison's smile disappeared. "John . . . does this mean you forgive me?"

"You! Forgive you!" John laughed. "I came three thousand miles to ask if you'd forgive me!"

Harrison beamed. "Come on, let's go take a walk."

They made their way down Waikiki Beach, shoes and socks in hand. The beach was never that packed in August anyway, and now that evening was approaching, only a few die-hard sun bunnies and romantics like our heroes were to be found out there.

"We should have done this a long time ago," Harrison said.

"You are right," John agreed. "I can't believe I'm thirty-three and I've never been here."

"I can't believe I'm forty-two and I've never been here!"

"We stopped doing stuff, you know that?"

"What do you mean?" Harrison asked.

"When we met, we'd go out on dates, remember? We'd go see a movie or a play, and if it was good, we'd get out of there all excited, and walk and talk for hours sometimes. Then we moved in and started . . . economizing,'' he said diplomatically. ''And I went back to work full-time and had to go to the gym after work, and weekends were about errands and cleaning . . . I should have said something about how I was still doing all the cleaning, even though I was back to work, but I didn't. I just seethed and held it in. Guess I was waiting for you to just . . . notice, I suppose, and volunteer to help out.''

''I should have noticed,'' Harrison said sheepishly. ''Absent-minded professor, you know, just assuming everything's all right if nobody says otherwise.''

''And I should have said otherwise,'' John said.

''Well, I'll . . .'' he trailed off. He'd wanted to say he'd pay more attention in the future, but that implied a future, and John hadn't gone so far as to say that was a possibility. ''It's funny, isn't it? Half the time I wasn't paying attention, and the other half of the time I was treating you like a kid, nagging you about saving money and taking your pills and not running up the charge cards. And you're a grown-up, John, I didn't need to mother you.''

''Maybe you did,'' John said ruefully, ''considering what a good job I did of managing my life on my own.''

''You had to find out a lot of things for yourself, though. Everybody told you that life was the glittering prize, the bestest and mostest, and could anybody have convinced you otherwise? It was your experiment, and you had to find the results for yourself.''

''I did,'' John admitted. ''You can tell yourself that's all shallow and meaningless, but all the while you'd be wondering if you weren't kidding yourself, if you were just telling yourself that to make yourself feel better, because you weren't hot enough to participate and so you pretended it didn't matter. Now I know. I even thought of a name for it—the Naomi Wolf Principle.''

''How's that?''

"Okay, Naomi Wolf writes this book about beauty and how corrupting it is to make women feel like they're shit if they don't look just so. So what's the first thing you do with the book—admit it! You turn to the author photo to see if it's some big lesbian in overalls! But it's not, it's this pretty girl who wrote this book, so you know it's not sour grapes and so you read it. The point is, you can't condemn it from outside, you know? You have to live it and only then can you say, there is no *there* there."

Harrison nodded. "There is no there there, is there?"

"There is not," John replied with a laugh. He wondered how Harrison could be so sure, and had to ask, but circuitously, "You really do look great, you know."

"Thanks. Matt took me on, made me over from head to toe."

"Helen didn't help?" John grinned. "She actually let Matt have a project all his own?"

Harrison smiled. "I think she knows where her expertise ends and Matt's begins. I really like working out; I feel so different— mentally, physically, everything."

"It's great," John agreed. "It changes everything. Obviously," he said ironically, referring to his own changes.

"I think I know a little of what you've gone through, if I may be so bold. I had no idea how different your life had become once your body changed, until I changed mine, changed my look—or had Matt change it. Everyone treats you differently, don't they?"

"They do. People who wouldn't give you the time of day before . . ."

"Are suddenly offering to make a watch for you," Harrison finished, and they laughed.

"Yep. So," he asked, finally asking the question on his mind since Harrison had displayed his intimate knowledge of the Naomi Wolf Principle, "have you used your new popularity yet?"

"Once. Went home with a stranger and can't say I liked it."

"Once is not enough, as Jackie Susann said."

"Once a philosopher, twice a pervert, as Voltaire said," Harrison countered, with a smile.

"I guess Jackie Susann is no match for Voltaire!" John laughed.

Harrison sobered. "He just . . . I felt like a sex toy. A blowup dolly or something. Like he wasn't really having sex with me."

John nodded, thinking of his own recent experience. "It's definitely better when there's some kind of attraction beyond drunken lust."

"Did you feel that for . . . the young man?"

"Brian? To be honest, I did. But I screwed it up."

"Matt mentioned something about drugs."

John sighed. "It was fun when I first did it, but it just kind of . . . took over. Another thing I had to try for myself, to see if it was true. Kevin was right, though. You totally love the drug until the day you wake up and realize you hate it and you can't get away. I don't know, even if it hadn't been for the drugs, to be honest I don't think I could have had a long-term relationship with Brian."

"No?"

"Nah. Like, we got this record and it turned out to be from K-Tel; I burst out laughing and he didn't get it."

"Could have been worse; could have been something from Ronco."

"The Veg-o-matic! I forgot all about that. But he just didn't *get* a lot of things that I grew up with. He's got a picture of that time, you know, but it's a picture from the shitcoms they run on Nick at Nite, like *that's* any reflection of reality! There's just a lot to be said for a relationship with someone who gets where you're coming from, you know?"

Harrison nodded. "Yes, I do."

They walked in silence for a while, both unburdened of the things that had pressed on them the most. The moon was full and lit their way down the beach; they could hear luaus and other festivities coming from the grounds of the hotels along the beach. "It's beautiful out," John said.

Harrison looked at John's profile in the moonlight. Older, and wiser, he thought, a little worse for wear but yet, somehow, that makes him more attractive. "John," he said, and John turned to him. The look in Harrison's eyes told him what was coming and he didn't resist. They kissed, softly; John put a hand on Harrison's startlingly different body, and Harrison at last touched John's muscular frame with all the ardor he'd felt—but had held back—since John had acquired it. Hands roamed slowly across new fields, and ended clasped together.

"All I want in the whole world is to make love to you," Harrison said.

"That's all I want, too." John smiled, hugging Harrison tightly. "That's all I want."

The covers were on the floor, the sheet tossed back, the air conditioner off, and the sliding glass door open to admit the moonlight, the sound of the waves, and the buttery warm air. They lay on the bed, naked and spent, sweaty but unwilling to get up.

"Oh . . . my . . . God," John said, laughing deliriously.

Harrison grinned. "I didn't think Hawaii had earthquakes."

If sex with Brian had been like swimming underwater, John thought, the sex with the new, improved Harrison had been like running with the dolphins. The body was new, but the face was still the same, the man he'd loved all this time. John had shut his eyes in a combined agony/ecstasy, and was transported to a strange place, only to open them and see the familiar. The *intensity* of it had astonished both of them—the way each had grasped the other, grappled with the other, brought together in violent, slamming passion as if trying to make one person out of two. Then they surrendered to exquisitely slow caresses, feeling each other's hearts hammering, droplets of sweat trickling off one onto the other. John had astonished Harrison with a few of the places he'd put his tongue, but he was willing to match his partner trick for trick. The condoms were the only barrier between them, and each was astonished to discover that they hardly interfered with the sensations. And it wasn't just Harrison's body, John knew that—it was the amazing sensation of making passionate *love,* of doing it with someone you ... *recognized,* that was the only way he could put it: someone who was made of amazing parts, yes, but who was more than the sum of his parts because he was ... well, your lover.

"Is it like this for you all the time now?" Harrison asked.

John laughed, thinking back. "Hell, no, baby. Jesus, that twenty-one-year-old couldn't hold a candle to you in the creativity department. Now," he teased, "he may have an advantage on you in the endurance department ..."

Harrison rolled over and pinned a laughing John. "We'll see about that."

In the morning, Harrison ordered a big breakfast. "All that food from room service, that's a little expensive," John noted when the food came.

"We're on vacation, aren't we? Time to loosen up the purse strings."

"You *are* a changed man."

"I think I've been a little too frugal in the past, don't you?"

"Well ..." John hesitated. "There's just one problem. I quit my job. It was just too stressful. I'm going to temp, find another job eventually, but I need to not work full-time for a while."

"That's fine. So we won't take any more trips for a while, but I think it's time we started going out on dates again. Dinner, plays, movies?"

"Yes! And I think that's how we should approach it. Dating, for a while."

"Ah," Harrison said, nodding. "You mean you wouldn't move back in."

"Not the minute we get back, no. I mean, I want a . . . what do they call it when you buy a car?"

"Buyer's-remorse period?"

"No! Not remorse, but do you know what I mean?"

"I think I do. Here we are on vacation, we're as happy as clams, we just had the best sex of our lives, no?"

"Yes," John enthused.

"And we shouldn't make plans for back there while we're still here."

"Just a week or two, to make sure it's right. And of course we still 'date' after that; we don't let ourselves get stale again."

"I can wait a week or two. As long as we're going to see each other during that time."

"Of course! Do you really think I could go two whole weeks celibate, knowing I could be having sex like that?"

Harrison buttered a muffin and put a piece into John's mouth. "Sometimes patience isn't a virtue." He smiled.

"So where are we headed?" John asked outside the hotel.

"I don't know," Harrison said. "I thought we'd just drive around, enjoy the scenery."

"Sounds good. You rented a car?"

"That one right there," Harrison said, pointing at a black Miata.

"A convertible!" John shouted. "This is definitely a new Harrison."

"A new John deserves a new Harrison." He opened the passenger door for his partner. "Shall we take it for a test drive?"

John beamed at his beloved before getting into the car. "I'd like that. "I'd like it a lot."